IN THE
BELLY OF
JONAH

WHAT'S NEXT IN SUSPENSE FROM SANDRA BRANNAN?

"Enjoy this library book as a personal thank you to all the book clubs who gave me my start in 2010."

Sandra Brannan, Author

Liv Bergen Mystery Series

IN THE BELLY OF JONAH

A LIV BERGEN MYSTERY

SANDRA BRANNAN

GREENLEAF
BOOK GROUP PRESS

Published by Greenleaf Book Group Press
Austin, Texas
www.gbgpress.com

Distributed by Greenleaf Book Group LLC

For ordering information or special discounts for bulk purchases, please contact Greenleaf Book Group LLC at PO Box 91869, Austin, TX 78709, 512.891.6100.

Design and composition by Greenleaf Book Group LLC
Cover design by Greenleaf Book Group LLC

Publisher's Cataloging-In-Publication Data
(Prepared by The Donohue Group, Inc.)
Brannan, Sandra. In the belly of Jonah / Sandra Brannan. — 1st ed.
    p. ; cm. — (A Liv Bergen mystery)
    ISBN: 978-1-60832-050-9
1. Serial murder investigation—Fiction. 2. Women—Crimes against—
Fiction. 3. Colorado—Fiction. 4. Suspense fiction. I. Title.
PS3602.R366 I68 2010
813/.6   2010925772

Part of the Tree Neutral™ program, which offsets the number of trees consumed in the production and printing of this book by taking proactive steps, such as planting trees in direct proportion to the number of trees used: www.treeneutral.com

Printed in the United States of America on acid-free paper

10 11 12 13 14 15   10 9 8 7 6 5 4 3 2

First Edition

TreeNeutral®

To Mom, who taught me to dream
To Dad, who proved I could dream BIG
To my brothers and sisters, who spent hours with me daydreaming
To my husband, who taught me how to dream in color
And to my boys, who made my dreams come alive

CHAPTER 1

A BOTTLE ATOP A tiny two-drawer cabinet next to a larger two-drawer cabinet. Where had she seen this before?

The cabinets were brown. The bottle was brown. The cork, brown. The gravel beneath her feet, the hills around Horsetooth Dam, the rowboats nearby, even the clouds in the dark sky. Brown. Differing shades of brown, as far as she could tell in the moonlight, but brown nonetheless. The dress he had made her put on—simple and old-fashioned, with eggshell-colored lace serving as trim around the collar and the tight short sleeves—was a warm chocolate brown.

Undressing in front of him had made her tremble. Not because of the cool June night in the Rocky Mountain foothills but because she dreaded what would come next. She was proud of having remained chaste and she didn't want to lose her virginity now. Not like this. But he hadn't raped her. Instead, he had just stared at her nakedness and smiled. His dark eyes were wild and still. They didn't scan her body as she would have anticipated; rather, his stare pinned her in place, rendering her useless to fight back or run or scream.

But she *was* strong enough, fast enough, crazy enough to fight back. Even after sleeping off the roofie or whatever it was that he had slipped into her drink, so disoriented when she had awakened that she had no clue what time or even what day it was. She had lain in the dark room for what seemed like hours, trying to clear her mind, regain her strength, calculate a way out of this mess. She had pretended she was with her mother, laying her head on her lap, feeling hands stroke her hair, and hearing her say everything was going to be all right. And she had felt strong again.

When she had tried the doorknob in the dark room, it didn't give. The only window was covered by a steel grate that had been welded on the inside of the frame. There was no escape. He had done this before, she had thought. She wasn't his first prisoner. Or his last. And then a second thought had come to her. She hadn't heard or read anything recently about women disappearing or dead bodies being found. A wave of relief had washed over her mind then. She wasn't going to die after all. She just had to do what her abductor told her to do.

So, here she stood, focusing all her energy on being still, obedient. Dressed like a settler, complete with a homespun apron, and standing amid the bizarre props he had pulled from the back of his truck.

He had promised her earlier that night that if she obeyed his every instruction, he would not harm her. But if she did not obey he would turn his attention to Julia. She would not let that happen. Even if it killed her.

Her frazzled nerves had paralyzed the part of her brain that was trying to recall where she'd seen this setting before. The odd cabinets they had both carefully placed near the water's edge at his instruction, the wooden cane he was carrying, the dress. It was somehow familiar, but she couldn't quite recall why. And why did it even matter whether she had seen this before? Something primordial demanded it of her, though. She *must* know the reason for all this.

Neither his stare nor his smile had changed, even after she had finished dressing. What was he fantasizing about her? Was she his maid? His pilgrim? His little woman in his little house on some stupid prairie out west?

But the shoes. They were the most confusing part of all. Her high-top leather basketball shoes and tube socks were heaped by the shoreline next to her blue jeans, T-shirt, and green CSU hoodie. Next to the heap was a pair of tan Converse low-top tennis shoes with no laces.

He told her to slip on the shoes.

For some reason, this was deeply disturbing. The shoes didn't match the dress. Not that she had any fashion sense whatsoever. That was Julia's talent, not hers. Something in the pit of her stomach lurched at the thought of Julia slipping on the shoes instead of her, making his threat and her compliance more important than ever. It was all much too surreal for her. Surreal.

Obedience, she told herself. Be obedient, and live. She slipped her feet into the shoes.

His smile widened. "Sit."

He hadn't hurt her. He had always been gentle, as well as meticulous, careful, prepared. As she sat watching, he spent a painfully long time positioning the props, particularly the bottle. She could see it better now. The combined shape formed by both the bottle and the smaller cabinet to the right was identical to the silhouette that had been cut away in the bottom door of the larger cabinet to the left. Or, seen another way, the shadowy cutout in the door of the cabinet on the left was mirrored in the posed objects on the right. A shadow of the small reflected on the large? Mirror images? Art mimicking art? The overpowering connection of this setting with a faint memory irritated her.

"Like my handiwork?" he purred.

She glanced away, disturbed that he had noticed her soaking up the scene, trying to figure out what this was all about. And why it seemed so familiar, yet elusive.

"Please. Why are you doing this?" was all she could manage.

"Recognizable, isn't it?"

Was he a mind reader too?

He turned his back to her and reached into the camper top of his pickup, which he'd pulled onto the rocky beach nearby. He was unwinding a long hose that looked a lot like the air compressor hoses she'd used at work. She hadn't seen this type before. Her eyes followed the hose to where it was connected to a large tank tucked toward the front of the truck bed. Panic swelled in her belly, constriction overtook her throat. She sprang to her feet, tears burning her eyes.

"Please, please, don't hurt me," she sobbed.

"Hush," he cooed, dropping the nozzle at her feet and touching her elbow lightly. "We had a deal. I won't hurt you or Julia if you just let me finish."

"What are you going to do?"

She wasn't really sure she wanted an answer to that question, but she was sure she needed to keep talking. She needed to hear her own voice, as if awakening herself from this horrible nightmare.

"This won't take long," he said as he guided her back onto the ground and walked behind her. He started fondling her hair, twisting and stroking it between the pads of his fingers and thumbs. "Now pull your lovely brown hair up in a knot, just above the nape of your neck."

She did as she was told, trembling with fright as she wrapped her long hair in a tight bun. He handed her a band and pins to secure the knot. She heard the gravel crunch beneath his feet as he backed away from her. She stole a glance over her shoulder and saw him staring at her, holding his hands to form a picture frame as if capturing a snapshot with her in the foreground and the cabinets and reservoir in the background.

"Look across the water, will you, Jill?"

She did as she was told. She heard him groan with pleasure.

"Now, please stand up and take the dress and shoes off again."

Trembling, she handed him the dress and shoes, and he set them aside. She was standing stark naked in front of him once again. The disconnect between his lack of interest in her nudity and his interest in her surroundings was like a cold finger dragging along her spine. He placed a folded towel in the shallow water and said, "Sit, please."

"It's . . . it's so cold. I can't."

"Yes, you can. Haven't you ever heard of the fable about Jonah being swallowed by a whale?"

"Yes," she said in a small voice.

"Then you know you can."

He was insane, she thought. Certifiable. Stay calm. And keep him talking. "What do you mean?"

"Jonah was strong. Very strong." He smiled. "Jonah lived in the belly of a whale for years, decades. And he never complained of the cold, now did he?"

Her eyes widened. She glanced down at the submersed towel, a ter-rycloth manta ray floating in the shallows, wings bending back and forth, back and forth. She felt sick.

"Did he?" he barked.

She shook her head and bent on shaky knees, lowering herself onto the soggy towel.

"Never," he answered.

She wrapped her long arms around her knees, hugging herself into a fetal position. He squatted behind her, placing his hot, sweaty hands on her shoulders to keep from tottering. He struggled to pull something from his pocket with his right hand.

"What's that?"

"Nutrition."

Just as she felt his hot breath on her bare shoulder, she felt the prick of the needle in her right arm and immediately relaxed. A sudden euphoria enveloped her. This was all going to be okay, she thought. He wasn't going to hurt her. She wasn't going to catch her death of cold in this frigid water. In fact, it felt more like a Jacuzzi now. She was beginning to feel drowsy. He wasn't behind her anymore, but she didn't remember him leaving. Her body was warm and tingly. Maybe he was gone. Maybe it was all over now. She had nothing to fear.

Then she heard the squeak of a knob turning and the hose on the beach wiggled to life with a hiss. Her heart raced and her mind willed herself awake. She sat erect, fighting gravity to keep her head from lolling toward her chest. He was coming toward her again, the hose hissing near his feet. Her instincts told her to run, but when she moved to stand, her legs were too heavy to pull from the water, her arms too heavy to throw a punch. It was hard enough just to breathe.

She felt him slowly lower her shoulders to the ground, her limbs too weak to fight the fatigue. The water tickled her ears. He had promised her that everything would go back to normal again. She wanted to believe him. She wanted to believe that she would wake up and this would all be over. She wanted to sleep. She wanted to laugh at the water for licking her ears. But a small part of her still wanted to scream.

Her mind drifted to Jonah in the belly of that stinking whale. To what her captor had said about Jonah not complaining even after years, decades, in the belly.

"Three days," she croaked, remembering what Allan had told her. After only three days, the whale spat Jonah out on the beach at God's command. It wasn't a fable; it was a story from the Bible. He had it all wrong. It was days, just three days, not years or decades. Her mind floated away with the tide, with the whale, Jonah free.

In a burst of clarity, she was back at Horsetooth. She wasn't sure if she said the words aloud, but they came out like an echo in her ears, thick and slurred. "Please, I won't tell anyone."

Through the heavy fog in her head, she heard him say, "Neither will I."

CHAPTER 2

THE VIEW WAS SPECTACULAR.

I hadn't climbed up to watch a blast in more than two months, and I'd forgotten how amazing the landscape looked from this vantage point. Standing near the piñon grove at the north end of the quarry on top of the hogback, I could see the Rockies, dark and inviting, to the right of me and the plains, stretching to the horizon, far to the left.

Directly in front of me was the best part of all. The smooth layer of limestone just south of the road was pocked with three-inch-diameter holes; a neat pile of bright white drill cuttings lay around the lip of each hole. I counted the holes and, knowing the spacing and estimating the height of highwall in that area, quickly did the math. Twenty thousand tons. Less than the past few months' average, but better than Joe and I had thought. We were almost as far west as we wanted to be—maybe two or three shots away from the buffer—and still able to maintain the beautiful hogback ridge. We'd be reclaiming this area by next spring for sure, another fifteen to twenty acres restored in this hundred-year-old quarry.

I was proud of the progress we had made in the past five years: preparing nearly thirty percent of the quarry for reclamation and having earned release on half of that already. That meant the state approved our accomplishments and released us from bonding requirements. I looked down at the ground where I stood, which had not been mined and never would be, so the piñons would be protected, and at the area to the north of the road cut, where we had finished reclamation three years ago. I couldn't tell the difference between the two landscapes. Neither could the fox that was trotting off into the valley to the northeast.

I imagined what would be left of the limestone a half hour from now, picturing in my head the progression of mining blocks in the coming weeks, followed by the reclamation effort. A tiny movement in one of the holes caught my eye. Ronnie must have tugged a bit on one of the wires during his final check. My eyes traced the wires that snaked from each hole in the same general direction, gathering at a single point where, sure enough, Ronnie was doing his final check. I saw him lift the radio to his scruffy face and heard a crackle from the radio clipped to my hip.

"Ready, boss," Ronnie announced.

I glanced to my right, easily spotting Joe as he stood by his white truck in front of the crowd that had gathered on the opposite side of the hogback beyond the mouth of the quarry down the entrance road. Haul trucks, pickup trucks, loaders, and nearly two dozen employees waited patiently.

I saw him lift the radio to his lips.

"Unit three to unit ten?" Joe's voice crackled.

"Unit ten ready," Paul's voice sounded.

"Unit three to unit seven?"

"Unit seven ready," said Manuel.

"Unit three to unit thirteen?"

"Yo, ready boss," Shawn, our youngest supervisor, replied. I knew Joe would be having a chat with him by day's end regarding blasting procedures and safety protocol. I saw Joe shake his head slowly, then looked to my left and saw Ronnie's shoulders shake with laughter.

"Unit three to base?"

Darlene's voice was the clearest on my radio handset. "All neighbors have been called. Hal has the seismograph ready. Base clear."

"Unit three to unit eight?"

Back to you, Ronnie, I mouthed silently. Ronnie was talking to himself, likely counting down his checklist items. He nodded once in approval and pulled the radio to his lips. "Unit eight ready."

"All units please stay off the air until after the blast," Joe said.

Ronnie knelt over the detonation control he had strung behind the back bumper of his blasting truck and awaited Joe's command. I moved behind the large rock, poking my head up to watch but able to duck in the unlikely event that a blasting mishap sent fly rock in my direction.

A flash beyond Joe in my far right peripheral vision caught my eye, what must have been a glint of sunlight bouncing off the windshield of a car turning off the highway onto our entrance road. Joe must have seen it too because I saw him motion to Manuel, who was blocking the entrance road with his loader. Safety first. Joe hesitated while Manuel talked to the driver and then Manuel signaled with his thumb that everything was okay, and the car stayed put on the safe side of the loader.

I glanced at Ronnie, who had become antsy about the delay. Because he was on the opposite side of the hogback downhill from me, he was the only one who couldn't see Joe or the car that had entered our quarry. But he had seen me perched atop the ridge and was looking my way. I gave him my own comforting "okay" sign from behind the rock and he smiled, returning the gesture.

Joe started the countdown on the radio. "Ten. Nine. Eight. Seven. Six."

We all did the rest of the countdown in our own heads, leaving the radio clear for an emergency abort by anyone on the team. With Joe having set the cadence, I counted down the rest of the way, and at precisely one second past zero, the ground rumbled, dust puffed, and rock crumbled as if Mother Earth had simply made a polite cough.

The sequential timing of the explosives was executed perfectly to minimize the ground vibration. The sky was cloudless and windless, which minimized any air blast. The dust settled quickly on top of the heap of limestone—perfectly blasted rock sized at twenty-four inches or less. The excitement I felt swelled into pride as I saw Ronnie rise to his feet with a grin.

Joe walked back to his truck and waited the agonizing minutes for any unwanted sound resulting from an unplanned, delayed detonation of a faulty blasting cap or misplaced wiring. The employees were anxiously and obediently waiting for the well-respected operations manager's signal that the shot had been denoted, the expended blasting material had been inspected and cleared, and everyone could safely return to work. But Joe always put his employees' safety ahead of their strong work ethic, taking the extra precaution of waiting out a mishap.

Within minutes, Joe was checking out the shot rock, inspecting the completeness of the blast and making sure that all holes were properly detonated. It reminded me of how my dad used to make sure all our fireworks had been expended before allowing the nine of us back outside to play the day after our Fourth of July celebrations. Safety first. With noses pressed against the big plate glass window of our living room, our mom telling us to be patient, we watched Dad as he wandered the driveway and yard back and forth, back and forth.

To my left, Ronnie was rolling up the electric cable and collecting the controls. To my right, the quarry employees patiently milled around near the entrance, awaiting Joe's clearance of the shot. The radio remained quiet. In my mind I quickly reviewed the rest of my schedule for the day, and although this was one of my favorite pastimes, I suddenly felt guilty about having taken the time to climb up the ridge to watch the blast. Guilt. Either you're guilty or you're not, and you shouldn't waste time wallowing in it. Wise words from a friend in my adulthood that would have been nice to hear earlier in my life, considering I was raised Catholic and attended Catholic grade school. Before I could declare myself guilty, Joe pulled me from my reverie.

"Unit three to all units. All clear."

The movements that followed were like a well-choreographed dance. Employees returned to their pickups, climbed ladders into their haul trucks and loaders, and wordlessly fell into a hierarchy behind the lead dancer. Manuel, at the wheel of the largest loader, drove through the road cut and into the quarry, followed by three haul trucks, the smaller loaders, and a half dozen quarry pickups. As if saluting the general as they drove by, the operators each gave Joe a nod as they passed the spot where he had parked between the road and the new shot. Manuel and the haul truck drivers went to work immediately on the humped-up shot rock.

I took a deep breath. Although I may not have had the time, I was glad I took it because observing this team in motion inspired me to be a better boss to them all. They deserved it. Guilty! I picked my way through the rocks, native grasses, and cacti and scrambled down the natural hogback ridge toward my office. Then and there I wished I could have teleported this image to Mom and told her, "This is why I still wear jeans and steel-toed boots to work. Sorry, Mom. A dress or a suit would never cut it out here, although either choice would be more befitting a division president."

As I walked across the fine grind plant yard and road, Bill popped out of his truck and approached me.

"Got a minute?"

Who was he kidding? It never took Bill a minute. He might be a hell of a trucking company owner and truck driver himself, but he always had a complaint about my people. Unjustified in most cases, I might add. The honest answer to his question right now was "Absolutely not," but instead I heard myself saying, "Sure."

"About yesterday," Bill started.

"It's behind us, Bill."

"Liv, please," Bill began again, struggling to keep up with my pace as I continued toward my office. "I can't make money unless your employees load my trucks."

"And I can't help you make money if your truck drivers get hurt wandering around the plant and calling my employees shitheads," I countered.

Bill's face puckered. "Knuckle heads," he corrected.

I sighed. "Bill, follow our rules, have your drivers stay in their trucks, and we'll get you loaded and out of here in no time, okay?"

We were both startled when Terry drove up and stopped beside us after pulling away from the office a few yards away. He rolled down his window and thumbed back at the office. "A detective's here to see you, Liv."

Bill's eyes widened.

"About?" I asked.

"Jill."

"Brannigan?"

Terry nodded.

I was puzzled at that one.

Jill Brannigan was one of the summer temps I had hired to bag material in the plant. Each year, I offer the athletic directors at the two nearby universities the chance to keep their athletes strong and in shape during the off-season and to help those college students earn some money. From my days on the University of Wyoming basketball team, I knew how hard it was to get into shape and stay in shape during the summer breaks. And we could always use the help. We had hired two from Colorado State University out of Fort Collins, twenty miles south of our plant, and two from the University of Wyoming out of Laramie, thirty miles north. A basketball player at CSU, Jill was the perfect candidate for our summer employment program.

"Well, she should be out bagging in the warehouse if she's not with Kyle. If you'll go get her while I finish up with Bill, I'll meet you in my office with the detective."

Terry swallowed and shook his head. "Jill didn't come to work this morning. I think that's what the detective's here to talk with you about."

"Damn. Wonder what this is all about. Find Joe. Please." I was more polite than I felt like being.

Nodding and apologizing, Bill turned abruptly and made his way back to his truck.

———

"She's a no-call, a no-show," Joe Renker explained to Larimer County Detective Doug Brandt.

"Ever happen before?" Brandt asked my operations manager.

"Never. Jill is reliable, hard-working. Bags more product than some of the guys twice her size," Joe added.

"When's the last time you saw her?"

Joe appeared calm, but I knew better. "She's on day rotation now. Six AM to six PM, Wednesday through Saturday. It would have been last Saturday. At six PM."

"You were here?"

Joe nodded. "Yep. Every shift change."

"Notice anything different about her?"

"Like what?" Joe asked.

"Was she agitated, upset, distracted, anything?"

Joe looked at me. I saw something behind his eyes that was not meant for Brandt. "Not that I can remember."

"Jill's been with us for only about seven weeks," I explained. "She's a seasonal temporary worker. Summer help."

He was jotting notes while I spoke. The pencil looked like a toothpick in his beefy hands. I wondered how the hell he got that index finger through the trigger guard or if he had to have a custom-made gun. "How many other seasonal temporary workers do you have?"

"Four temps, total. Jill is one of them. We also have two football players from UW and a men's basketball player from CSU."

"Jill also being from CSU," he said.

"Yep, women's basketball player," I said. "Don't you usually wait twenty-four hours before investigating a missing persons case?"

Brandt nodded. "Jill's roommate called us yesterday. She said the last time she saw Jill was Monday night when she left for the library to study."

"Study? I thought all the kids were on summer break."

"According to the roommate, Jill is taking an independent study for credit this summer. That and one art class. She apparently wants to get ahead for the fall. She had a paper due and headed to the library to do some research." When I observed his discomfort as he leaned back in the chair, I resisted the urge to wince, afraid I'd be pummeled by buttons popping off his shirt.

"And she just never came home? Disappeared?" I asked.

Brandt nodded.

"That doesn't sound like Jill," I said, turning to Joe.

Joe let out a breath. "No, it doesn't."

Brandt continued. "That's what her roommate said too. We've checked the library, Jill's home in Wisconsin, places she hung out with friends, the entire campus. We're concerned—" The detective's pager sounded. "Excuse me."

Brandt stepped out of my office, walked past the scale dispatcher, and left through the front door. Joe and I watched him through the windows, his face sagging within seconds of answering the cell phone. The conversation was short-lived. For such a large man, Brandt moved like a cat. He bolted for his car and took off without explanation, lights flashing.

Joe said, "Huh. Well, that's not good."

CHAPTER 3

"DETECTIVE BRANDT? THIS IS Special Agent Streeter Pierce from the Denver Bureau."

"Fudge," the man said.

"Pardon me?" Streeter looked at the phone receiver as if he could see the man on the other side.

"Oh, hell. It's just that my plate is heaped plenty full already. More than I have the stomach for, and I don't need one more thing. I don't need you Bureau guys coming in here and pulling rank, you know?"

His honesty was refreshing, Streeter thought. "I know. But notice that I didn't jam my credentials down your throat. I heard a rumor from the coroner's office concerning your vic at the reservoir up there, and I have a couple of questions if you have a second."

"Okay, okay, but we haven't come up with a complete game plan up here yet, and already the television crews are begging for a press conference so they can get this on the late night news."

"Don't," Streeter said, his gravelly voice steady and confident.

"Don't?" asked Brandt.

"Don't. If you're not ready, don't let them push you faster than you're willing to go. Even if your police chief agrees with them."

"How'd you know . . . ?"

Staring out at the city lights, Streeter kicked back in his chair and put his feet on the corner of the desk. He knew everyone else had gone home hours ago, leaving him alone in the sanctuary of solitude. Streeter also knew that Brandt's office was probably swarming with people. Poor bastard.

"Let them all know you have scheduled a press conference and set it for tomorrow morning at nine. That will get them off your back and give you time to formulate your strategy. Plus, by nine, most people will have already completed their commute to work, which means your audience will be minimal. Facts will change and evolve between now and tomorrow's five o'clock news when most people will see it," Streeter coached.

"Except for the articles in the morning papers," Brandt added.

"Which will have minimal information since you haven't given anyone a statement yet, right?"

"Right," Brandt said. "What did you say your name was?"

Streeter rested his head back on the chair. He had the detective eating out of his hand now. Cooperation between departments was always the biggest hurdle in any case that crossed jurisdiction, and Streeter knew exactly how to clear it.

"Special Agent Streeter Pierce from the Federal Bureau of Investigation in Denver," he answered. "I need some information from you and I see I caught you at a bad time. Why don't I call you back in twenty minutes and give you a chance to make a few phone calls about that press conference you're going to hold tomorrow morning."

"Hey, thanks," Brandt sighed. "I'll be here."

Streeter glanced at the clock, took a deep breath, and called the state coroner. "Berta? It's Streeter."

Berta was one of a handful of people he called by their first names. Although everyone—with just a few exceptions—called him by his first name, Streeter was accustomed to using last names as a reminder to keep distance between himself and most people. Bad things tended to happen to those who were close to him. Berta, on the other hand, called everyone by his or her first name, regardless of whether she was at home, in a grocery store, or at work as the chief coroner for the state of Colorado. She probably even called the governor by his first name. The thought brought a smile to his weary face.

Her hushed whisper was reproachful. "Damn it, Streeter, it's eight o'clock. I'm helping my kid with her math homework. Don't you have something better to do than work?"

"Nope," he answered. "Are you on it?"

"On what?"

"The murder vic found west of Fort Collins," he said calmly.

She sighed. "I heard about it, but no. I didn't see the point."

"The point is I need you," Streeter said.

"So what? So, do my kids. And my husband," she said defensively.

"Berta?"

"She was assigned to Mark. He's scheduled to start tomorrow morning after the ID."

"Berta," Streeter pleaded, switching the phone to his other ear and pivoting his chair for a different view of the snowcapped Rockies in the distance.

Her sigh of concession spoke volumes over her protests. "That's why I hired Mark and Eddie and Shayla. They're all capable, bright, young assistants."

"But they're not you," Streeter said.

He could hear the young girl in the background singing a Room Five song, and he pictured her bopping to her iPod, tapping a pencil against her schoolbook. A pang of guilt stabbed his gut for having made this call.

"All right," she said. "But not until Hannah's off to school in the morning."

"Great choice."

"You know I'm trying to retire, don't you?"

"Mmm."

"Jackass," she whispered. This brought him another smile. "You know, *you* should think about retiring, old man."

"Come on, Berta. I only just hit the big 4-0."

He could hear Hannah croon a few more bars while Berta mulled over the situation. She finally connected the dots. "You think this has something to do with our de Milo?"

"Don't know for sure yet, but something in my gut says it does. I'll be talking to the detective assigned to the case in a few minutes and I'll know for sure. Just a hunch, but I think we may have a serial on our hands. That's why I need you."

"Then meet me at ten. I should be in the middle of things by then."

"I'll be there," Streeter promised.

"Frank's going to kick your ass," she promised back.

"As he should," Streeter said before hanging up, knowing her husband would do nothing of the sort.

He leaned back in his chair and rubbed his eyes, and then he raked his fingers through his butch. He could see his ghostly image in the windows and noted the similarity between himself and the snowcapped mountains. Neither seemed right being capped in white, this being June in the Rockies and he being only forty. "As old as the hills and twice as dusty," according to his goddaughter, whom he'd seen last weekend. She couldn't possibly know he'd gone prematurely gray—or white, as luck would have it—after Paula's death. At least she had made her father, Tony, laugh.

Having Berta at the table reviewing the results eased his mind. Having Tony Gates rather than Doug Brandt as the lead detective would make it even better. But that wasn't going to happen. It wasn't Denver Police Chief Tony Gates's jurisdiction.

Streeter filled his coffee cup, looked at the clock, and made the phone call to Brandt.

"Better now?"

"Yeah. Hey, thanks for the tip," Brandt said, sounding more confident. "What can I do for you?"

"I need some confirmation on a few details. The word down here is that the perp—how do I put it?—cut a window into the girl's body. Is that true?"

"That's what the guy who found her keeps saying. We can't muzzle the guy. He's a mess. We held him for six hours going over and over his story. But we finally had to let him go."

"Not a suspect?"

"Nah," Brandt said. "And believe me, he's an emotional basket case over this. Kept babbling about the window. We tried to keep him away from the press, but I won't be surprised if his story hits the AP within hours."

"Tell me about the 'window.' What are they talking about?"

Brandt's voice became a bit shaky. "It was like someone took a cookie cutter and punched a hole right through her torso."

"How big?" Streeter was jotting down notes, trying to suppress the repulsion and shock that ripped through him. Remaining calm was critical to keep Brandt talking, but Streeter's mind was already racing toward a connection with de Milo.

"Oh, about six inches high and four inches across. Her stomach, lungs, heart were gone. Looked to me like the guy tossed her guts into the reservoir as fish bait."

"Why do you say that?" Streeter swallowed hard, tasting a bit of the bile that had crept up his throat.

"I waded out into the shallows and found some bits of bone and stuff in the rocks. Too much to be fishermen gutting and deboning their catch of the day."

"Did you bag and tag?"

"Uh-huh," Brandt answered.

"Tell me about the scene," Streeter pressed.

"I got there at . . . oh, I'd say about 9:30 to 9:40 AM. I'd been out at the quarry talking with the vic's boss on the missing persons call when I got the call from dispatch. That was at 9:10. The fisherman had found the vic just ten minutes before and had called it in immediately."

"And tell me what you saw when you arrived."

Brandt took a deep breath. Streeter imagined the detective was leaning back in his chair at his desk, just like he had been doing earlier. The ultimate thinking position. But now Streeter hunched over his desk and wrote as fast as Brandt was speaking.

"It was awful. Worst crime scene I'd ever been to." Brandt blew out a breath. Streeter didn't fill the uncomfortable silence that followed, allowing Brandt time to gather his thoughts and composure. "Okay. The first responders had cordoned off the entire south shore of the reservoir. There were just four officers trying to keep dozens of looky-loos away from the beach. It was kind of crazy because we had some fishermen returning to the nearby dock, unaware they had slipped off in the early morning darkness right next to a gruesome murder scene."

"Did you question any of them?"

"All of them were detained and interviewed at the station. We thought one of them might be the perp," Brandt explained.

"And now?"

"Doubt it."

"Okay," Streeter said, sketching a time line at the top of his paper. Predawn, fishermen launch. Nine ten, call taken by Brandt. Nine thirty to nine forty, Brandt arrives at crime scene.

"Interviewing the fishermen kept us busy. Securing the crime scene tied up a bunch more of our guys' time. So, I was the one investigating the crime scene. It was a circus out there."

Streeter knew Brandt was stalling. Recalling a crime scene as gruesome as this one must have been a strain, to say the least. Streeter felt sorry for the poor guy, knowing he'd need months, even years, to get to the point where the images were blurred from memory. If ever.

"There were these cabinets near the water's edge. Two of them."

"Cabinets?" This was a detail Streeter had not heard from the coroner's office.

"The kind that have two doors in them. One had an empty brown bottle sitting on top. We hauled all that stuff off to the lab right away to dust. Didn't want any more commotion out there than we already had."

"Smart," Streeter said. "You think the killer put the cabinets out there?"

"Know he did," Brandt said. "There was a stream of blood running across the rocks from the girl to the water that pooled around the base of each of the cabinets, like the guy planned it that way."

"All right, good eye." Streeter was impressed. He had also earned Brandt's trust and therefore was getting more information in a shorter time frame than he would if he pulled jurisdiction from him and took over the case. "What else?"

"The boats nearby kept rocking around, knocking into each other. Every time I looked that way, I about lost my lunch. Kept it real, if you know what I mean."

Streeter knew. It was the girl, the blood, the smells that were making Brandt sick, but the mind has a powerful ability called transference. It was easier for Brandt to blame the rocking boats, which symbolized seasickness, for his urge to throw up.

"She . . . the girl was sitting up, hands in her lap, legs straight out, facing the reservoir," Brandt struggled.

"North? The body was facing north?" Streeter asked, drawing Brandt's attention to details so his memory would be sharp. Plus, Streeter had sketched the reservoir in relation to Fort Collins and was marking areas as Brandt spoke.

"Yes, north. It was weird, Pierce. She had a . . . a wooden stick shaped like a T propping her up, stuck under her collar bone. Kind of like where her spine should have been . . ."

His words trailed off.

Streeter was losing him to the world of nightmarish memories. "What kind of stick, Brandt? A tree branch? A walking stick? A pole?"

"More like a crutch, I'd say. It was a wooden crutch with a T . . . no, more like a U-shaped handle. The shaft was about three feet tall."

Streeter ruminated on this image. "One piece or two?"

"You mean was the handle attached? No, it wasn't a separate piece. The shaft and the handle were both hewn from one piece of wood."

"Same wood as the cabinets?"

Brandt paused. Streeter heard a clicking noise and imagined Brandt tapping a fingernail or a pen against his tooth or something.

"No. Different wood. Maybe the same wood as one of the cabinets. I can't remember. I'll have to check."

"Anything else around? Other furniture, weapons, cigarette butts, clues, anything?" Streeter had diverted Brandt's attention from the girl for the time being, trying to extract as much as possible before getting back to the emotionally draining images.

"We're still combing the area. We've picked up boxes and boxes full of crap off that beach. Bottle caps, cigarette butts, candy wrappers, fishing hooks and line, you name it. It's a really popular spot for locals."

"Anything catch your eye that might fit with the murder?"

Brandt hummed. "Nope. Well, just that . . . nope."

"What?" Streeter urged. After a long pause, he added, "Trust your instincts."

"Well, the odd thing to me was what *wasn't* there," Brandt offered.

"How so?"

"Like, where was her middle? I mean, I know I found bits of bone and gunk in the shallows, but where was the spine? Did he take it home as a trophy or something? There wasn't anything nearby except a lot of blood, and even that wasn't as much as I would have expected considering the damage that was done to her."

"So you think this wasn't the spot where he killed her?" Streeter switched the phone to his other ear and shoulder and kept writing.

"My gut says it was, but not where she sat. The gravel looked wet all around her body and to the water's edge, like she'd been in the water and dragged up on shore or something. Maybe the water washed away most of the blood. The stream of blood from her body was more like a trickle, and the pooling around the cabinets was minimal considering the wound. Least ways that's how I figured it."

"Maybe he tossed the spine, the bigger chunks into the deeper water."

"Maybe."

Streeter's mind imagined the gray rocks on the beach at Horsetooth Reservoir. He had been there before with his late wife. The reservoir was long and narrow, running north and south, with a road encircling the water. It was a stunning, rocky area with pebble beaches, not sandy ones. The pebbles were smooth and round after decades of being polished by whitewater rapids spilling from the peaks of the Rockies and varied in shades of gray, dark brown, and black. If the victim had been in the dark waters and dragged onto the beach, the pebbles around her would be much darker than the surrounding dry areas. Darkened by water, blood, and bodily fluids. And if the killer had carved out a chunk of the girl in the shallow waters, they should have found some remnants, even if the fish had chummed for a few hours before the girl was found. The waters were still and little would have washed away in that short a time.

"Was she found naked?" Streeter asked.

"Nope. She was wearing a dress and shoes."

"Can you get water samples from her clothes to compare to the reservoir?"

"Well, that's the thing. Her hair was damp, but her clothes and shoes were dry."

"He dressed her *after* she was in the water?"

"Seems so."

Streeter's mind processed all the information he had assimilated. He flipped back through his notebook. "So, he cut her torso after she was out of the water?"

"Don't think so. Not based on the area around her. The rocks were pretty clean, like I said, except for the blood that trickled from her. She had to have been cut while she was in the water," Brandt concluded.

Still flipping through his notes, Streeter's eyes landed on the first note he wrote. "If she was sliced up in the water, dragged back up on shore, and dressed afterward, then how did the fisherman see the window through the girl?"

Brandt slurped what Streeter imagined was a hot cup of coffee. "That's the thing. The dress had been cut to mimic the torso. Looks like a carpet knife or something crude."

"The killer took the time to drag the victim back on shore, dry her off, dress her, and cut the dress to shape only to leave her propped by the water's edge?" Streeter summarized. "That's just weird."

"It gets weirder," Brandt said. "Remember, he moved the cabinets between her and the water, placed a bottle on one of the cabinets, and then wrapped her face in a piece of cloth."

"Why? Was her face bruised? Cut?"

"Nope," Brandt said. "And as far as the why, you tell me? The perp's insane."

"Very meticulous, prepared, organized. Mind if I get the BU involved?"

"BU?" Brandt asked.

"Behavioral unit out of D.C. They might be able to help if you'd like," Streeter suggested.

"Are you trying to pull rank on me, Pierce?" Streeter was about to protest when Brandt added, "Because I'd welcome the intrusion. Just don't tell the chief I said so."

CHAPTER 4

THEY FOUND JILL.

The newsboy's perfect aim at my front door alerted me to the morning paper at precisely 5:50 AM, just as I was getting the milk for my cereal.

The Coloradoan headlines read "CSU Student Found Dead."

I almost choked on my Rice Chex.

Two small pictures of Jill—one taken as a studio portrait, the other in her CSU basketball uniform—underscored the large picture of the crime scene. The photo was of Horsetooth Reservoir as seen from the road that winds along the south side. Crime tape in the foreground blockaded the south beach. Dozens of criminalists, police, and emergency personnel huddled east of the dock area. Dozens more crowded the cars stacked along the roads to the east and west overlooking the gruesome scene. Everyone in the photo was watching a tall form on a gurney being carried to an ambulance.

A blanket draped the form. No flesh uncovered. No rush.

The story was even more sickening than the initial shock of Jill's death. She had been butchered on the south beach sometime during the night. A fisherman had found her around nine o'clock yesterday morning when he returned with his early morning catch. That was about the time the detective had been interviewing Joe and me up at the office. No wonder he had left so abruptly.

The fisherman had left before dawn, as did three other boaters. None of them had seen anything unusual or suspicious on the beach until returning. All of them noted it had been too dark to see anything at the hour of their departure. The police gave no indication that any of the fisherman were "persons of interest" at this time, meaning those poor bastards were probably all suspects for the moment, even the unlucky guy who found her. He was quoted as saying, "Oh dear God, it was horrible. That poor girl was just sitting there and she had a window sliced out of her body. I've never seen anything like it. A perfect rectangle. You could see right through her."

I lost it.

Made it to the bathroom in time, but I lost it. Too much information, *Coloradoan*.

I rinsed my face and brushed my teeth, opting not to finish reading the story. Jill was too good for this, too kind. Whatever happened to her, she did not deserve this. What kind of monster would do this to such an innocent young woman? A woman with hopes, dreams, ability; a long life ahead full of promise and purpose.

Poor Joe.

He had worked closely with Jill for the past seven weeks, mentoring her, shepherding her, helping her through the unavoidable obstacles of being a new hire at our company. As if mining and mineral processing were not a hard enough industry to work in as a summer temp, Jill had it doubly tough being an attractive college girl. Joe had made sure the uphill battle of acclimation, indoctrination, and acceptance was as painless as possible for the four athletes, particularly for Jill. And Joe had already decided he would invite Jill to return next summer because she was such a strong, reliable worker.

I dialed the number knowing Joe had likely been at work since at least five and had probably missed the early morning news.

"Joe, it's Liv. Are you sitting down?"

He didn't respond right away.

"Sitting?"

"Yeah. What's up?" he asked.

There was no easy way to say it. "It's Jill. She's been murdered."

"Oh no," he said, his voice sounding small.

I wished I could have told him in person, face to face. But the plant is almost forty minutes from my house, and I was afraid someone would get to him before me. I knew he'd need time to recover from the news, and he'd be embarrassed if one of his employees witnessed his reaction.

"It's bad, Joe. It's all over the news. She was butchered by some monster near Horsetooth."

He said nothing.

"I know you're in the middle of a shift change right now. You'll need to pull it together quickly and tell the employees. Have them take a minute of silence for Jill and her family. The guys are going to need it. Tell them the authorities are working the crime scene and that we'll know more later. But for the moment, all we can do is pray and cooperate any way we can with the authorities to help them find the bastard who did this to Jill. Tell them we will have a counselor up at the site from four to eight tonight for anyone needing to talk about it in private."

I waited for his response. Nothing.

"Joe?"

"Yeah, I'm here," he croaked.

"You okay?"

"Hell no."

That took me aback. It was the first time I had ever heard Joe swear. Ever. "I'm leaving now. I'll be there by six forty and I'll cover for you with the quarry and maintenance employees when they come to work at seven. Are you okay to talk with the plant employees right now or do you want me to do it via speaker phone?"

I heard him clear his throat. "I've got it. I can handle it."

"I know you can. See you soon."

═══════════

After fielding some questions from the quarry and maintenance employees, which it turned out I had no answers for, I cornered Joe.

"How are you doing?"

"Not so good, Liv," Joe said, sporting a sickly shade of green.

"I'm so sorry, Joe. I know how close you two were these past few weeks." Did I see him blush? "Do you need a little time for yourself? I can cover here."

"No, I'll be okay. Besides, I want to be here for Detective Brandt."

"He'll let us know when he's coming back," I added. "He has his hands full with this one and it might be a while. His missing persons case just turned into a homicide."

I saw him wring his hands, something else I had never known him to do before. It reminded me of the odd expression on his face when he had looked at me yesterday during Brandt's interview with us. "Joe, what was different about Jill last Saturday night at shift change?"

"What do you mean?" His eyes gave him away.

"When Brandt asked you if you noticed anything last Saturday night at shift change, the last time you saw Jill, you had that look in your eyes," I explained.

"What look?"

I pointed at him. "That look. The one you have right now. You're not a good liar. Something's up. Give."

He shook his head and wrung his big, callused hands, which sounded more like sandpaper blocks rubbing against each other. I knew he wouldn't lie to me, so I waited until he was ready to tell me whatever it was he thought I didn't need to know.

"It's just that . . . "

Still I waited. He stopped wringing his hands and sat up in his chair, looking me straight in the eye. "I got there a little late on Saturday night. Cathy and I had been quarreling and I lost track of time. It was almost six when I got to the plant. The team leaders had already started the walk-through inspection, and the assistants were grabbing pre-shift and post-shift samples together. The loader operators were doing the equipment inspections, and the material handlers were off looking at truck arrival schedules."

There was more to this, but I knew Joe well enough to know he would tell me in good time. We were in his office near the quarry shop, away from the constant bustle of the scalehouse activity and out of earshot of any other employees. This would be the only way Joe would tell me the story he was so desperately trying to avoid.

"I was alone with Jill. No fifth man on nights to bag," he stammered.

I nodded. "And?"

"I was asking her what she had accomplished for the day and for the week. Her numbers were great. Better than any other worker's bag-per-hour ratio in the past year. I was just trying to build her confidence."

Was that an apology in his voice? Justification? He was taking way too long to spit this out. My patience was spent and I blurted, "What the hell happened, Joe?"

His expression hardened. "She kissed me. On the cheek."

That I hadn't expected. Jill had just turned twenty this spring and Joe had grandkids. Knowing Jill, she had been genuinely grateful for the compliment Joe had paid her and probably had shown her appreciation with an innocent kiss. She was probably more like me than I thought. A hugger. Nothing meant by that quick kiss other than showing another human being that he was worth it, worth a hug. An attitude of gratitude.

"I swear I didn't kiss her back," Joe protested. "Cathy and I may have been quarreling, but it wasn't what you think. I told Cathy all about it."

The beads of sweat popped out on Joe's brow and his cheeks burned red. He was not a touchy-feely kinda guy, to say the least, and very much appreciated at least two feet of buffer area around his body as his personal space. When someone had invaded that space, it was obvious by the way Joe's body stiffened and his lips tightened. Much like he looked at this moment. I knew firsthand; on several occasions my celebratory gratitude had catapulted into a hug, making my operations manager uncomfortable. I learned to refrain from what was otherwise natural for me.

"What a relief."

Joe's head snapped back and his eyebrow arched with confusion.

"I thought something ominous had happened between you and Jill."

"Something *did* happen, Liv."

"Something *innocent*, Joe. It was just a young girl thanking a gallant cowboy for all his kindness over the past month. She had no idea how shy, guarded, and painfully old-fashioned you are, Joe. Jill is—was—just trying to show you her gratitude. Nothing sexual was meant by it."

Joe was surprised by my response. He grimaced as he struggled with the word. "Sexual?"

"I'm sorry, Joe. This new generation just has a different way of interacting. Lots of hugs, lots of physical contact."

He shook his head. "That's what Cathy said. And she laughed at me."

"Sorry, Joe, really, but it struck me as a bit funny too somehow."

"Funny," he scoffed.

"Well, maybe not funny. More like relief. Like I said, I really thought something ominous or horrible had happened that night."

"That wasn't horrible enough? She kisses me on the cheek, says 'Thanks,' I walk away from her saying nothing, and now she's dead. I see no humor, no relief. I see nothing but horrible."

He was right. Jill was dead. There was nothing funny about this situation.

"You did nothing wrong, Joe. Neither did Jill. She was just thanking you and—"

Joe's speakerphone interrupted us with an alarming beep. "Boss?"

"Yes, Terry?" I answered.

"There's a woman here to see you. Says it's urgent."

I looked at Joe, who was already shaking off his earlier confession. "Did she tell you what it's about?"

Terry's tinny voice came across the wire. "She said it's about Jill Brannigan."

CHAPTER 5

THE BAR WAS ROCKING.

For a college town, Fort Collins had a downtown scene that was as diverse as the students who attended the university there. Normally they would have hung out at Washington's or Nate's, grabbed a pizza at Sporty's, or quaffed a margarita and a platter of nachos at Tia Louisa's when a change of scenery was in order. But today was different. Habits were discarded, caution thrown to the wind. The whole gang was hanging out at Martini's, a bar that was usually frequented by the business set on Mondays through Fridays and was never a college haunt.

Those of the female persuasion were already halfway to drunk; the males, halfway to horny. He himself was admittedly already aroused. What a day. What a trip. What a life.

The atmosphere on campus, still teeming with eager students despite its being a summer session, was morose because of the news of Jill's death. Yesterday morning seemed like lifetimes ago. Well, at least one lifetime ago, he thought. The saving grace for this dismal morning of unproductive, ill-attended classes was the rush of adrenaline from rumors that had raced throughout campus. It was the hot topic of conversation in the commons, the halls, the classrooms. It was so hard to concentrate. He wanted to hear every juicy detail that was being discussed. Every class had centered on what had happened to Jill Brannigan. One of *them*. One of his gang.

She was missing her own party. The partying, the drinking—this was all for her. A celebration of her life. And, of course, it was a way to drown the gang's sorrows over her death.

"Jill will be missed," the crowd would chant, then chug-a-lug.

"Jill will be missed," he had added quietly.

Kari Smithson had started all of this. Between her and Julia's roommate, the entire school had known about Jill by the start of one o'clock classes yesterday, causing the school to cancel classes today until Monday. Now his Thursday had turned into the gang's Friday. The authorities had notified the family and Jill's roommate. And it took everything Kari had not to stop everyone on campus and individually share the story of her roommate's disappearance and eventual murder. Discretion was not one of Kari's fortes. Nor was vanity, since crying turned her otherwise comeliness into homeliness. Snot and tears smeared her blotchy cheeks. At least grief added some color to her pallid complexion. This was Kari's fifteen minutes of fame, he realized, as some of the students told and retold the story that it was Kari who had reported Jill missing on Tuesday.

By comparison, Kari's roommate was gorgeous. Jill's body had been rock solid. Her skin, smooth and clear. Her long hair, brown. A perfect shade of brown. He had been able to spend many hours with Jill between Monday night and Wednesday morning. Several of those hours had been glorious, the crescendo the fisherman's discovery later that same morning.

He took a sip of his water, to which he'd asked the bartender to add a twist of lime. The rest of the gang always believed he was drinking a vodka or gin and tonic.

He also took in the scene. Females gyrating to the music while expertly keeping their martini glasses upright; males straddling them from behind, leaving their drinks at the bar so as not to distract their focus.

"Hey," the redhead said as she sidled up to him at the bar. "Buy me a drink?"

"Absolutely," he said to her, signaling the bartender. "You look like a chocolate martini girl to me. Am I right?"

"Right as rain, big guy," she said, flashing a dazzling smile.

He was indeed fully aroused, both by her curvaceous body and with the euphoria of brilliance and power.

"Aren't you in my eleven o'clock class?"

"Tuesdays and Thursdays," she said, accepting the chocolate martini from the bartender and taking a delicate sip.

"I thought so," he said, turning his wrist to note the time. Lifting his glass to her, he added, "To skipping class."

She giggled. "To skipping." She polished off the entire chocolate martini.

With her long red hair, her impish grin, and her devious green eyes, she reminded him of his model near Platteville. She was a firecracker.

He loved women. Truly loved them. Every one of them. He enjoyed their uniqueness and their sameness. Every woman he'd ever met was like a precious snowflake. No two were quite the same, yet they all brought much needed relief into his desert-like life with their individuality. Women were a gift from God. A blessing. Just as Eve was a gift for Adam. Few men regarded women with such delicate wonder and gratefulness.

He did.

Women were his life, his passion, his motivation. They were a vision to him and should be regarded as if each were a fine piece of art to behold and admire. His mother had taught him that. She herself was a magnum opus.

He sipped his water and ordered her another round.

"I love chocolate," she said. "Do you like chocolate?"

He hesitated. Chocolate was brown, he thought. Twirling the ice in his empty tumbler, he answered, "Depends on what kind."

She leaned in close enough to whisper, "Let's start with chocolate syrup. My name is Tina."

It took just one more chocolate martini before she suggested going to his place. He wasn't sure what she intended, but he had a good idea and was eager to find out. He slid off his stool, gave a wave to the gang, and placed his hand on the small of Tina's back.

"Let's ride," he said.

"I intend to," she giggled again.

Noon rides are quite pleasant, he thought to himself later, and he wondered if that was every coed's interpretation of a lunch date. After insisting that he crank up the stereo in his car, she had expertly performed a striptease, placed her mouth on him, and worked both of them into an explosive orgasm before offering a "Toodles" on her way out the door and back to her car. Wham, bam, thank you ma'am. And he was truly thankful.

After her departure, he drove to his house—which no one knew he owned and certainly would never think he could afford. Blaming a roommate and lack of privacy, he never brought women home to have sex. He had good reason. Parking in the two-car garage, he hurried through the door and escaped to his darkroom in the basement to retrieve his latest work.

He slid the print into an eight-by-ten frame and carried it upstairs to his bedroom.

"Masterpiece," he said, admiring the photograph as he added it to the gallery of five other framed prints hanging on his bedroom wall.

The photo had been taken of the girl from behind. His attention was drawn to the knot of brown hair, noticeable beneath the cloth wrapped around her face and head despite the gaping rectangle cut in the girl's midriff.

"Breathtaking."

He moved quickly down the stairs into his den, where he sat at his computer and typed the word "Nutrition" on the keyboard. Then he placed a sheet of labels in the feed while the printer whirred to life. He peeled the label from the sheet and went back into his bedroom, affixing the label at the base of the new photo.

He stood back to admire his work. All expertly matted and framed, two rows with three pictures each. Ordered, labeled, and perfectly displayed. Self-Portrait. Mother. Sister. Masturbator. Bather. And now Nutrition.

He picked up the glass of scotch he had placed on his dresser and lifted it toward the gallery. "To perfection," he toasted.

CHAPTER 6

"I DON'T UNDERSTAND WHY I have to do this," I protested, trying to keep up with her.

"The family is traveling from Wisconsin and won't be in until later this afternoon," the policewoman said. "Jill's roommate upchucked before she ever left the waiting area, and Jill's little sister, Julia, refused to come in at all. We need to move on with the investigation and have a positive identification."

I was feeling froggy. "Well, how in the hell do you know this is Jill if no one has identified her yet?"

From her expression, I knew I wasn't earning any brownie points.

"Look," I continued, "I get motion sickness, *really easily*. I rode with you all the way from the quarry to Denver in the back of your cruiser like I was some criminal or something. I'm not at my peak here. I am constantly ralphing up my socks whenever I travel. If Jill's roommate and sister didn't want to be here, then maybe I shouldn't be here either."

"Well, you're in luck. Only a few more feet to travel and we're there," said the officer as she slid her card in the ID slot beside the door. The lock clicked open and a buzzer sounded. The policewoman held the door for me and motioned me inside.

"Shit," is all I said, which brought her a smile.

The room was large and tiled in grays and white. A few chairs were clustered in both corners; there was a window on one wall. I could hear it before I saw it. The gurney was being wheeled around the corner of the concrete divider splitting the room, presumably from the body refrigerators located on the other side. I didn't want to find out if my presumptions were right. I just wanted to get the hell out of there.

The man pushing the gurney wore a gown, gloves, cap, booties, and mask, as if he were a surgeon. My eyes just kept staring at the masked surgeon, refusing to fall to the gurney. All I kept seeing in my mind's eye was the Humpty Dumpty character falling off the wall at Storybook Island in my hometown of Rapid City. And for some sick reason, what crossed my mind was to demand that this guy put Humpty Dumpty—my friend Jill—back together again or I was going to have to kick his sorry ass.

The policewoman touched my arm just above the elbow, and suddenly I was back in the room again. This gray-and-white antiseptic locker room of sorts. Except it didn't have lockers, it had body refrigerators. And it didn't smell of sweaty clothes and moldy shoes, it smelled of formaldehyde and ammonia. I didn't want to look away from the surgeon's face any more than I had wanted to see my naked teammates taking showers after practice or games. I was indeed going to be sick.

For the first time, the policewoman's voice was tender. "Liv?"

I stood staring at the man in the mask and said nothing.

"Liv, this is the coroner's assistant, Mark Blumenthal."

Not one of the king's men?

Mark asked, "First time?"

I nodded.

He smiled. "She is still completely covered. I have pulled back the sheet just enough for you to see her face."

Like that would help.

I had avoided funerals all my life, and at those I was forced to attend, I made sure I had a reason to disappear when it came time to walk by and gawk at the deceased. So yeah, it was my first time ever to see a dead person. Shit. I am almost thirty and I've never seen a corpse. How I had managed to avoid that all these years I'll never know. It freaked me out when at age sixteen I saw my grandpa lean down to kiss my dead grandma while she lay in her casket. Romantic, yet creepy at the same time. I must have watched too many *Creature Feature* episodes when I was a kid.

I slowly lowered my eyes down Mark's torso, not really noticing where my eyes were so much as focusing on where they were not. I willed myself to rein in my peripheral vision so I wouldn't have to see Jill before my eyes were ready. What must have seemed like eons later, my eyes finally rested on Jill's angelic face. She looked like she'd just stepped out of a cold shower, her long brown hair stringy, her skin gray, her lips slightly parted, her bulging eyes closed as if in deep, childlike sleep.

An incredible calm settled in my chest, my mind resting on the images of Jill during her interview, bagging fifty-pound bags of pulverized limestone one after another, eating lunch with the other employees on her shift, smiling and laughing at their stories and jokes. Jill so full of life, now so empty of it.

"That's her," I said. My words sounded distant and small.

The policewoman nudged me. "That's Jill Brannigan?"

"That's Jill Brannigan."

Joe was waiting for me in the lobby and he walked me to his truck. Thank God for small favors and thank Joe for following me down here!

"I'm taking you home," was all he said.

I didn't argue with him. I was feeling unlike myself: unsure, dizzy, a little out of control. I don't remember what or if he said anything to me during the long drive back to Fort Collins or while walking me to my front door, but I was thankful he was there for me. I couldn't go back to work. I just couldn't. It wasn't like me to miss work. Ever. But I'd never had someone I knew be a murder victim before. Never had an employee die by a butcher's hand. Never seen a dead body. I just sat in my living room, staring at the television for what must have been hours. The television wasn't even turned on. The ringing in my ear turned out not to be my imagination as I first thought.

"Hello?" I answered.

"Liv?" asked a voice that was vaguely familiar.

"Who is this?" I asked.

"Lisa Henry. From UW."

My mind quickly scrolled through my college days—the faces of teachers, roommates, classmates, and friends—and landed successfully on a picture of my teammates. I had played basketball with Lisa Henry in Laramie. She was two years ahead of me, and the most intelligent athlete I ever met during college. Lisa was nearly six feet tall, had long black hair and striking robin's-egg blue eyes, and could have been a model. Plus, she was a helluva starting forward.

"Do you remember me, Liv?"

"Of course I do, Lisa," I said, even though I hadn't seen her since I walked off the court my sophomore year, which would have been almost ten years ago. "How's Elsa?"

Elsa, a guard like me, had been Lisa's roommate and best friend during college.

"Great! She has two kids already," Lisa said.

"Jeez, and I'm not even married," I remarked, not knowing why I found it so important to share that tidbit about my life. Maybe it was because I'd always wondered if Elsa and Lisa were an item. Being so surprised by the news that Elsa was married, with kids, I wanted Lisa to make no mistake that my sexual preference was for men, too. I truly felt in those undergrad days, especially when I was with fellow athletes, that I was in the minority when it came to that particular issue.

"Me neither," Lisa added. "Liv, I was wondering if I could talk with you."

"Talk? With me?" I was confused. I had been giving my money to the alumni association ever since graduating from the University of Wyoming, but I hadn't responded to any of the special invitations to come back and play demonstration basketball games or to help get donations for the athletic department. "Hey, Lisa, I just don't have the time to do more fundraising than I'm already—"

"No, no," she laughed. "This isn't about the Cowgirls, Liv. I'm getting hounded, too, believe me."

"Then what's it about?"

"Jill Brannigan."

I opened my mouth, then shut it. I eventually managed, "How did you . . . why did you call *me*?"

"Because you were her boss. You and Joe Renker. I want to talk with you about her if you have time."

My mind had trouble computing. Lisa Henry, Jill Brannigan. Both basketball players, but at different colleges and years apart. Different last names. Nothing was adding up. "Are you related to Jill somehow?"

"No," she said. Before I could protest that I would not talk with her about this if she were a journalist or part of the media in any way, Lisa added, "I'm with the FBI."

"FBI?"

"Federal Bureau—"

"I know, I know. My question was more along the lines of how the hell you got from the court as a UW Cowgirl to the FBI. I would have expected you to be a model or an actress or something exotic."

That made her laugh. "I'm serious, Lisa."

"Thanks, Liv," Lisa responded. "You always could make me laugh. And you're now running your own mining company. Good for you."

"Not quite," I corrected. "I'm just a division manager for our Colorado sites."

"Same, same. You always were goal-oriented, not to mention being the one who brought the team's grade point average up."

"I thought that was *your* role."

If I remembered correctly, Lisa had been almost a straight-A student who then studied for the LSATs with her heart set on being accepted into UW's law school. No easy feat even for someone with her intelligence.

"Will you meet with me, Liv?"

"Sure, Lisa," I said. "What day works for you? I'm at home so I don't have my schedule here in front of me, but I could—"

"I'll be over in ten minutes," she said.

"But you don't even know where I—"

The dial tone buzzed in my ear before I ever finished my sentence.

She must have been at the corner of Drake and College, because Lisa was at my door within five minutes. I swung the door wide and gave her a big hug. She was a vision of beauty, as always: tall, lean, with a timid smile, yet her face revealed confidence because of her piercing eyes.

"Come in, please," I told her.

It took us a few minutes to catch up on the past ten years and everything we'd been up to. I talked her into having lunch, and we made turkey and avocado sandwiches with a smear of cottage cheese.

"I thought you were in pre-law?"

Lisa finished her bite. "I was. I took as much psychology as I could to be a better trial attorney, which is what I thought I wanted to do, only to find out I loved psychology."

"So you got your doctorate in psychology instead?"

"Behavioral. This sandwich is good."

"Help yourself."

She made herself a second one.

"You were always forgetting to eat. That's how you stayed—and stay—so slim," I said.

"And you were always so thoughtful and well prepared. That's why you had a cabinet full of good food to eat no matter what time of day or night we all crashed at your dorm room," she countered. "Nothing ever changes, huh?"

"Yes, it does. You're an FBI agent. Amazing." I worked the last few bites of my cottage cheese as she devoured her second sandwich. "How long have you been living in Fort Collins?"

Lisa shook her head. "D.C. Five years. Profiling as part of the Behavioral Assessment Unit of the Special Investigations Branch. I'm just working with the Denver office on a case they've been following. Ever heard of Special Agent Streeter Pierce?"

I shook my head.

"He's a legend. And incredibly handsome," Lisa added. "I'm lucky to be working with him on this case."

He must have been something special because, although Lisa was a stunner, I never saw her date and never heard her mention any interest in men. She never seemed to stray from her goals, which didn't seem to include marriage or children.

"Cool," was all I managed.

I'd always wanted to be an FBI agent. My softball coach in high school was an FBI agent, and I had a deep admiration for him both as a coach and as a human being. Class act.

"So how does that fit with Jill Brannigan? And when did it become the FBI's case?"

"It's not, yet. And me first," she said, dusting the crumbs off her hands and pushing her plate aside. "I have some questions for you."

She pulled out a pen and a pad of paper from her satchel and dated the top of the sheet, writing my name beneath and the time of day. Organized.

"When did you last see Jill?"

I looked over at the clock. It was three. "About four hours ago." Lisa stopped writing and looked up at me. I added, "I had to ID the body."

Her face collapsed. "So sorry, Liv."

"Me too. Before that, the last time I saw Jill would have been . . . what is this, Thursday?" I was struggling to remember anything since this morning, let alone how to count backward. "About five days ago. Last Saturday."

"Where did you see her?"

"At work. She is—was—on day shift Wednesday through Saturday, so it would have been the last day of her shift last week. I went into the plant to talk with Allan, our team leader for that shift, around two o'clock. I must have talked with Allan about an hour, then did a quick inspection around the plant during which I stopped to talk with Jill. That would have been around three thirty or so."

"Where was she?"

"In the warehouse. Bagging," I said.

"What's bagging?" Lisa asked.

"We mine high-grade calcium limestone at our quarry between here and Laramie on U.S. Highway 287. At the plant, we pulverize the lime-stone so that it's small enough to be suspended in liquid. You know, like flour or face powder. Our smallest product is called #325, which means there are three hundred and twenty-five holes in a one-inch square and the material is fine enough to pass through those holes. At least that's the basic concept."

I caught myself delving too much into the details, like always. I kept hearing my little brother Jens saying, "Forty-thousand-foot view, Boots. Give me the forty-thousand-foot view." Translation: stick with the big picture, sister.

To my surprise, Lisa's eyes hadn't glazed over out of boredom; instead she asked, "Why does it need to be so minute? Why do you need to suspend it in liquid?"

I smiled. "Our biggest market for the high-grade limestone is for agricultural feed as a calcium supplement. The limestone has to be so small it suspends in the liquid feeds for the cows that drink it. Make sense?"

"Perfectly," Lisa said, jotting notes as I talked.

"We either ship the limestone to the customers in a pneumatic truck, meaning a container that can be pressurized so the material can be blown into and out of the vessel, or it can be shipped in bags. We bag the materials in fifty-pound paper bags up to one-hundred-pound paper bags or as much as one thousand pounds in a canvas bag."

"Wow. Nearly half a ton?"

"Sometimes almost three-quarters of a ton is bagged for the customer in the super sacks, as we call them. Just depends."

Lisa shook her head. "And Jill was filling these bags? By herself?"

"Well, the super sacks can be tricky for one person to handle because they require a forklift for each bag, but she could manage the paper bags, sure. She filled and palletized most of those by herself."

"All with the aid of machines?" Lisa pressed.

"Well, not really. We have an antiquated system, so Jill had to man-handle each bag onto the pallet. Four to six bags to each layer, with about ten to twelve layers high on each pallet."

"Whoa. So Jill did this all day long? Moving fifty- to one-hundred-pound bags onto pallets? Twelve hours a day, four days a week?"

"Not all day long, but a large part of it. To give her a break, the team would ask her to charge the bins with feedstone, meaning she would drive the loader for a while, or to help with maintenance or loading the pneumatic trucks."

Forty-thousand feet, Liv. Give Lisa the big picture.

Based on her expression, I wondered what industry jargon I had used that didn't sit well with Lisa.

"So let me get this straight. Out of forty-eight hours a week, how many hours would you say she was manhandling bags?"

I thought about that. "I would say approximately twenty-four to twenty-eight. Why?"

Lisa sat back in the chair and tapped the pen against her chin. "Think about it, Liv. Jill was a basketball player. Six feet, six one. Weighed a hundred and eighty pounds, all lean muscle mass, right?"

"Dripping wet," I said. "I don't understand these coaches. They want their players so thin nowadays. How do they hold their positions under the net?"

"Right," Lisa said. "And you've got her moving how much weight in a day? What did you say, palletize?"

"Palletizing. You know, putting stuff on pallets, the kind you see at warehouse-type grocery stores? The super centers? Things are stored on them and they're maneuvered easily by a forklift. Jill was palletizing the bags, which means she was twisting and stacking those bags to position them on the pallet. The pallet sits on a spring about waist high. Let's say twelve to eighteen bags an hour for fifty-pound bags. Take fifteen bags times fifty pounds times twenty-five hours a week and—"

"That means she moved over nine tons a week," Lisa calculated. "For the past . . . how long did you say she had worked there?"

"Seven weeks," I said. "Shit, you're still a human calculator, aren't you?"

"And you've never succeeded with your New Year's resolution to stop swearing, have you?"

"It's my *perpetual* resolution," I grinned. I was watching her jot the numbers we had just discussed into her notepad. "Where are you going with this, Lisa?"

"My point is that Jill was strong. Extremely strong."

"And?" I pressed.

"And she didn't fight back. Think about it. Ten years ago, when we were in great shape, we were strong. Wouldn't we have fought an attacker?" she asked.

"Maybe she *knew* him," I suggested.

Lisa blinked. "Could be. Maybe she didn't think she was in danger because she knew the guy. Or maybe he sedated her before she knew what was happening."

"Sedated? She was poisoned to death?" I asked, wishing I had read the entire article this morning.

Lisa leaned forward. "It was a drug overdose. Please don't repeat that. It's not public knowledge. I'm just brainstorming here."

I gave her the zipped-lip signal and encouraged her to continue by saying, "So, there was nothing under her fingernails, no defensive wounds on her hands, considering she was hacked up with a knife or something?"

Lisa pushed away from the table and walked into the living room. I stacked the dishes in the sink while she paced. I joined her in the living room and plopped myself on the couch. She walked over to me and leaned over, pointing an accusing finger. "Did the coroner tell you all that while you were identifying the body today?"

"No, I just . . . well, you said she didn't fight back. I guess I read too many crime novels or something. Watch too many of those police and court shows. I was just asking."

Lisa's face softened and she plopped on the couch beside me. "Sorry. This case is just driving me nuts and I've been at it way too long. I'm starting to let paranoia get the best of me."

"Too long?" I asked. "Jill was just found yesterday."

Lisa sighed and rose to her feet. "I've got to go check into a hotel before they're all snatched up by the media."

"You can stay here," I offered. I was confused by the exasperation I sensed in Lisa. And curious.

"I'm sorry, Liv," she said. "We just got started on the questions and I have to go."

She was out the door before I was able to lodge a single protest.

CHAPTER 7

AS I FINISHED MY last stretch after an hour and a half of lifting weights and doing the treadmill hill climb, I heard the knock. I took the stairs from the basement two at a time, feeling the ache in my hamstrings, and jogged to the front door midway up the stairs of my split-level house.

"Hi," Lisa said, appearing a bit sheepish.

"Hotels are all booked," I surmised.

"You got it. Offer still good for me to hang with you?"

I smiled and swung the door wide. "Only if you let me take a shower before I cook you some dinner."

She heaved a duffle bag off her shoulder and said, "I'll do you one better. How about I make you dinner while you're in the shower?"

"Sounds like a deal," I said. I led her up to the main floor and down the hall and pointed to the room on the right. "Spare bedroom. It's all yours. Bathroom is right next to it and I'm across the hall."

The warm shower relaxed the tight muscles in my shoulders and neck. I felt like staying in there forever, but I knew Lisa was knocking around in my unfamiliar kitchen and probably needed some help preparing dinner. I towel-dried my hair and pulled on some jeans, a T-shirt, my boots, and a Rushmore hockey team hoodie. I looked in the mirror and told myself I was getting too old to wear hoodies and needed to invest in some big-girl clothes one of these days.

The aroma wafting through the hall was amazing. I was mistaken to have thought I needed to cut my shower short. Lisa clearly knew her way around any kitchen.

"What's that heavenly aroma?" I asked as I entered the kitchen.

I hadn't smelled food this tantalizing since the last time I was home. My mother was an incredible cook. Nine hungry kids to feed and I guess you learn quickly what sells and what doesn't. Her food was always made from scratch and rivaled the finest meals from any gourmet chef.

"Broiled chicken with lemon pepper and stir-fry mixed vegetables," Lisa said, popping a raw mushroom into her mouth while she fixed our plates.

"I could have sworn I smelled melting cheese," I said, gawking at the colorful dish of hot, healthy food.

Lisa pulled the cookie sheet from the oven. "Parmesan cookies for our salads."

"Yum," I drooled. "Where did you learn how to cook like this?"

"My mom," Lisa said, flipping two crisp cheese cookies onto the top of each green salad.

"Wish I'd paid more attention with mine," I said.

I tended not to take the extra step of putting effort toward an appealing presentation of whatever I prepared. This looked, smelled, and tasted incredible—perhaps *because* I hadn't had to cook it myself.

Over a bite of chicken, I asked, "Okay, Lisa. Give. What's up with the drug overdose? Jill wasn't the kind who'd use drugs. And how long have you been working this case? Are we talking serial killer here?"

Lisa carefully speared a strip of yellow pepper and cut it in half before eating it. She was stalling. Maybe she was thinking about what she was going to say. Or whether she was going to let me in on the story at all. Buckled brows, tight lips, she chewed—at a rate of about thirty chews per bite. I couldn't see how a small piece of pepper could withstand such a grind. More stalling. I could almost hear the wheels turning in that unbelievable brain of hers.

"A bit too much, I think," she said.

"Excuse me?"

"Soy sauce. I put a little too much soy sauce on the vegetables, didn't I?"

She was messing with me and I wasn't in the mood. I ignored her and drained my Coors Light. I got up from the table and washed my dinner and salad plates, as well as the cooking pots. By the time I was done, Lisa had brought her dish to the sink and started drying.

"Do you still like brownies?" I asked. Even though I wasn't quite finished with my sulking, I wasn't about to let her in on my shame for feeling that way toward her for shutting me out. After all, it was none of my business.

She said, "Uh-huh."

I pulled a box down from the cupboard and poured the mix into a bowl. I was fuming. And I was avoiding Lisa. I don't know why. I knew Lisa couldn't jeopardize the case by divulging to an old college friend any information she'd gathered as an FBI agent, but it still bugged the living shit out of me. Strategizing and solving puzzles was my passion, and I wanted to help. Taking my aggression out on the poor batter, I finished stirring, spooned the batter into a pan, and popped it into the oven. I set the timer for twenty-five minutes, determined *not* to overbake them. Then I grabbed two more beers and joined Lisa in the living room, reminding myself that what Lisa needed from me right now was a friend, not a whiny brat.

"Okay, so what can I do to help?" I proffered.

"This is a good start," she said, grabbing the beer I handed her and taking a long pull. "Tell me about Jill. When did you meet her?"

I took a long swig, too. My mind flashed back to a moment I shared with Jill about a week after she started. She was wrestling with a half-filled bag of limestone against the air blowing from the load spout. I showed her how to position the bag sleeve on the spout and get a tight seal, and I was rewarded with a wide smile of relief that brightened her face. We spent the next fifteen minutes comparing notes about the conflicts unique to a student athlete and marveling at how many of the coaches in the conference were still the same. And the agony of waiting to be asked out on a date by guys who aren't totally repulsed or intimidated by female athletes.

"She was great, Lisa. I met her about three and half months ago. Mid-April. Every spring we interview candidates that the athletic directors from both CSU and UW select for our summer internships. They ask companies like ours to find physical work at higher pay to help their athletes, many of whom are less wealthy students on scholarship. Like I told you earlier, bagging limestone at our plant is great strength training in the off-season. We had four interviews set up at UW, all football players, and six interviews set up at CSU. We narrowed the field to two from each school and Jill was one of them."

"The lone woman?" Lisa asked, grabbing her pad and pen off the kitchen table.

"One other candidate was a female volleyball player, but Jill was the only one hired." I took another drink of beer. "Being a woman in the mining industry is no cakewalk. Guys giving each other shit, pushing each other to the limits to see if one will crack or break. With women, it's an even tougher initiation. The men don't like whiners, geeks, or wimps and assume women won't carry their weight. Most can't. Or at the very least, most of the guys think women working in these tough conditions will run whining to the supervisor the first time things get tough. Jill took it all in stride. She dished it right back to them and fit in like one of the guys. They all liked her. I liked her. She didn't complain about the conditions: how dusty it was, how tough the work was, how much work had to get done. She just got it done, you know?"

We drank our beers in silence. The room was beginning to smell like freshly baked brownies. It was nice to have someone to talk to for a change. Made me think Frances—my closest sister, both in age and in friendship— was right, always asking me when I planned on getting married. Maybe I should consider at least getting a dog.

"She was strong, took no guff, so why didn't she fight back when she was abducted?" Lisa finally asked.

She was once again confiding in me. It felt good. She was beginning to trust me. I rattled off some brainstormed thoughts that came to mind. "She didn't feel the need to fight because she was with a friend. Or she didn't have the opportunity to fight because she was blindsided. Or she was so drugged up she couldn't do anything but drool all over herself. Or she refused to fight because he threatened her with something worse."

"Worse than death?"

I could think of a few things, not the least of which was someone going after my Achilles heel—my family.

"What's worse than what she went through?" Lisa asked.

"I don't know. What did she go through?" I'd pushed too far again. Lisa clammed up and drank her beer in silence. Brainstorming again, I added, "Maybe she took a bullet intended for someone else? Metaphorically speaking. Do you have anyone in your life you love so much you would give your life for them?"

Lisa blinked and stared at me.

"How about that Pierce fellow?" I pressed.

She grimaced. "Are you crazy? I just said he was handsome. We're not dating or anything. He's not like that."

"Gay?"

She shook her head.

"Now me, if someone threatened my mom or dad or even one of my brothers or sisters, I would be willing to lay down my life." I'd never been in that situation, but I wasn't exaggerating. But who's to say? Especially when your life is on the line. I added, "I think."

She smiled. It got her thinking about it anyway. It was my turn to go silent. It turned out to be an excellent strategy.

Lisa spoke quietly. "She doesn't have one single bruise on her body, Liv. Nowhere. And you were right. She had nothing under her fingernails, no broken fingernails. She never scratched her attacker or struggled in any way. She had no defensive wounds on her hands. Just one large chunk cut from her center."

I gasped, nearly choking on my beer. I still couldn't wrap my mind around that one. "Shit. I just can't get used to that thought. I threw up this morning just reading the guy's account of how he found Jill's body."

"Yeah, kind of crude, wasn't he? He didn't mean to be. Shock can do that to some people. He just couldn't stop babbling, ruminating over the image."

"What's the cause of death? Do they know?"

"They got started late because they were waiting on the ID," Lisa said.

"Oh," I said, embarrassment rushing to my cheeks. I hadn't realized I was holding up the show. I was so reluctant to look at Jill's face. It still haunted me. The gray, waxy skin. The dark lips. The bulging eyes. It just wasn't Jill at all. And yet it was.

"Agent Pierce and the coroner were waiting until you finished identifying the body. I was there with them, but I didn't realize it was you on the other side of the wall; otherwise, I would have stayed with you through that terrible moment. As soon as you were done, the coroner started her initial assessment, which is why I know there were no visible defensive wounds. Pierce will let me know what the coroner finds after it's all done. Other than toxicology. That takes days, sometimes weeks."

"What are you hoping to find?"

"What do you mean?"

"Well, you're here for a reason. This is an unusual murder. There must be something about it that's pulling you toward similar cases. What's the common link?" I asked.

She snapped on the television with the remote control that was on the coffee table and channel surfed. Settling on a country music video channel, she set the remote down. Staring at the set, she asked, "Have you ever thought about joining? Seriously?"

"A band?" I asked. Such a smart-ass.

"The FBI," Lisa said.

"Yes and no," I said, grabbing the remote and turning off the television. "Yes, I've thought about it. No, not seriously."

"You should." Lisa stared at the blank set, just as I had a few hours ago. "Okay, here's a puzzler for you. Why would you cut a chunk out of your victim's body and then prop it up on a crutch so she's sitting up? What does that mean?"

"Jill was propped on a crutch?" I asked, trying hard to fight the bile that was crawling up my throat.

"More like wedged. The perp stuck the crutch—or cane or whatever the thing was—behind the girl and wedged the handle beneath the shoulder blades where the spine should have been. That poor girl."

I felt sorry for Lisa. I had had trouble simply looking at Jill's face and couldn't imagine how I would have felt seeing her body, let alone having to study it as Lisa must be doing.

"Maybe it's a symbol or a message to someone. Like he was tired of carrying her, supporting her," I speculated.

She gave a nod of approval. "That's a thought. I was thinking more like the perp ripped her heart out, her guts, her being, then propped her up for the whole world to see he'd conquered her."

"You're the psychologist. Why a square?" I asked.

"Actually a rectangle. And that's the fifty-thousand-dollar question," she said, draining the balance of her beer.

"So, why do you think Jill didn't fight back, Lisa?"

"That bothers me the most. I've been wracking my brain trying to figure out a scenario where I would not fight for my life."

"And?"

"And I can't come up with one. Except if I were unconscious," she concluded.

"Was she? You mentioned drug overdose earlier," I pressed.

"Still too early to know for sure. Coroner suspects she was. Jill had a needle mark on the upper part of her right arm. Lab results aren't ready yet. But the coroner is sure we'll have something to work with," Lisa assured.

The oven timer alerted me that the brownies were ready. I pulled the pan from the oven and set it on a cooling rack. I retrieved two cold beers, handing one to Lisa and setting the other down on the coffee table in front of the couch. A few minutes later I went back for the pan of brownies and two forks. I folded my long legs underneath me on the couch beside Lisa, handing her one of the forks. We both dug in.

The pan was half empty and our bellies were full. Lisa tossed her fork aside and leaned back on the couch, holding her stomach. I did the same.

"She was wearing a weird dress," Lisa said in a small voice.

She was staring out the window, and I slowly leaned forward, straining to hear her.

"It looked like a costume. At this point, we don't think it's hers. Did you ever see her wear a dress? No, of course not. What was I thinking," Lisa said, her voice regaining strength. "She had on a pair of tennis shoes, but we don't think those were hers, either. They were way too big for her and there was no sand or mud or anything on the soles. They looked brand new, like they were just slipped on her feet after the fact."

"Strange," I said.

"That's not all. There were these weird little cabinets on the beach between Jill and the water. It looked like they were staged there for her to be looking at, if it wasn't for the fact that her face had been covered with a tea towel."

"You mean like a dish rag?"

"Yeah. I don't know what this guy was thinking, but the whole scene was bizarre, macabre, unreal . . ." Lisa's words trailed.

"And you're thinking this might be the work of a serial killer? You mean there is more than one body with the center hacked from the torso?"

Lisa's cell phone rang. She looked at me before answering the call and said, "Yes and no."

CHAPTER 8

WHILE THE PHONE RANG, Streeter looked at his watch. It was eight o'clock. He and Berta had been into the autopsy for nearly seven hours when he had decided to cut out, take a shower, and head back to his office for a few. Lisa Henry had left a message for him that she'd arrived in Fort Collins and was planning on finding a room in a local hotel. She would assess the situation and then talk with Doug Brandt and some of the key players before reporting to him on her findings.

Henry answered after two rings.

"How's it going?" he asked, popping the top off a cold can of soup and taking a swallow.

"The hotels are booked up here. I'm staying with a friend from college who happens to be the vic's boss."

"Is he on the up and up?"

Henry cleared her throat. "*She* didn't kill Jill Brannigan, if that's what you mean. I can vouch for her."

"Oh, you mean the Bergen woman, not Joe Renker. Is she sitting right there listening?" Streeter said, guzzling from the can a second time. It was the only thing he'd eaten since breakfast, and despite the day he'd just experienced, the tomato soup appealed to him.

"I'm outside now. Spent about two hours with Detective Doug Brandt. He is happy to have the FBI's assistance and confirmed that even if you didn't find what you were looking for during the autopsy, he'd love for us to take the lead."

"Can't unless we can find a jurisdictional reason," Streeter reminded her.

"He knows. He's trying. What did you find?"

Streeter took a deep breath. "Pretty sure it's heroin again. Berta wants to confirm some of the findings and will be spending the next two days or so with the scope. And multitasking by planting her foot so far up the laboratory's backside that they'll want to expedite the tests."

Henry laughed. Streeter imagined her clear, bright eyes and shy smile while she stood on some woman's porch. What he couldn't imagine was being a houseguest while working a case. It would drive him crazy not to have his solitude in the mountains to gather his thoughts, having instead to feign the enjoyment of company and being polite about it.

"Is the weather cooperating for Brandt?"

"It hasn't rained yet. They have the crime scene secured. I spent about half my time with Brandt on the scene. It's so darn cold up here compared to D.C., even this time of year. I almost forgot."

"Are you freezing standing outside? Because I can call you later if you'd rather," he offered, though he was hoping she would not accept.

"No, I'm fine."

"We'll go through all the evidence they've collected and review the photos. I'll meet you tomorrow morning at Brandt's office, and you can take me to the scene after we're through. Might as well make a day of it," he said, tossing the empty soup can into the wastebasket.

Streeter frequented Fort Collins from time to time as cases and leads found him in the area. He hadn't been there since the Jaspar case three years before. And the opportunity to meet Brandt had never presented itself then. What he dreaded was the return to Horsetooth Reservoir, because the only other time he'd been there was to watch a sunset with Paula. And she had made it a memorable sunset for him. Moon rising as the sun was setting. Spectacular.

"I take it that means you and Dr. Johnson confirmed your suspicions," Henry said.

"We have a serial case on our hands," Streeter answered. "Whatever the killer used to sever the core from Jill Brannigan was the same instrument used in the de Milo case last October."

"So you're the new lead?"

"Appears so."

"Doug Brandt will do cartwheels," Henry said.

"It's more important than ever that you're working with me on this, Henry. I need this guy's profile. I need you to reach deep and tell me what this bastard is up to." The pencil Streeter had been tapping snapped in his fingers. He tossed both ends in the wastebasket and plowed his thick fingers through his hair.

"Does Dr. Johnson have any idea, yet, what made the cut in either this case or in the de Milo case?"

Because of the way the killer had left one of the vics' torsos near Platteville, just north of Denver, the FBI had referred to the case file as the "Venus de Milo Murderer," shortened to the de Milo case. In the de Milo killings the cuts were all made in one direction. Streeter spread the pictures of today's autopsy across his screen, zooming in on the tissue of Jill Brannigan's midsection. The cuts were in one direction, no sawing motions. The motion was from front to back, as if a hunk of skin, bone, and organs had been forced out of her by a blast of some kind. It reminded Streeter of those horrible images he brought back in his tortured mind after his time in Mogadishu. Jill's skin hadn't been singed or burned in any way, and the force of whatever had torn through the tissue was strong enough to nearly cauterize the blood vessels, which staunched the blood flow. As Brandt had said, it truly was as though a giant hand had come down and punched a cookie cutter into Jill Brannigan's torso.

Whatever it was, it was strong enough to cut through her spine in two places and her ribs, although what bones she had left in her midsection had been shattered by force. As Streeter studied the photos, what amazed him was the precision. Just as in the de Milo case, the killer was meticulous with each cut, careful not to damage any other part of the victims' bodies. It made Streeter wonder if the killer was a surgeon, a welder, a butcher, or an expert in some other profession that demanded such precision. But he didn't want to share his thoughts with Lisa Henry. Not until she had a chance to draw her own conclusions. Then they would talk, compare notes.

"We have forensics trying to mimic the cut pattern and have been for the past nine months. No knife or saw-blade patterns we've tried can replicate the patterns in the de Milo case so far. They've even tried blow torches and saw blades," Streeter answered.

Henry added, "That means you've narrowed down the weapon to something unusual, which is bound to help you locate whoever made the purchase."

"If we ever figure out what it is that's making the unusual cut pattern," Streeter reminded her. "Look, let me send you these digitals so you can study them tonight. I'll bring my files up and we can compare notes after we've drawn our own conclusions on this thing. I have enough that if you can compile some kind of profile for me by tomorrow night, I can fire a battery of questions your way so we can get this thing hemmed in."

"Shouldn't be too tough since I have my profile from the de Milo case. I want to see if my conclusions for you on that case morph or focus any more clearly after tomorrow," Henry said.

"That's what I was hoping," Streeter confirmed. "Thanks, kiddo. I'll see you at Brandt's around eight."

Lisa came through the door and shrugged out of her jacket. "Brrr. I forgot how cold it gets here."

"It's June."

"It's cold."

I gave her a look. "You *have* forgotten, because Laramie is a helluva lot colder than it is here in Fort Collins. Don't you remember stealing away on the weekends just to mall crawl or movie hop to warm up indoors? We used to think Fort Collins was like some tropical island for us compared to Siberia."

"We did have a tendency to exaggerate, didn't we?" Lisa said, plopping beside me on the couch.

I put my book down. "Exaggerate, my ass. During the five o'clock news, I saw where the high in Laramie today was fifty degrees compared to seventy here in Fort Collins. Can you imagine how cold it must have been six months ago?"

Lisa shivered. "I used to schedule my classes according to where the underground tunnels reached and how far away the buildings were from the tunnels."

"No wonder you dropped the law dream. That building was a mile away," I laughed.

"With no tunnels."

Her words trailed and I could see that although she was trying to be relaxed, she was distracted by what she'd learned from her phone call. I wanted to give her the space she needed, but I was dying to know what she meant during our conversation just before she took the call.

"Lisa, you said 'yes and no' when I asked you whether the other victims had been cut the same way Jill had been. Did you mean yes and no about this being the gruesome handiwork of a serial killer, but this might be a copycat, or did you mean yes you have a serial killer on your hands and no there is not more than one body with a chunk cut out of it?"

"Uh-huh," Lisa said, reading through the notes she had taken earlier in the day.

"Which uh-huh?" I asked.

"The second."

"So this is a serial killer, but the other murder or murders did not exactly match Jill's?"

"Right," Lisa said. She peered over her notebook. "But remember, this is not for public consumption, Liv. You can't be telling anyone what's happening here."

"I won't, Lisa. I know you don't want to panic people or incite the media. Tabloidic journalism is already an epidemic," I opined.

"Tabloidic? Is that even a word?" Lisa grinned.

"No. But it should be. Was it good news?" I pointed to her cell phone on the coffee table.

"What? The call? Yeah, it was good news. The autopsy was done after you left, and Special Agent Pierce was giving me a brief update. He's coming up tomorrow morning to spend the day."

I have no idea what overtook me in the moment, but I was struck with a brilliant idea that I would reflect on ruefully days later. "Well, since you don't have a hotel room, do you guys want to use this house as your base camp?"

"Headquarters, you mean?" Lisa said.

"Why not? I'll be at work all day, and I won't bother you guys a bit. I can stay out of your way and simply need a place to crash each night and shower in the morning. Otherwise, I'll just camp out at work."

Lisa laid her notebook on her lap. "You'd do that for us?"

"For *you*, and for Jill. I don't know these other guys."

"Thanks. We might take you up on that. I doubt it, though. We're hoping to use Detective Brandt's office as our makeshift headquarters, but it all depends on how dicey it gets with his boss."

"Chief of Police Mel Richardson?" I asked. "Of Fort Collins? Well then, I better go buy more coffee and food, because both your FBI asses will be kicked to the curb as soon as you pull jurisdiction," I said.

Lisa simply stared at me.

"Control freak," I explained. "Even Detective Brandt may need somewhere to light after your meeting in the morning. Invite him along too. *Mi casa es su casa.*"

"You're insane."

"Like you said, some things never change."

I pushed myself off the couch and went back to my bedroom, bringing out my desk chair and placing it in the kitchen. I went back to retrieve my computer, then my monitor, and set them on the kitchen table.

"What are you doing?" Lisa asked.

I motioned to her. "Come help me a minute."

She followed me back to my bedroom, and together we carried the large desk into the living room. I set my end of the desk down next to the bare wall by the fireplace. She followed my lead. We pushed the couch against one wall and put the easy chairs opposite the couch centered by the coffee table. Within minutes, we had a war room.

"Local stations are on channels two, four, seven, nine, and fourteen. Fox News is on Channel 31, and I can never find CNN."

I grabbed my coat and billfold and headed for the garage.

"Where are you going?"

"To the grocery store to stock up. When I get back, I expect you to have your car parked in the garage. I'll be parking out on the street."

"I can't do that to you. This is your house," she protested.

"It's the least I can do for you. And for Jill, remember?" I leveled my gaze. "I want to help. This makes me feel a bit more useful."

Lisa was dumbfounded. She stood, mouth agape, and stared. Shaking her head, she said, "You're already letting me sleep here. I'll eat your food, Liv. But I'm not using your garage. Okay?"

"You're still stubborn. Thanks for letting me help by feeding you. It's the very least I can do," I said.

With that I was down the stairs and out the door that led into the garage.

My Explorer wasn't there, and for a moment I couldn't for the life of me recall what had happened to it. Then I remembered I had driven to Denver with the policewoman, leaving my SUV at work. I turned to go back inside when I saw through the garage window that someone had parked it in my driveway. Joe. He had given me a ride back from Denver and must have arranged to have someone bring the Explorer to me from work. I thought for the thousandth time that I didn't know what I'd do without him.

As I drove away, I realized how the lights in my living room made the place come alive.

CHAPTER 9

FRIDAYS ARE GREAT DAYS at work. Although several of our customers operate seven days a week, twenty-four hours a day, three hundred sixty-five days a year, like we do, many don't. Fridays tend to be the most relaxed days for those with a normal five-day workweek. The weekend allows us time to replenish our empty silos, as well as our tired bodies and overworked minds, and Fridays provide a perfect springboard to end the week productively with customers, vendors, and haulers.

I slipped out of the house before five-thirty, hoping to let Lisa sleep. I had heard her up reading, studying, and typing notes until two this morning. I prayed she and Agent Pierce would have a rewarding and successful day.

My first stop was at my office. After all, I had been at work for just a few hours the day before when I was whisked off to Denver by that awful policewoman. I had barely had enough time to call Brethren Social Assistance to arrange for an on-site grief counselor to be available yesterday afternoon for my employees. Probably could have used some time with them myself.

Speed reading through my e-mails and answering those that couldn't wait until Monday, I focused on the stack of mail, reports, invoices, and requests in my inbox, quickly sorting and prioritizing my workload. After collecting all my voice mails and jotting down numbers so I could return calls, I glanced up at the clock. Eight fifteen. Lisa was at Detective Brandt's office with Agent Pierce and Chief Richardson. Joe would be done with plant shift change and having set the direction for the quarry and maintenance crew. By now he'd be well into digging through his morning pile of invoices and messages.

I bounded down the hall, out the door, and nearly jogged toward Joe's office trailer across the lot.

"How'd it go last night with BSA?"

Joe looked up from his pile of invoices. "They sent Cindy."

"Great," I answered. The employees were comfortable with Cindy; she was the one who conducted the annual Employee Assistance Program speeches each January. "Any major issues?"

Joe shook his head. Wounded, I thought as I read his eyes.

I offered a conciliatory smile, "Besides you?"

He offered a sad smile. "Everyone was thankful you brought Cindy in. No one wanted to ask her for one-on-one time, but they all hung pretty tight around her from about six to seven. Mostly plant guys."

"Makes sense. The quarry guys didn't know Jill as well as the rest of us."

He nodded.

"And you?" I already knew the answer, but had to ask.

"Did I talk with Cindy? Nah," Joe said. "I'm fine."

"That's what Jim Bowie told Davy Crockett at the Alamo," I argued. That earned me a smile. "Have you cleaned out her locker, yet?"

Joe shook his head. "Didn't know if Detective Brandt or Officer McDouglas would want to go through it first."

Officer Jan McDouglas. The pushy policewoman. My cheeks burned. "Officer McDouglas can go—"

"Liv," Joe warned. "Watch your language. New Year's resolution, remember?"

I didn't have the heart to tell him it was a lost cause.

I knew that Lisa wanted me to keep up the illusion that Detective Brandt was the lead on this case and figured she and Agent Pierce would want anything we had of Jill's that might help them piece things together.

"I doubt if Brandt or McSmarty-Pants will be back anytime soon. I wouldn't want Jill's stuff to get misplaced or rifled through by anyone but her parents. Let's at least box it up and give it to the Brannigans."

Sounded logical. The reality was I intended to take the box home, to the new FBI headquarters, considering it would be a cold day in hell before Chief Richardson ever let the FBI use Brandt's office. Lisa and the Denver agent she was assigned to could go through all of Jill's personal belongings and glean whatever they could.

"You really think Detective Brandt won't be back up here? To question me?" Joe asked.

"No worries, Joe," I answered. His secret about Jill's thankful kiss on his cheek would be safe with me. "They may be back, but we can stick with what we know of Jill's work and who she gravitated toward on breaks. Okay?"

Relief washed over his lined face.

"Come on," I waved. "Let's go clear out her locker."

On my way out the door, I grabbed an empty box from the lab. Joe was close on my heels. We walked across the gravel road toward the plant, bypassing my office. Joe led me to the lower break room next to the unisex bathroom and tapped on the third locker from the left on the bottom row, indicating the one that had been assigned to Jill. The locker was padlocked.

"Cut it," I said.

Joe disappeared next door to the plant maintenance shop and returned with bolt cutters. One hardy snip and we were in. Jill had left her hard hat and her coveralls hanging on the hooks. The coveralls were dusty but had no rips or tears in them yet. Her hard hat was adorned with three stickers: one that said "Safety First," one that had our company logo, and one that said "Go Rams!" On the floor of the locker, Jill had placed her steel-toed boots side by side with the laces neatly tucked inside each boot. On the top shelf of the locker cabinet, we found a blue bandana, a paperback edition of *Crime and Punishment*, and a silver chain necklace from which some heart-shaped charms hung. I placed the boots in the box first. After carefully folding Jill's coveralls, I laid them atop the boots, scooped the contents from the shelf onto the coveralls, and placed the hard hat in the box last.

The whole process was more emotionally challenging than I had imagined it would be, and Joe must have experienced the same weightiness I had felt, if his sigh was any indication.

"She turned in her time card Saturday night," he said.

"Let me guess," I added. "On time and completed without a single error?"

"Yep."

"The Jill Brannigans of the world are hard to find."

"And even harder to lose."

I placed the lid on the box and hefted it from the ground. Joe closed the locker door and ceremoniously peeled the sticker bearing Jill Brannigan's name off the front. We both bowed our heads for a minute and quietly left the change room.

He stayed beside me as I walked to my Explorer with the box. "She didn't mean a thing by that kiss, Joe, other than to thank you and tell you how much she appreciated your kindness."

I had told him before, but I sensed he needed reminding.

"Thanks," he said, opening the door to my backseat.

I set the box down and closed the door. "Anytime. Want to make a round through the plant with me?"

He nodded. "Kyle's taking this the hardest."

"Think he had a crush on Jill?"

"I think the entire team had a crush on Jill. What's not to like about the girl?"

We took the catwalks along the conveyor and the steps up to the highest reaches of the plant, listening and looking at every piece of equipment as we passed. We pulled some samples along the way and shook them through sieves to check for quality. When we got to the top of the silos, we looked down below at the scale and the trucks waiting to be loaded, over to the quarry, and beyond the pit to the Rocky Mountains.

"Where are all the guys?"

We hadn't seen any of the other four plant team members for this shift. Normally we would have at least seen the material handler loading trucks or the assistant charging the hopper for the dryer with feedstone, but we hadn't seen a single soul for the past thirty minutes.

Joe said, "Maybe after sleeping on it, they're struggling more today over the news than they were yesterday."

"Think we should bring Cindy back?"

"Let's find Allan and ask what's up."

We finally found Allan, Greg, and Oliver in the control room. Looking a bit sheepish, they started to scatter when Joe and I came through the door.

"Hey, guys," I said, stopping their retreat. "Sorry about Jill and not being able to come see you about it yesterday."

They made rumblings, but nothing coherent.

"Did it help to have Cindy here?"

Allan nodded. The other two kicked at invisible rocks on the control room floor. Not the boisterous, opinionated guys I had grown accustomed to. I hadn't seen them this mulish since the Christmas party following the summer when I had hired a stripper as a material handler because she said she wanted to turn her life around. Night-shift workers' spouses were not real thrilled with me that year. Not one of my finer moments. Tough on the guys as well.

"I'm thinking about seeing if she could come back again today," I suggested. I wanted to send out the trial balloon to gauge their reaction. I got some subtle head bobbing but nothing definitive until I added, "For me, of course, since I didn't get to talk with her."

Cindy would be coming. They still needed her. Or something.

"Where's Kyle?" I asked.

"Over with Terry," Oliver said. "They're talking with some of the drivers."

"About Jill?"

More nods.

"What are you guys hearing? Besides a bunch of bullshit rumors," I asked.

That brought them around a little bit. Fleeting smiles, at least.

Greg looked at the imaginary rock and kept kicking and swaying. "Heard she was cut to bits, boss. Heard she was hurt bad."

He never looked up. I scanned the other faces. None of the men would look me in the eye. I was no psychologist, but I couldn't help but wonder if this was about me being a woman and them having heard something about Jill being raped. So I asked, "Are there rumors that Jill was raped?"

Allan nodded and elbowed Greg. "Go on."

"Well, we heard she was raped," Greg began, "and that she was cut bad all over her body. And her face. And that's why they aren't showing nothing on the news except those basketball pictures of her."

"Well, none of that's true. At least the part about her being cut all over her body and face," I said. "And as far as rape goes, they haven't even received the lab results yet, so whatever you're hearing are unfounded rumors."

"Ask her," Oliver whispered to Greg.

Allan jabbed Greg again with his elbow.

"Well, you always told us that you hate rumors and that if we heard something that bothered us, we should just ask you and you'd tell us the truth. Straight from the horse's mouth, you said."

"And I meant that," I said.

I braced for what might come. I chose not to lie to my employees, and I encouraged directness to combat rumors. But in this situation, I was obligated to Lisa to keep quiet about what I knew and was walking a fine line between not lying and not divulging too much about what I knew of the case.

"We heard you saw Jill yesterday," Greg finally blurted.

I hadn't noticed I'd been holding my breath. Relief allowed me to blow it all out before answering. "I did. Officer Jan McDouglas from the Fort Collins Police Department stopped by yesterday morning to escort me to Denver to identify Jill's body. Her younger sister is also a student at CSU and was still torn up by all the news. The authorities wanted to start the autopsy as soon as possible, but Jill's parents were in transit from Wisconsin. So they asked if Joe or I would identify the body."

"How'd she look?" Greg asked.

The control room was as quiet and still as I'd ever heard it. All four men were rigid, awaiting my answer. My mind went to that lifeless face, so unlike Jill's, which was always full of life. I wasn't about to describe her deathly pallor, so I grasped whatever I could from the truth of what I saw.

"It was Jill, no doubt. She looked like . . . like Jill. There were no cuts or bruises that I could see on her face, neck, or shoulders, so I can tell you for sure, some of those rumors you're hearing are not true."

Their eyebrows were still highlighting the concern in their eyes. They collectively held their breath. What did they want from me? I didn't have the power to take away their concern that Jill suffered. She was dead. What suffering is worse than losing a life? Their faces told me the answer: what's worse might be the survivors' suffering over a lost life. I knew if I saw Jill's sister or parents' faces, I'd know for sure their suffering would be the worst of all.

"Look. I'm no doctor or psychologist. But I was struck by the sense that Jill died quietly, despite the hole. Something in her face. It wasn't terror or pain. I can't describe it," I answered, as honestly as I knew how.

At some point while I was speaking, Kyle had walked into the control room behind me. The others' eyes landed on him, and I turned to see what they were seeing. Kyle's eyes were wide and bloodshot.

"Kyle? Are you all right?" I asked.

Kyle's voice was unsteady, incongruous with his sturdy six-foot-three, two-hundred-fifty-pound frame. "It's all over the news. The drivers. They told me and Terry."

"What did they tell you?" Joe asked.

I couldn't imagine what would have made the news by this early in the day. Maybe it was leaked to the press that the Fort Collins Police Department no longer had jurisdiction over the case and that the FBI was taking over. Maybe the coroner had released some of the early findings. It would be too soon for Lisa to make any conclusions on the behavioral profile or for Agent Pierce to be making any statements or release anything to the press. Maybe it was about Detective Brandt turning in his resignation because Chief Richardson was a pompous, egocentric ass. But it turned out to be none of my various speculations.

"It's de Milo, the serial killer. The Venus de Milo murderer killed Jill."

CHAPTER 10

AS HE SIPPED HIS water with the twist of lime, he read the captions as fast as they flashed on the muted TV above the bar. The anchorwoman was describing the breaking news that Jill Brannigan, the popular CSU student who was murdered west of Fort Collins, was indeed the third victim of the Venus de Milo murderer.

How he hated that stupid moniker.

And how completely asinine the FBI had been for choosing it. They weren't even close. The least those idiots at the Bureau could have done was to name him the "*Aphrodite* murderer," a more accurate and poetic name than the more popular name—Venus de Milo—for the same statue.

Upon further reflection, though, the parallels between who he was and what they were calling him began to come sharply into focus. Yes, the Venus de Milo was missing her arms. So were many of his models.

The ancient statue of Aphrodite had limbs originally, just as his models had. Only he intentionally removed the limbs from his models, something Alexandros never intended to do with Venus, arms breaking accidentally while being loaded on a ship. He was proud of his superiority in that his art was intentional, not accidental.

And the sculptor, Alexandros of Antioch, was a copyist, creating bizarre and striking images of life, just as he did. The brilliance of Alexandros's ability to add original twists to his work was similar to his own. Although, he mocked life with far superior ability than Alexandros dared to do.

And finally, he would be revered in centuries to come, just as Alexandros, both men living in decadent periods of history.

He studied the images of the stony-faced man with a white butch haircut and the lovely girl with long black hair leaving the Fort Collins police station with Detective Doug Brandt. He followed the captions to find out who the people accompanying the detective were. But his instincts already told him. Those two were FBI, the idiots who were calling him the Venus de Milo murderer. Simply because of the way he had staged, more like molded . . . no, *carved* his models.

He grinned at the thought of his Great Masturbator. That poor, unsuspecting couple lying along the riverbank outside of Platteville had been quite perfect for his purpose. He had spent the entire evening enjoying his models and molding them into the surrealism of his own sexual neurosis. Not that he, too, suffered from nightmares that *his mother* might one day devour his penis but, rather, that such a horror could exist in the brilliance of his sculpture. Fascinating.

The work gave him a sense of validation and comfort. After all, he did suffer from a fear of being brutally chomped by one of his sexual partners, yet neither being able nor wanting to deny himself the pleasure of sexual intimacy. Resisting but always yielding to erotic release, like he had experienced the day before with Tina from Martini's. Not to challenge his hero's brilliance, but the Great Masturbator should have been more aptly titled "Succubus" or "Incubus."

And why had they seen his models as the Venus de Milo? Because of the pretty girl's face, perhaps? A likeness to the Greek goddess of love and beauty? Or maybe it was because she no longer had arms. Or legs. But didn't they find the locust? The tongue? And his male model was quite Apollo-like, particularly in his tighty whities. But mostly, he suspected, the FBI bestowed the name upon him because of his genius, his carving. Yet they hadn't truly seen it. They hadn't grasped what he was attempting with his five masterpieces to date.

In fact, the imbecilic FBI agents hadn't even associated his other three works of art with these two. He understood why they had made the connection between the latest and likely greatest of his works so far—Nutrition, or as others knew it, the popular CSU student Jill Brannigan—and that nice couple he molded into his Succubus. No, he should be respectful to the master. The couple would remain the Great Masturbator. But why hadn't the investigators seen it in his personal favorite, the hermaphrodite, his Bather?

A smile slid across his lips. Hermaphrodite. Aphrodite. Maybe the FBI weren't so far off after all? The moniker, considering the juxtaposition, was starting to grow on him. So close, and yet so incredibly far. He would need to do better; show them more, lead them closer. An example, a clue. Maybe two.

Squinting, he committed the faces of the man and woman standing next to Detective Brandt to memory. The man was menacing, stern. He reminded him of his own father, a perfect William Tell, trying to shoot an apple from his head, the threatening presence that he so wanted to eliminate. The girl pleased him. She was lovely and soft, but her steps were sure and quick. She would be a wonderful model. He imagined her sleeping—a dreamless, timeless sleep. A sleep so deep that the bitch would forget about her schedules and calendars and deadlines. The woman walked with purpose and precision, which detracted from her beauty and prohibited her from being his perfect model. His Awakening.

Time was running out for him, and it seemed as if this woman was turning up the volume on the ticking time bomb of discovery he had worked so carefully to avoid. It was time for him to find out who she was. If he was right, and these two with Brandt were FBI, they were likely going to the crime scene.

─────────────

"Hello, Awakening," he murmured. Within minutes of parking in a remote area alongside the reservoir on the eastern shore, he spotted them through

his binoculars. William Tell and Awakening. Detective Brandt was showing them around, pointing out something in the rocks and showing them
what appeared to be photographs.

"I've got better ones I could show you," he whispered.

He watched Brandt tap one of the pictures and point toward the
water's edge. He lowered the binoculars and glanced first at his watch and
then around him to make sure none of the many other spectators and news
reporters had come anywhere close to where he had positioned himself.
He counted dozens of cars along the road where he had parked and twice
as many along the western side of the reservoir. He figured there must be
at least a hundred and fifty people camped on the shores, on the rocks, and
along the road, each with a front-row seat to the biggest show to hit Fort
Collins in years.

No one would take note of him. And even if they did, he was no more
guilty than the rest of these rubberneckers were. He settled back into his
car and decided to wait this one out, watching William Tell and Awakening until he could find out for certain who they were and how he should
cast them in his next little scene.

A woman and a man interrupted Brandt's discussion. He lifted the
binoculars. The man had a camera on his shoulder with the call letters to
a local television station stenciled in bright red above the lens. He shifted
his binoculars to the right and recognized the blonde as a local anchorwoman for the evening news. He saw Brandt wave his arms and yell something at them. William Tell grabbed Brandt's arm and leaned toward him,
their heads close, to whisper something to him, perhaps. William Tell then
shook the hands of the news team, and Awakening followed suit.

"Chummy," he mumbled.

Nevertheless, Brandt launched into a diatribe of some sort, and the
anchorwoman looked like she was apologizing to him. William Tell then
led the two newspeople aside and eventually under the yellow crime scene
tape toward their news van.

"Clever. He just escorted them politely to the exit and the blonde is still
smiling about it. Doesn't even know what hit her. Good one, Mr. Tell."

He swung the binoculars down to the shoreline and saw that Awakening was cajoling Detective Brandt and he too was smiling.

"You're clever too, eh, Awakening? I'll have to be very careful with you two. Treat you with the special care your intelligence deserves. And make sure your de Milo remains faceless."

He settled in for a long afternoon, careful not to doze. He watched Tell and Awakening study the pictures, reports, and maps, and then talk to Brandt, the criminalists, the technicians. He watched them comb the rocky shore in a tight grid, back and forth, back and forth. He watched them sit, think, write, and study the entire scene.

Eventually, his eyes caught the news van pulling away from the road-side and lumbering up the hill to the east of the reservoir. They were coming his way. He pulled his truck out in front of the van as if not noticing their approach and heard it screech to a halt and blare its horn. He feigned alarm and jumped out of his truck.

As he approached the van, he saw the cameraman rolling down his window.

"I am so terribly sorry. I didn't see you coming up the road. Please accept my apologies."

The cameraman scowled.

"Truly. Forgive me. This is such a distraction, a circus." He waved toward all the parked cars. "More like a nightmare, actually."

The cameraman nodded. "It's okay. No harm, no foul."

"I just flew into DIA and was on my way home when I ran into all of this. What's going on here?"

The anchorwoman leaned over. "The Venus de Milo struck again."

He gasped. "No. In Fort Collins?"

She nodded.

"Who? When?"

"A college student. They found her yesterday morning," the blonde answered.

"Oh, dear Lord. Please tell me the proper authorities are working on this," he said.

The cameraman nodded. "FBI arrived today."

"Oh, thank God. Do they have an SAC designated yet?"

"An SAC?" the blonde asked.

He chuckled. "Sorry, old habits die hard. My father was with the FBI. Special agent in charge. The one who's lead on the case."

"Oh, that would be Special Agent Pierce," the cameraman answered.

"Streeter," the anchorwoman added.

"Streeter Pierce," he repeated. "A man?"

The cameraman nodded. "He's got a hottie tagging along with him."

"He brought his wife?"

The anchorwoman scowled. "Lisa is a behavioral profiler."

"Lisa?"

"Special Agent Henry," the cameraman added.

The car pulling up behind the news van sounded its horn.

The cameraman waved. "Better get going."

"Oh, hey, please. Again, so sorry."

"Don't sweat it," the cameraman said, rolling up his window.

He jumped back into his truck and pulled back into his parking spot alongside the road, waving timidly as the news van passed him. The driver in the car behind the news van flipped him the bird as she drove by.

He returned the favor and grinned. He turned off the car and resumed watching the scene at the shoreline. He'd been right. They were FBI. William Tell was in charge of the case. Awakening was in charge of finding *him*. She was indeed the ticking time bomb he thought she was.

Ticktock. Ticktock.

Awakening would need to go first.

He studied her for the rest of the afternoon. As darkness stole the sky, the FBI agents found their way to their cars. Awakening pulled onto the road and William Tell fell in behind her. They were coming his way up the hill. He nonchalantly pulled in behind them, careful to keep his eye on Awakening's car the entire time. He was not going to try to find out where both of them were staying tonight. Just Awakening.

But as luck would have it, William Tell stuck close to Awakening's tail, not that he blamed Tell for that. Awakening had quite the tail. He followed them into a nice, quiet neighborhood ten minutes from the reservoir. Awakening pulled to the curb of a two-story blue house on a small cul-de-sac. William Tell parked behind her.

He kept driving and circled the block to make sure they were both still at the blue house.

They were. He glanced at his watch and saw that it was too late to get the homeowner's name from the courthouse. Then he thought of the library. He could access the county's mapping system to find out who lived here. That could help him figure out why these two were staying at the house. First, he would wait to see if this was a short visit or something more. He leaned back in the driver's seat and watched through the big picture windows as the two settled next to what looked like a desk with computers and monitors in what should have been the living room area.

Three hours later, William Tell, aka Agent Streeter Pierce, emerged from the front door and took off down the street. Within fifteen minutes, another car pulled onto the street. He ducked down as the lights swept through his windshield. He poked his head up in time to see a white Ford Explorer pulling into the garage of the blue house. After a few minutes, a woman appeared in the window with Awakening, aka Agent Lisa Henry. Again the two huddled around the desk, staring at whatever Agent Henry had pulled up on the computer screen. The woman was not as striking as the FBI agent was; this one was shorter and not as thin, her hair brown. She walked with the same confidence as Awakening had, however, strong and sure.

That must be the owner, or at least the wife of the owner. He decided to pull online information about her tonight at the library.

"I'll be right back, ladies," he clucked as he pulled away from the curb.

CHAPTER 11

"YOU JUST MISSED HIM, Liv," Lisa said as I walked into the kitchen.

"Shoot, I was really looking forward to meeting him. I stayed late tonight at work hoping to give you guys time to work, if you decided this was home base."

"Headquarters. And it is. You were right. Police Chief Richardson blew up when Streeter took over the case. Held a press conference against our wishes and told the whole fricking world that we were looking for the de Milo murderer."

"I heard that," I admitted. "What an SOB. Nothing like putting Pierce's ass in a sling before he even gets started."

Lisa nodded. "That's what I said. Just not quite that colorfully."

I opened the lid of the box I had brought with me. "Hey, I've got some good news, I think."

"What?"

I pulled Jill's hard hat from the box and set it aside so I could show Lisa Jill's personal belongings. "Joe and I cleared out Jill's locker today. Thought it might help with the investigation somehow."

"Thanks," Lisa said. "Did you happen to find a necklace?"

"With three heart-shaped charms with *Mom*, *Dad*, and *Julia* engraved on them?"

"That's the one," Lisa sighed. "Her mom called. Said Jill wore it everywhere. She wanted it back if we recovered it."

My chest swelled.

"And I thought this was the best part." I grabbed the book from the box with my hand tucked in the sleeve of my shirt. No prints of mine would mess up this case. With my other hand, also tucked deep in my sleeve, I fanned the book until it fell open to the page where a folded letter was stuck tightly in the binding. "I thought this might help."

Lisa stared at the letter. "What is it?"

"We didn't touch anything with our bare hands. As a matter of fact, we tried to touch as little as possible. I saw this sticking out of the book right away and noticed that the handwriting doesn't match Jill's. It's a letter from someone. Maybe it's a clue."

Jinkies, Velma, *maybe*? I was so out of my league with Lisa.

Lisa cocked her head to one side. "Possibly. But it's not likely we'll find a letter from the killer stashed in Jill's belongings stating he intended to murder her or anything."

"Oh, don't be a dullard. I know that. I'm just saying that maybe there's a name on that letter of someone close to Jill who can help answer some questions."

Lisa pulled on some gloves she had stuffed in her pocket.

"You carry latex gloves in your pocket? Damn, this girl's prepared."

Lisa chuckled. "They've been there since this afternoon. From when we were out at the crime scene."

"How was that?"

"Interesting. Strange. Sad."

"I'll bet."

"And helpful."

"Good," I said. I looked at the clock. Eight twenty. "Want me to make you some dinner, or have you already eaten?"

"That would be great," she said, her fingers delicately unfolding the penned letter.

I washed my hands and got to work. I diced some onions and peppers, tears streaming down my cheeks. "How about stir-fry and rice?"

"That sounds perfect," she said. "Mind making some for Streeter too?"

"He's coming back?" I wiped the tears from my face and tossed the peppers and onions in the frying pan I'd coated with some olive oil. "I just assumed he went back to Denver when you said he'd left."

"No, he went to interview Jill's little sister, Julia. It was the first chance he'd had."

"So he's planning on staying here?"

"Hope that's okay. Still no hotel rooms."

"I'm thrilled to be able to help."

I pulled some precooked and shelled shrimp from the freezer and ran cold water over the bag. I poured a box of instant rice into a bowl, added the butter and water, and popped it in the microwave. I opened a bottle of white wine and poured some in two glasses, taking one to Lisa. She was still reading the letter, her brows furrowed.

"What is it?"

"Sounds like a love letter. Kind of," she said, flipping to the next page.

She read quietly for another few minutes, so I retreated to the kitchen to stir the sautéed vegetables and the rice and to check on the thawing shrimp. I grabbed my glass of wine and returned to the living room. She set the letter on her lap.

"Ever hear Jill mention someone by the name of Jonah?"

I shook my head and sipped my wine.

"It sounds like this Jonah character overstepped a friendship boundary with Jill and made a pass at her or something. It's kind of like an apology; a please-give-me-another-chance letter."

"Nothing unusual about that. So why the concerned expression?"

"I don't even know the guy, yet he freaks me out with the way he's gushing about her and pleading for her to get to know him better. It goes on and on about what a great guy he is and how his father worked so hard to provide for his mother, and how he wants to care for her in the same way."

"Think they were dating?" I asked.

"No." She picked up the letter again and scanned through the pages until she found what she was looking for. "Here. It says: 'Not that it was a real date, but I thought it was proper to give you a good-night kiss when I dropped you off. My intention was just a kiss, and I see my mistake now.

Hindsight is a great teacher! I am so sorry. I should have waited until we went on our first date to make such a bold move,' and it goes on and on."

"Do you suppose he tried more than a kiss?"

"Don't know," Lisa said, laying the letter carefully on the desk. "Thanks for this, Liv. It may be a clue after all. And if we need to lift some prints from this, you did the right thing by not touching it."

"Why would she be carrying the letter around with her? Was it dated?"

"No, but it did say 'Midnight Friday,' as though it mattered what time he wrote the stupid blathering."

"If he wrote it the night before her last day of work, Jill would have had to be at work Saturday morning at six. And Saturday was her last day of work. Is it possible she saw this Jonah guy sometime between midnight and five thirty?"

Lisa cocked her head to one side. "Or he left it for her somewhere to find as she left for work: in her car, under a wiper blade, against the door of her dorm room. Somewhere so that she grabbed it and took it to work with her."

"Or he could have given it to her some other Friday, an earlier week."

"Let me call Streeter so he can add that to his list of questions as he interviews Julia Brannigan and Kari Smithson." She pulled her cell phone from her pocket and started punching numbers.

"Who's Kari Smithson?"

"Jill's roommate."

I finished making dinner while also eavesdropping on Lisa's call with Agent Pierce. I'm such a competent multitasker. She relayed the information about the letter and suggested he ask the girls if they knew a Jonah.

"Tell them we found Jill's necklace." Lisa offered me a smile. "Liv did, at work. In Jill's locker along with the letter."

From Lisa's comments, it sounded like Agent Pierce was in the middle of talking with Julia and Jill's parents, who had arrived from Wisconsin. Poor bastard. Lisa mentioned I was making dinner for them, and she fell silent for several minutes before closing her cell phone and shoving it in her pocket. She took a drink of wine, draining half of her glass.

I handed her a plate and offered to refill her glass, only to be waved off.

"I have to finish my profile while Streeter's gone. He won't be back for quite some time. He said he had his hands full with the Brannigans, and he had told Kari Smithson he wanted to talk with her later tonight when she got off work at ten."

"Too bad. Well, go ahead and eat his share. You need to keep up your strength, right?"

"Do you mind making him a plate for later? He told me to tell you thank you for dinner. He hasn't eaten since breakfast."

"No problem."

We both shoveled our food as fast as we could chew. Lisa talked around each bite. "This Richardson press conference is really going to screw up our investigation. The only one that his stunt helped was the de Milo murderer."

"It's really another de Milo murder?"

She nodded. "The coroner has concluded that the strange cuts on the couple found at Platteville were the same as on Jill's body."

Curiosity getting the better of me, I asked, "What happened at Platteville?"

She lifted a file from her satchel, flipped through some pages, and pulled out the glossy eight by tens, splaying them across the coffee table. I would have thought my stomach would have lurched at the sight or my appetite for dinner would have been spoiled, but miraculously, neither happened. Mental note to self: Avoid gruesome details about tragic events involving loved ones and friends. Objectivity is possible when strangers are involved.

As I scanned the photos, some close-ups of the victims and some of the areas surrounding the crime scene, depicting roads and farmhouses nearby, my eyes locked onto one particular photo. The tall grasses along the riverbank were matted down around the man and woman. The woman had no arms, no legs, no clothes. Her wavy red hair was splayed behind her head, which was turned to the left. Her lips were painted ruby red and nearly touched the groin of the man lying next to her. He had no arms, no head, and his legs were cut off at mid-shin. His chest was hairless, his stomach cut with six-pack abs. He was wearing nothing but tight white cotton briefs that revealed his bulge. Surprisingly, there was not as much blood as I would have expected.

"She's young," I said.

"Seventeen," Lisa said. "He was eighteen. They were high school sweethearts."

"What's this?" I pointed at the spot where the girl's genitals should have been.

"A locust."

"What? Like a grasshopper locust?"

Lisa gave a nod.

"And is this a cat?" I pointed to the chunk of meat between her left shoulder and his right thigh.

"A cat's head and tongue. We found the cat's body in the weeds nearby."

"And this?" I pointed at the girl's right hip.

"A fishhook."

"Shit. He sank it into her flesh." Like that was the worst of this girl's problems. I could imagine having a fishhook sunk into my flesh and knew it would hurt like hell. The rest of it was too mortifying for my mind to comprehend.

"He's sick, Liv."

"That's an understatement," I said, studying the array of photos.

Lisa finished her dinner and took her dish into the kitchen. "He's what we call an organized murderer. Jill's situation confirmed what I already knew. He's probably a white male between the ages of twenty and thirty-five and of above-average intelligence; the first born, he was most likely subjected to inconsistent discipline as a child, had a father who worked in a stable job; this guy is very controlled, works in a professional capacity, and is probably married or living with a partner. Our perp has dramatic mood swings but keeps a tight rein on them. Evidence suggests he's extremely controlled during the murders. And he was probably soaking up all of the news today like a sponge. Wouldn't be surprised if he was one of the bystanders out there on the road watching Detective Brandt work the crime scene yesterday or at Chief Richardson's press conference today."

"You got all that from these photos? Damn, you're good."

"If I was good, I could give Streeter this creep's name and we could bust the guy and go home," Lisa remarked.

"Anything new you learned from Jill's murder that changed your profile from the Platteville murders?"

"Well, I was thinking he might have a sexual neurosis of some sort, but now I'm not so sure."

"You mean he can't perform?" I asked.

"No, not really. People with one or more sexual neuroses often have normal sexual experiences. But at times they have unusual or abnormal fears or concerns that may or may not affect their performance. I suspect this guy is quite sexually competent."

"Did he rape Jill? Or the girl from Platteville?"

She shook her head and I breathed, not realizing I had been holding my breath.

"This guy is playing with us. He thinks he's smarter than we are. Brilliant, actually. And he's sure he won't get caught. I'm afraid if we don't get a line on him, the murders will become more frequent. And possibly more bizarre."

"Any clues?"

"Not at this point. He's smart enough not to leave any body fluids so that we can check DNA, no fingerprints, no boot prints, nothing. We were able to lift some tire treads at Horsetooth that will come in handy to link the murderer to the scene once we find him. Forensics are following that lead and trying to match them with the treads we lifted in Platteville."

She lay back on the couch and stared at the ceiling. I cleared the dishes and cleaned up the kitchen, making a plate for Agent Pierce and putting it in the refrigerator for later. Stir-fry was never better the second time around, particularly when it was made with shrimp. Satisfied that the kitchen was clean and having made sure there were fresh towels in Lisa's bathroom, I turned my focus on straightening up my bedroom and bathroom. I had decided to give Agent Pierce my room and I'd sleep on the basement couch. I'd fallen asleep there a time or two, and it was comfortable enough. My treadmill, a television set, my shelves of books, and a three-quarter bath were down there, so I had everything a girl could need. I put fresh sheets on my bed and fresh towels in my bathroom, tidying the counter. I was a neat freak anyway, so surprise houseguests never ruffled me much. I threw some clothes in a duffle and slung it over my shoulder.

I took the duffle downstairs and tossed it near the couch. I glanced around the room, and my eyes landed on a shelf full of my favorite classics. I pulled Fyodor Dostoevsky's *Crime and Punishment* off the shelf and flipped through some pages to refresh my memory on what the story was about. It came flooding back to me. The young college student who enacted in the real world his theory that a community would turn a blind eye to a crime if the murder victim was so abhorrent that they deemed they would be better off without that individual. Turned out that the young man killed a second person in order to conceal his identity as the murderer; the result was he suffered a self-induced illness that nearly killed him. The cause of his illness was his own remorse, guilt, isolation, and paranoia after the crimes.

It was a tough read as I remembered it, but in the end the murderer does the right thing. He turns himself in to the authorities and does his time for the two crimes he committed. Rather anticlimactic.

Why would Jill have been reading it? Was it a requirement for the independent study she was taking over the summer? Was she anticipating a need for reading it for a fall or a winter class and she wanted to get ahead because of her busy schedule once basketball practice began? Or was she reading it for fun? The paperback I had found in Jill's locker at work appeared new and unopened save for the makeshift bookmarker, the folded letter. No cracked spine. No dog-eared pages or creases. Maybe she hadn't started to read it yet. But why bring it to work with her? It's not like anyone has time to read out at the mine. Not even on breaks. I would ask Allan and the other team leaders if any of them had ever seen Jill read on breaks or at lunchtime.

Lisa was at the computer, waiting for a printout of her final report profiling the Venus de Milo murderer. She was staring out the front windows as I topped the stairs.

"What's wrong?"

"The weapon. It's the hardest part to figure out. And probably what's keeping us from piecing this together."

"What about the weapon?"

"We can't figure out what instrument de Milo used on the victims. Forensics have been cataloging all the various tools they've tried over the past nine months, including every variety of knife and chainsaw they could find." She rounded the desk and moved toward the coffee table.

"Does it take that long for the FBI to figure out what makes a cut like that?"

Lisa nodded. "Hundreds of cases, thousands of boxes of evidence, too much to do and too little time to do it in. Honestly, within a month they had exhausted their inventory of weapons and related cuts. The rest of the time is spent on dreaming up other possibilities not cataloged in our weapons inventory."

The close-up pictures from the Platteville case and Jill's torso were side by side. If I didn't think of it as Jill's body, I'd be okay.

"Look. See the regularity and single direction? On all three bodies. Identical."

The notching of tissue indeed looked identical on all three bodies. It reminded me of Yosemite Sam's cowboy hat after the cartoon cannonball went through it. As if a giant finger had poked through Jill while she was impersonating the Pillsbury Doughboy.

"Huh," was all I could say. Very clever *and* efficient. I could see why it was bothersome. Something familiar began to tickle the far reaches of my mind; I'd seen that kind of evenness before, but where? My mind was getting fuzzy and the hour late.

"Lisa, I'm bushed. Mind if I call it a night?"

"No problem. You going into work in the morning?"

"If you need me to. I don't want to be a bother here while you and Agent Pierce are calling this home—"

"Headquarters," Lisa groaned through clenched teeth, miming strangling me as she did.

"Okay, okay. I don't want to be a pest while this is your headquarters."

"We don't want to crowd you out either."

"Oh, I know. Listen, I'm sleeping downstairs so I can stay clear of your space. I put clean sheets in the master bedroom for Agent Pierce. He can stay there. I made a plate of dinner for him and covered it with blue Saran Wrap and put it in the refrigerator. Just have him nuke it in the microwave for a minute or two, but warn him that it probably won't taste so great the second time around."

"Liv, you're too much. You didn't have to give up your bed."

I didn't really want to hear what arrangements she'd prefer, and they could make whatever decisions they chose, which is why I opted for the basement. Away from it all.

I ignored her and added, "Help yourself to anything in the fridge and whatever else you find in the cabinets. Good night."

"Good night."

It took me all of five minutes to brush my teeth, put on my pajamas, and crawl onto the couch under the comforter. I've been accused of falling asleep before my head ever hits the pillow and tonight was certainly no exception. Maybe it was a defense mechanism learned while living among eight other siblings.

I could have sworn I heard a noise at two o'clock in the morning and that I saw what I thought were two legs standing at my basement window. The windows in my basement are at ground level, allowing me in this instance to see just a pair of shoes and halfway up the shins. I blinked, rubbed my eyes, and looked again, only to see the silver light of the moon casting shadows on my neighbor's yard. I must have been dreaming, but something good came of it later on, as it turned out.

Those slivers of moonlight gave me a tether into the deep recesses of my mind, and I suddenly remembered where I had seen incisions like those on Jill's torso before.

I dreamed I was Velma, adorned in an unflattering turtleneck, knee-highs, pixie haircut, and glasses—the best birth control a girl could ever use—staring up at the ghost hanging from hooks on the ceiling, Scooby Doo and Shaggy by my side. I was one of those pesky kids who foiled the Swiss Cheese Specter's million-dollar scheme, the Specter being Mr. Jenkins in a rubber mask.

As to Velma's other sidekicks, Daphne's last name was Henry and Fred's was Pierce.

CHAPTER 12

GENEVIEVE L. BERGEN.

He had found her name on the Larimer County website, specifically the page that listed the owner, the purchase price, and the date of purchase and showed the property boundaries. Everything anyone wanted to know about a particular piece of property at any address in the county. They had made it so easy for him. What made it even better for him was that the local commerce directory allowed him to find out what Genevieve Bergen, aka Liv Bergen, did for a living. It was all right there, at his fingertips, in no time. All he had needed to do was log onto the library's computer using a false identity and then he was surfing the Internet anonymously.

Liv, he thought. How appropriate. At first he thought it was a typo. But then he realized Genevieve L. Bergen must be Genevieve Liv Bergen. To Liv, or not to Liv: that is the question.

Liv Bergen had been the chairperson of the local chamber of commerce the year before and was division manager of a mining and mineral processing company north of Fort Collins.

Small world, he thought after putting two and two together.

Jill had worked at a mining company. How many mining companies could there possibly be in one area like this? He realized Liv Bergen must have been Jill's boss. Interesting.

But what connection did Awakening or William Tell have to Liv Bergen besides the dead Jill Brannigan? Why would the three of them be hanging out together sipping hot toddies and singing "Kumbaya"?

Liv was the woman Jill had told him and the gang about that night back in April when she had first heard she'd landed a summer internship. Jill had been so excited. Her eyes had sparkled; her dimples had deepened. On reflection, it was the moment he had realized he was going to have her—one way or another.

But sadly, she had refused him, rebuffed his advances. Who did she think she was? He could have any woman he wanted. Didn't she know that? She should feel lucky that he had directed any attention her way. She was nothing more than a jock. A stupid one at that. She had said no, so he took control of the situation. And it had been wonderfully magical for him.

Ah, Nutrition.

He admitted to himself that he had made one mistake, however. He had written that letter, thinking Jill would see the error of her ways and apologize to him. He had poured his heart out to her, shared his deepest thoughts—something he had not done for his four other creations. He hadn't found the letter. She didn't have it with her, and it wasn't in her car or in her dorm room. He had checked both places, naturally.

Jill had told him she had thrown it away, along with the book, even after he had threatened to cut her while they were in his garage, demanding the truth or he'd inflict more pain than she could imagine. He'd had to sacrifice his neighbor's cat to make his point, taking the nozzle from the back of his truck and showing Jill what he was capable of doing with it. Her Mona Lisa smile, the smile that belied her insistence that the letter and book were gone for good, had so infuriated him he had made quick work of her on that shoreline. It was better that way.

It didn't really matter if she had lied about disposing of the letter.

So few people knew his real name, but he had shared it with his sweet Jill. He was almost positive she had not revealed it to anyone else. He had simply asked her not to, and she was a person of her word. He liked the simplicity in her approach to life. Why couldn't all women be so uncomplicated, he thought. But why couldn't she have been smart enough to see they were meant for each other? It was her fault Nutrition had been added to his gallery. It was all Jill's fault.

He enjoyed a double cheeseburger from the drive-through and chased it with a fistful of fries after returning to Genevieve L. Bergen's house at ten. Awakening's rental car was still parked out front. William Tell's Jeep was gone. He could see Awakening sitting at the desk in the living room, working at the computer. She was a vision: an ever-present calmness; kind, bright eyes like Jill's; raven black hair. She truly was stunning. A bit on the lean side to be playing the role of Awakening, but she would do.

No sign of the other woman he'd seen earlier. She must have been Genevieve Liv Bergen, he supposed, but he would need to confirm that.

Around midnight, Awakening went to the back of the house, and he did not see her again. He was about to head home when headlights appeared down the street and headed his way. He ducked down as the headlights swept across his windshield. When the vehicle had passed, he sat up again in time to see William Tell emerge from his Jeep and step into the house. He didn't use a key, so they had left the door unlocked for him. That will make things easy, he thought.

He didn't see Tell for a few minutes until he entered the living room from the left, carrying a plate of food. So, the kitchen was on the left, the bedrooms and bathrooms at the back of the house. A split-level, the front door and garage were midway between the living room—visible in the windows—and presumably the basement.

William Tell walked to where Awakening had been sitting, picked up some papers from the desk, sat down in an armchair, and began to read. He ate and read for what seemed like fifteen or twenty minutes. It was nearly two o'clock in the morning now. He imagined Tell was reading a profile about him that Awakening had composed. He couldn't afford to give them time to figure out much more.

Finally, the SAC retreated to the back of the house after turning off all the lights. He was heading to bed too. The stalker quietly opened his door, thankful he had dismantled the overhead light last year, and climbed out of the truck, being careful not to let the door slam. He crossed the street, hopped the small fence, and walked around the blue house to find out which room William Tell was staying in. The light was on in a room at the back of the house on the southwest corner. Two lights, actually. A bedroom and a bathroom. He walked around the house twice, noting the second room in the northwest corner of the house. Probably the bedroom where Awakening, Bergen, or both women slept. He noted that the basement had two small windows on the downhill side of the building, to the west. He also noted the feel of the grass beneath his boots, realizing that Genevieve L. Bergen likely didn't own a dog or was impeccably neat about it. No squishy mess. No odor from his shoes. She was making this so easy for him.

Sometime between his first and second pass around the house, William Tell had called it a night and turned off the lights in his room. In the moonlight, the fingers of his outstretched arms slid along the base of the windows for any opening and his strong hands tested the window locks. The house must have air-conditioning, since none of the windows budged in the kitchen, living room, and second bedroom. He avoided Tell's bedroom since he was probably still awake.

Lastly, he tried the basement windows, neither giving an inch. Trying both the kitchen and front door, he noted the knobs turned easily but the doors didn't give way. Deadbolts. Everything was locked tight. So, they locked up after all three were home.

He made mental notes of everything he had observed and decided to call it a day. As he passed under her window, he whispered, "Sleep tight, Awakening. Tomorrow will be a busy a day for us both."

CHAPTER 13

MY SATURDAY MORNING RUN was spectacular.

Four colorful hot air balloons were floating low in the sky at sunrise with the Rocky Mountains and clear blue skies as a backdrop. The typical afternoon winds and thunderstorms this time of year were nonexistent in the early morning hours. I ran down to City Park and back, stopping at the corner coffee shop a block from my house to buy a bag of fresh bagels for breakfast.

By the time I'd come home, taken a shower, dressed, and made coffee, it was nearly six thirty. Lisa came padding down the hall, having been awakened by the smell of freshly brewed "breakfast blend."

"Morning," I whispered.

"You're up early," she mumbled, not quite awake yet.

"I'm going to head up to work this morning for a few hours. Get out of your hair so you guys can work."

"Is Streeter here?"

"I assume so. His Jeep's parked outside."

"Good."

"I've got bagels and cream cheese for you guys whenever you're hungry."

"Thanks, Liv. Brandt's coming by at seven thirty, so I'm sure Streeter will be up soon."

"Did you get your report for him done?"

She nodded and yawned. "Everything but what's motivating this guy."

"Lisa," I began, "I was thinking." Suddenly I found myself feeling a bit silly. The idea had sounded so brilliant at two o'clock in the morning, particularly to Shaggy, but it seemed to have cooled in the warmth of my sunrise jog. "Like I told you before, after finishing at UW, I worked for Boeing for awhile."

She looked at me as I poured a cup of coffee and handed it to her, putting my empty cup in the dishwasher.

"In Everett, at the 747/767 plant. Because I was with the Industrial Engineering group I was able to see a lot of the plant, unlike so many of the tens of thousands who work there. I mean, you wouldn't believe how big this plant is. I don't know how many city blocks it consumes, but I'd heard that at one time it was the biggest building in the world."

"Big enough to hold a 747," Lisa quipped. She sat down at the kitchen table and sipped her coffee, never taking her eyes off of me as I paced.

"Or two or three," I countered.

I swallowed hard and hoped that my idea wouldn't sound as stupid as it was starting to sound to me. "One time I came upon the department responsible for cutting the carpet for all the planes. I had been following up on a concern that management had about some planes seemingly being expedited through the system at a faster rate than scheduled, and they wanted to know why. So, it gave me a chance to follow up on every aspect of building the planes. Long story, but my point is, I was fascinated to learn about how the guys in the carpet department worked so quickly with minimal waste."

Lisa put her coffee cup down and was leaning forward, intent on where I was headed.

"Those pictures you showed me last night got me to thinking about Boeing and how those guys cut the carpets there." I pulled out the chair next to her and sat down at the table. "I know it sounds silly, but maybe it could help you somehow. You're the expert, not me. And I hate when someone tells me how to reclaim after mining when I do it every day of my life, so it won't hurt my feelings if—"

"How did they cut the carpets?" Lisa interrupted, placing a hand firmly on my forearm.

"With water," I said. "They used a super-high-powered stream of water. You know, like an air compressor hose and nozzle? Only smaller and more powerful."

"So the stream of water cut through carpet?"

"And wallboard and plastic and just about anything. They had to design the room with really tough alloys or something because when they hung the carpet from the ceilings so the patterns could be cut from them, the water would shoot right through the carpet and hit the walls. At least that's what I remember. But it's been a while."

"Water," she said, looking out the kitchen window.

"And the cutting was in one direction. Like your victims' skin and tissue," I continued. The room was quiet. I could hear the morning birds chirping in the trees out front and in the backyard. I stood up. "Look, maybe that's impossible, but I just thought I'd throw it out there as a possibility that might help you guys brainstorm."

Lisa nodded. "Water. Interesting."

I grabbed my keys and headed for the garage. "Good luck."

Lisa stood and said, "Liv?"

I poked my head around the garage door.

"Thanks. For everything. You're a good friend."

"So are you, Lisa. And by the way, for what it's worth, I could have sworn I saw someone outside my basement window around two o'clock this morning. Maybe it was my imagination, but I don't think so. Just be careful."

It was a moment I would think back on often. I wasn't sure what it was I saw in Lisa's eyes. Premonition. Resignation. Something.

She smiled. "And *you* have an incredible mind. You should really consider a career with the Bureau."

"Maybe in my next life."

Lisa laid the toasted bagels with cream cheese in the middle of the table. Streeter and Brandt both helped themselves. She took the one that looked the healthiest, if there was such a bagel. Tasted like a sun-dried tomato with whole grains or something.

They had been at it for nearly an hour.

Brandt explained what had happened at the station after the two FBI agents had left. The rumors were flying around about Chief Richardson wanting to fire him. Richardson was also protesting the jurisdiction of the FBI.

"He just wants credit for catching this guy, if you do, and someone to blame, if you don't. It's an election year. Don't take it personally," Brandt said, wrapping his meaty hands and mouth around the gigantic bagel and making it look more like a Cheerio.

"I don't," Streeter said simply. Turning to Lisa, he added, "I read your report last night. Great job. And the letter Liv found in Jill Brannigan's locker. I agree with you about getting it dusted for prints immediately and running the prints through AFIDS. I left a message for my office to send a runner up this morning. They should be here within the next half hour."

She nodded. "How did that letter strike you?"

"We need to find out who this Jonah character is."

Streeter was eating his bagel much more delicately than Brandt was, which was to say he needed no backhanded sleeve wipe for trails of cream cheese dribbling down his chin or out the sides of his mouth. She marveled at the differences between the two men and how one mountain of a man was so overshadowed by the other. She resisted a grin, thinking about how Liv had mistakenly thought she and Streeter were an item, then wondered why they couldn't be. She watched him as he sipped his coffee, studied his eyes. She could have sworn they were green yesterday and now they were blue.

"Jill's sister and roommate weren't able to shed light on who Jonah might be?"

"Never heard of him. Neither had the parents," he added.

"Who's Jonah and what letter are you talking about?" Brandt said, swiping at his lips with his sleeve again.

Streeter nodded at Lisa and she retreated to the living room, where she donned a pair of latex gloves. She returned with a pair of gloves for Brandt and the letter. After wiping his hands on his shirt, he squeezed his fingers into the gloves, pinched the corner of the letter, and began to read. Lisa offered Streeter another cup of coffee and bagel, but he declined. Brandt, on the other hand, looked up across the letter, nodded, and held his empty cup up to her. She filled it and toasted another bagel for him.

"We've definitely got to find out who this Jonah guy is," he agreed after finishing. "Strongest lead yet on this case."

"That, and the fact that both Julia Brannigan and Kari Smithson mentioned Jill was dealing with someone she had rejected," Streeter added.

"A stalker?" Lisa asked.

"Not quite," Streeter said, "although the roommate said their room had been ransacked the day after Jill was last seen. When pressed, her story changed from her room being ransacked to the room 'feeling' like someone had been there and rifled through their belongings."

"She never told me that," Detective Brandt argued.

"It took several hours and a lot of tears to get to that point," Streeter admitted.

"I didn't have the patience for it," Brandt admitted.

"If not a stalker, then what did Jill say to her roommate?" Lisa asked Streeter.

"Kari Smithson says that last Friday night Jill went out after work with some friends, and she later complained that someone at the bar where they hang out hit on her. She told the guy she wasn't interested, but he kept pressuring her and even kissed her. Jill got mad and came home early."

"Did the roommate get a name?" Lisa asked hopefully.

Streeter shook his head. "Afraid not. Julia Brannigan told me a similar story, same time frame. She mentioned that the guy kept calling Jill's cell phone for the next day or two and Jill wouldn't answer his calls."

"We can get phone records," Brandt said.

"Already on it. Disposable cell. Whoever this is knows what he's doing. Anyway, Julia said the guy left a letter inside some book for Jill last Saturday morning right outside her dorm room. Julia says it bothered Jill more than when he'd made a pass at her."

"But she didn't file a police report," Lisa concluded.

"Julia said she told Jill to do that, but Jill didn't want to. And she didn't tell her roommate because she would have 'freaked out' about it, according to Julia. Apparently, Julia and Kari are not on the best of terms," Streeter said.

"We've *got* to find this Jonah," Brandt repeated. "It's the only lead we've got."

"Not the only lead," Streeter said. "We have a match on the tire tread from Horsetooth with Platteville."

"And we might have another clue," Lisa said. Both men looked at her. "Liv had a thought about the weapon. I jumped online this morning and sent a few e-mails. Jack Linwood answered me from Ops. You know him?"

Streeter nodded. "Good, too."

"He's working on it now. Then I did a little research of my own."

She pushed the computer-generated photo across the table toward the men, enjoying their expressions.

"It's the same as the marks on the victims. What did this?" Streeter asked of the cut marks on the material in the photograph.

"Water," she told them and explained what Liv had learned at Boeing.

"We've got to get this to Berta immediately," Streeter said. "And I've got to meet Liv Bergen."

To her surprise, Lisa felt a pang of jealousy.

CHAPTER 14

SHE WAS STANDING SO close to him, Jack Linwood could feel Dr. Berta Johnson's breath on the back of his right arm. He had been working up the prototype for the last three hours. Ever since she had arrived an hour earlier, Dr. Johnson had been on him like flies on honey, waiting for the demonstration. He had told her he wouldn't be done until after lunch, but that hadn't deterred her from watching his every move.

So, he had put her to work.

Yes, he knew she was the chief coroner for the state of Colorado. Yes, he understood that by telling her to pick up the crescent wrench and hook up the canister to the frame he had built he might have been making a fatal move in his career. The delicate hands of a learned woman at the highest attainable surgical position in the state holding a wrench rather than a scalpel? Calvin Lemley was surely going to fire him.

It probably *was* a sacrilege, but no sense wasting a perfectly capable pair of hands, strong back, and quick mind.

Rarely had he seen the coroner grace the halls of the Bureau offices, let alone come down to Investigative Control Operations on the seventeenth floor. He had seen her picture in the newspaper numerous times through-out the past year since he had arrived at the FBI's Denver office, and although she was probably close to his age, she looked closer to retirement, the demands and controversies of her job having aged her by twenty years. Some would say she was a handsome woman, but he found her attractive because of her drive and dedication.

She hadn't shirked her duties one bit in the past hour. And after all that work, they were about to make their first trial with this contraption. She hadn't hesitated or indicated any resentment about following his orders. She stayed right with him and assisted in every way possible. And here she was, leaning over his right side to see the information he was studying.

He reviewed the diagram on the computer screen one last time to make sure everything was in its proper place. It had taken him no more than twenty minutes searching the Internet to locate a source for the water tool and to place the call to the engineers who constructed it for Boeing. Within half an hour, the blueprint was alive on his computer screen and soon thereafter he was assembling the parts that he had sent a runner to pick up. Twice, actually, and both times the businesses were open even though it was Saturday.

Linwood scanned top to bottom, right to left, glancing at every major component of his prototype and comparing it to the blueprints and notes. When he was confident they had followed the diagram to the letter, he said, "Ready, Dr. Johnson?"

"Ready," she said. "And call me Berta or I'll have to clock you with this wrench, Jack."

Linwood offered a rare grin. Boy did he admire this woman.

He stepped away from the computer and into the padded room reserved for ballistic testing, snapping off the pads from the back wall. He handed the pads to Dr. Johnson, who scuttled them out of the room. He yanked a frozen dog carcass into the room and hung it on clips from the ceiling.

"How much does that thing weigh?" Dr. Johnson asked as she stepped in behind him, studying the large dog.

"About a hundred ten pounds. It was the largest carcass in our freezer. I could probably find a cow somewhere if you think it's important, since Jill Brannigan probably weighed more than this dog did."

She arched an eyebrow. "Jill was solid muscle. It's just a guess since we didn't have all of her, of course, but we're estimating about a hundred and seventy pounds. So the dog is close in size."

"Shall we try this?" he asked, attempting to change the subject before Dr. Johnson pressed further.

He didn't wait to get her answer before retreating from the room and hauling the frame into the ballistics room. Then he waved, signaling her to follow.

"Are you okay with lifting this thing with me?" Linwood asked.

"I'll try," Dr. Johnson said.

It must have weighed at least two hundred pounds, Linwood thought, as he and Dr. Johnson struggled with the awkward contraption. They had to set it down three times in the short distance to the ballistics room. Hearing Dr. Johnson's heavy breathing, Linwood decided to leave it where they had set it down for the last time, just outside the door.

"The hose will reach," he said, handing Dr. Johnson the rubber hose and wand as he hooked up the hose from the lab sink to the contraption.

"You want to try it?"

Dr. Johnson's answer was to hand the wand back to the FBI agent.

"Okay," he said. "Let's see what it can do."

Linwood cranked the release two full rotations on the air compressor and the hose stiffened and hissed. As if he were watering his lawn, he pointed the wand toward the dog carcass at the other end of the room and squeezed the trigger. Water shot from the nozzle in a constant stream, knocking the dog toward the ceiling. The wand broke from his grip and tumbled to the ground with a clatter, the flow of water stopping abruptly as he released the lever. The dog swung back and forth at the other end of the room. Linwood rubbed his wrist.

"Why do you think I made you try it first?" Dr. Johnson grinned as Linwood continued to massage his wrist. "Haven't you ever heard of the axiom that for every action there is an opposite and equal reaction?"

Linwood regarded her. A challenge might be in order, but he decided to make things interesting. "Full throttle, Doc," he said with a nod toward the compressor release.

"Lean into it this time," Dr. Johnson offered.

He pulled the wand with him as he closed the distance between himself and the dog carcass. He came to within six feet.

"Wait!"

Linwood turned to see Dr. Johnson approach him with a pair of safety goggles.

"If you're going to stand that close, at least put something over those brown peepers of yours," she said with a wink.

She tiptoed back across the wet floor to the doorway and gave Linwood a thumbs-up.

He braced himself by angling his tall, lean body forward, one leg bent in front of him, the other anchoring him from behind. He gripped the wand securely with both hands, pointed it at the center of the large dog, and pulled the trigger. This time the water went straight through the dog's side, leaving a hole the size of a dime.

Linwood released the trigger, pulled off the safety goggles, and stared at the hole in the swinging carcass.

Dr. Johnson whistled. "That's amazing." She moved past him and tackled the dog until she had brought it to a standstill. She studied the hole from both sides. "Ready for the cadaver?"

Her partner nodded.

Snapping open her cell phone before she was even out of the room, Dr. Johnson told someone with the Denver city morgue to bring the cadaver downtown to the Federal Building.

Within an hour, Jack Linwood was helping Dr. Berta Johnson position the cadaver against the back wall of the ballistics room in a seated position, arms hoisted overhead and tethered to the ceiling hooks. When they were ready, Linwood instructed Dr. Johnson to release the compressor to wide open. He moved to within six feet of the cadaver, positioned himself, and pulled the trigger, making a circle in the cadaver's torso. Water, tissue, and bone fragments sprayed in all directions, the cadaver jerking from the initial pressure. He didn't remember dropping the wand once again or hearing the clatter as it hit the floor.

He had performed dozens of tests before in this lab, but never one like this. The destruction he had caused was staggering, and he would not soon forget the sight, the sound, and the smell that had resulted. Unfortunately. He stood staring at the cadaver for several seconds, shocked by what he had just done.

Dr. Johnson was crouched by the cadaver, poking and prodding and studying this creation. She was kneeling in the carnage. The room was designed for ballistics, not for water tests, and they would have to mop up the room when they were done. Water, bones, tissues, and all.

The absurdity of seeing the petite woman in her navy blue suit and matching pumps kneeling in the mess next to the naked cadaver with a hole through his chest was almost too much for Linwood to comprehend. Then she looked at him and smiled.

"Jack, you did it! This is it! The Venus de Milo killer is using *water* to butcher his victims," she concluded. He would have sworn ten years fell away from her face with that single statement. "You're a genius."

He didn't feel like a genius. After all, he'd been so busy trying to build the contraption, he hadn't thought about the real objective of matching up water slices with cadaver tissue or correlating how that must have played out with the teenagers at Platteville or the college basketball star in Fort Collins. What that monster de Milo must do, see, smell, and touch when he's butchering his victims. Horrid.

"You okay, Jack? You're looking a little green."

He nodded, warding off the bile that rose in his throat. Dr. Johnson was used to this. He was used to seeing presliced tissue, bone, and matter samples neatly placed between slides or growing in petri dishes. He wondered how Dr. Johnson managed to disconnect from all this and how he could learn to do the same in time. And he better be quick about it.

One good thing about Bureau work was that he could always find someone who could teach him more than he thought he was capable of doing.

"Look at the bone fragments. Same as the ones collected at the crime scene in the shallow waters at Horsetooth?"

He nodded.

Dr. Johnson added excitedly, "Well then, let's call the photographer in on this and cut off the arm and leg. We're going to need the comparison as evidence in court when we catch this guy."

CHAPTER 15

I HADN'T BEEN OUT in the plant all morning.

Knowing that Jill's coworkers would be here until their shift ended at six tonight, I had plenty of time to catch up on paperwork and still see them later in the day. I hadn't even seen Joe because, like me, he often used Saturday mornings to catch up on all the paperwork.

It was nearly noon, and I'd finished my variance report on the quarry and plant for the first six months of the year, comparing the budget to actual financials and relating my findings to my predictions for the balance of the year. It felt good to get something accomplished with no interruptions for a change.

As I walked over to Joe's office, I enjoyed the fresh air, heat, and sunshine on this glorious June day. The trailer was empty. Joe was not in the office. He's probably making his rounds through the quarry or talking with the plant guys on their lunch break, I thought. I walked back to the scale, through the warehouse, and out to the plant, climbing the metal stairs up to the control room. Joe was reading the operational reports near the control panel while Allan, Greg, Oliver, and Kyle ate their lunches at the small lunch table.

"Hi, guys."

The door closed behind me with a soft bump, shutting out the noise of the plant behind me. I pulled my earplugs out and stuffed them in my pocket.

"Hey, Liv," Joe answered. The others grunted their hellos. Still down about Jill's murder.

"Mind if I chew the fat with you while you eat?" I asked the four men at the table.

Joe looked over at me and I gestured to him to come have a seat with us. He did.

"How are you guys? I mean, *really?*"

Mumbles and groans—all noncommittal.

"Oliver?"

He lowered his sandwich and raised his eyes. "Not worth shit."

The others got a kick out of that. So did I.

"Me neither," I added. "Greg?"

"I think Oliver said it all."

"Allan?"

He was the team leader for a reason. I needed him to set the pace before I asked Kyle, knowing he had been the closest of all of them to Jill.

"It's kind of like a bad dream for me. Sometimes I can just go about my day, get my work done, and think about what I'm going to have for dinner or do with my kids on my days off. Then I start feeling guilty, and it's like I'm being selfish or something, all wrapped up in my world and not really giving Jill the credit she's due by mourning and stuff."

The others nodded, eyes cast down in the direction of their sandwiches.

"I feel the same way. I just finished my budget review this morning and was feeling pretty proud of myself until I thought of you guys and Jill. I was embarrassed that I took a moment to celebrate and feel happy about something so petty in the big scheme of things. But then on my way over here, I was thinking that if I were Jill and I'd been the one who was murdered, I wouldn't want you guys wasting a whole lot of time mourning over me. In fact, if you did anything but enjoy life all the more, squeeze those kids harder, and kiss your wives more often, I'd have to come back and kick your asses."

That made them laugh.

Oliver said, "And you're not telling stories there."

"That's right," Allan said.

Joe nodded. "Jill wouldn't want us to be all mope and sorrow about this."

Kyle continued to eat in silence, avoiding eye contact with any of us.

"Kyle?" I pressed.

He put his sandwich down and crossed his arms. "Well, she sure as hell wouldn't want us partying about it either. I mean, shit, guys, the monster who hacked Jill up is still out there running free."

"True," I said.

The mood darkened once again. I let it. It was better to let them stew in it a bit longer. "Any of you know if Jill had any enemies?"

"Who would be an enemy of Jill's? She was nice and sweet, kind-hearted and gentle . . ." Kyle drifted.

"Anyone who she was mad at or afraid of this summer?"

Most of them shook their heads.

"It wasn't like that, boss," Allan said. "We don't talk about those personal things much around here. More like where we went hunting, a game on TV, or what movies we saw."

"Ever talk about books?" I asked.

"Books? We don't read no stinking books," Oliver said, mimicking a line from an old western. The others chuckled and the mood began to lift again.

"Did Jill ever read during lunch or on breaks?"

"Never," Kyle said.

"I never saw her reading," Allan added.

Oliver and Greg shook their heads.

"Did Jill ever mention a book called *Crime and Punishment* to any of you?" I asked.

They all nodded, sat a little straighter in their chairs, and stared at me.

"Yeah, last week," Allan said.

"Saturday, at dinner break," Oliver mentioned.

"Noon?" I asked, making sure his dinner was my lunch, and my dinner was his supper.

He nodded.

Kyle asked, "How did you know about that?"

"Found a paperback copy in her locker," I said nonchalantly, trying to make it look like it was nothing. Joe was on to me. I could tell he knew there was something more to my questions. "What'd she say about it?"

Kyle was the first to answer. "She asked if any of us had read it before."

"She was trying to find out what it was about," Oliver added.

"Anybody tell her?"

They all looked at Greg.

He shook his head. "Not me. I told her it'd been a while since I read it, but that it was about this thieving, murdering college boy who thought he was above the law and clever enough not to get caught. He hadn't counted on the fact that his conscience would nearly kill him and that his mind ended up being worse than prison."

I was impressed by his simple yet accurate synopsis. "How did Jill respond to that?"

"She freaked and said she was going to, quote, 'burn the wicked book,'" Allan added.

"She freaked?" I asked.

Oliver nodded. "She didn't even finish her lunch. She grabbed her hard hat and went back to work before break was even over."

I looked at Kyle, knowing that when he was loading trucks under the silos he was the closest, physically, to where Jill worked over in the warehouse. "Did you talk to her later that day about it?"

Kyle cocked his head. "Not about that. She was upset. In between trucks, I went over to the bagger twice to check on her. She was still mad the first time I went over."

"Mad at Oliver?"

"No, about the stupid book. It set her off. She made a big deal about throwing the book away or burning it. She even mentioned tossing it in the dryer."

Our dryer drives off the moisture from our rock but would more than likely incinerate a book, I thought.

"Burning it?"

They all nodded.

It was making sense. The guy named Jonah must have given the book to Jill with the note in it. I wondered if the guy, Jonah, was a college student who also thought he was above the law, smart enough to get away with murder. If I were Jill, I would have been mad at a veiled threat like that too.

"When did you see her that afternoon, Kyle?"

"Around two, then again around four thirty. She was much better at four thirty," Kyle said.

"And great at quitting time," Allan added.

They all nodded.

"What did you think, Joe? You were the last to be with her," Greg said.

"I agree," Joe said, his cheeks reddening. "She was in a good mood that evening. Didn't seem angry at all to me. Not even a little."

Yet she had left the book and the note behind, in her locker, not to have access again to them until the following Wednesday. So, she must not have intended to report the incident to the police. Or maybe she just forgot it. Like she had her necklace. The necklace her mother said she took everywhere. She must have been really shaken up by the book and letter. Maybe she did forget the book after all.

Not likely, though. Especially considering how all the guys said it had consumed her all day.

Maybe she was worried her roommate would find it and ask a lot of questions she wasn't willing to answer. Maybe she was trying to keep it safe from someone trying to retrieve it. Maybe she was deciding whether or not to report it to the police and wanted it out of sight, out of mind, so she could have time to make her decision. Maybe she didn't want a jealous boyfriend stumbling across it and getting the wrong idea about her and this crazy guy.

And it made sense as to why, after a long day of stewing over the book and the letter, Jill would take the opportunity to thank Joe, to kiss his cheek, to reach out to a good, thoughtful man who wanted nothing from her but to do her best at work.

All speculation. I'd never know why now. It wasn't like I could ask her. Jill was gone.

"Did she ever mention a boyfriend?"

Everyone shook his head. Kyle blushed.

"What?" I asked Kyle.

"She didn't have a boyfriend."

"You're sure?"

"I'm sure," he said. Because of the awkward silence, he was compelled to add, "She told me she broke up with a guy last summer who she'd been dating for over a year and hadn't dated since. She was more interested in getting through school."

"Ever talk about friends?"

"Not much," Allan said.

Kyle added, "I saw her once at Washington's with a bunch of other kids on a Saturday night. They looked like college buddies."

"Washington's. Huh," I said. "A bunch of girls?"

"Girls and guys. Seemed like a tight bunch. About ten of them or so," Kyle added.

"Ever mention anyone named Jonah?"

They all sat up again, staring at me. I had hit another nerve.

"Again, last week," Allan said. "At lunch. Before the book."

Oliver jerked a thumb in Allan's direction. "She asked the reverend here about Jonah the biblical character and what he was famous for."

"What'd you say?" I asked Allan.

Allan looked around at his other team members. They nudged him to tell me.

"I told her . . . I said that Jonah was one of the prophets in the Old Testament. He was a reluctant prophet that God had a lot of trouble convincing to do his will. A troublemaker of sorts. So, God convinces Jonah to obey him by sending him some not-so-subtle messages, like strong winds and violent storms to change the direction of his ship because he went the opposite way God told him to go. The sailors throw Jonah overboard, thinking he's the trouble, and God makes a big fish swallow him.

"So, Jonah lives in the belly of this whale for three days, until it pukes him up on shore. Jonah finally obeys God and gives the gloom and doom warning he's supposed to give to this city. But the people actually listen and change their ways, so God doesn't punish them like he told Jonah he would do. So Jonah gets all pissed because he really wanted to see these people suffer, not change. He goes off and pouts, whining about being angry at God and wanting to die, missing the whole point of God being omnipotent, benevolent, and forgiving. I don't think Jonah ever gets it, because most of the time it's all about his big diva attitude."

"And you told Jill all this?" I asked.

"Yeah, before she asked her question about the book. I told her that everyone remembers the story in the Bible about Jonah being swallowed by a whale, but few recall that Jonah was a jerk and God didn't save him from the whale. God told the whale to eat him so God would have Jonah's full attention. But it didn't work."

"In the belly of a whale," I said, and wondered if there were a connection between the story and the letter from Jonah and Jill's belly having been removed. The peal of the phone near the control panel startled me. As Allan moved to pick it up, it stopped mid-ring. He settled back into his chair, and the room settled into silence.

"Why all the questions?" Kyle asked.

"Just curious," I added. "Joe and I cleared out Jill's locker yesterday and it was harder than I thought to touch her personal items, knowing what happened to her since she was last here. I was just hoping you guys could lift my spirits by telling me something I didn't know about her. So thanks."

"No problem," Allan said.

Greg offered Joe and me a Twinkie. I ate both Joe's and mine. I tend to eat when I'm stressed, nervous, or in this case, anxious. Joe tends to do the opposite—namely, not eat at all. The fellas finished their lunches and were about to go back to work.

"Detective Brandt called and left a message that he'd like all of us to be available to talk with him about Jill sometime on Monday. It's your day off, but would you be willing to come in around ten or so that morning?"

Each one nodded without hesitation.

"Plan on a few hours, because they may want to talk with you individually." More nods. A few of them donned their hard hats and made for the door. I added, "By the way, guys. Don't tell anyone this, because the police aren't releasing the information yet. It might be helpful in their investigation, and we don't want to screw it up for them. But you all should know, if it gives you any comfort at all, Jill was not sexually molested in any way."

They were all relieved by the news, even joyous. Kyle's eyes filled with tears, and he gave me a thankful nod before hurrying out the door to load trucks.

Joe hung back with Allan to go over the week's production reports, and I walked back to my office. Terry was cleaning the glass on the reclamation and environmental awards our company had earned over the years. When I passed by and patted him on the back, he asked, "Did you get your call?"

"What call?"

"The one I forwarded up to the control room," he added.

"When?"

"Just a few minutes ago."

I shook my head. Then I remembered the call where the caller apparently hung up before giving Allan the chance to answer. "Did they say who it was?"

"Nope," he said. "Some guy asking for Liv Bergen. I told him you were in the plant and that I'd transfer him to you."

"Recognize the voice? Customer? Vendor? Employee?"

"Nope, nope, nope, and nope," he said with a grin.

"Salesman," I grinned back.

"Probably."

"Thanks, Terry. When are you getting out of here today?"

"Pretty soon."

"Thanks for coming in. Go enjoy your family and this wonderful weekend."

I decided I had better let Lisa or Agent Pierce know about Jill's last conversation with the guys last Saturday in case it had some bearing on their investigation. Particularly, I wanted them to know about her reaction to *Crime and Punishment*, that she wasn't reading it, and that she'd asked about the name Jonah, as if it was a pen name, a veil, not the real name of the person who had written the letter.

I dialed my home number, but no one answered. I hung up when I heard my own voice at the message center. I made a mental note to let Lisa and Agent Pierce have my message center password and to change the message if they needed to use that phone. I dialed Lisa's cell phone number and it rang several times before going into her voice mail.

I left a long message, telling her all about the book, about Jill's conversation a week ago with the guys here at work, and about the biblical references to Jonah that Jill had asked about. I asked Lisa to call me as soon as she got my message.

And I never got the call.

CHAPTER 16

HE ENDED HIS PREPAID cell phone call and tossed the card into a Dumpster behind the commons.

Everyone was accounted for now that he had confirmed Genevieve Liv Bergen was thirty miles north at her workplace. She was the only one he hadn't been sure about. Her SUV would be parked in the garage if she was home, but he couldn't get close enough to the garage windows to see for himself. Close enough without being noticed, that is. He hadn't seen her all morning, but even so, he had assumed she was not in the house. He had had to make sure.

He had slept soundly last night, enjoying his dreams and the thought of his adventure today. He had awakened with a morning missile that ached to fly a mission, so he indulged as he studied his wall, his gallery of masterpieces, and imagined his Awakening soon joining them.

When he had arrived this morning, Agent Streeter Pierce was work-ing at the computer with Agent Lisa Henry. Now, nearly four hours later, was the first opportunity he'd had to act. William Tell had left shortly after lunch when Detective Doug Brandt stopped by with what looked like some files. They had been in a hurry. Such a hurry, in fact, that they hadn't even noticed his truck, even though both men had seen it parked here the night before. He imagined them thinking it belonged to one of the neighbors. And they would be wrong.

It was a stroke of luck, actually, that none of the neighbors had complained of his old truck being parked in front of their home. It was also a stroke of luck that none of the press had parked outside Liv Bergen's house in search of an exclusive story or to glean information from those closest to the case. After all, it had been so incredibly easy to learn who the lead investigators were and where they'd been staying. He puzzled through why the press hadn't done the same. For a town as small as Fort Collins, it wasn't as if there were too many competitors in the media. If one got the scoop they all got the scoop since they were largely one and the same. He sighed and snapped the latex gloves over his delicate-looking yet strong hands.

Broad daylight. He was about to do this in broad daylight.

That was new for him. A frisson of ecstasy quaked through him.

Arousal was accompanied by opportunity, which had presented itself like a long-lost friend. He had already seen the three other neighbors in Bergen's cul-de-sac leave this morning. One little man and lady in their late sixties, living to the south of Bergen, had left just after he'd arrived. One car full of screaming kids, a weary father, and a haggard mother had pulled out of the driveway to the north and east of Bergen around eleven. A young man decked in the brightest spandex he had ever seen practically skipped out of his garage toting his bike helmet, a water bottle, and a sporty yellow mountain bike, and was on his way west to the mountains.

Unless he had miscalculated somehow—and he was certain he had not—no one was home. Just Awakening.

He would wait until she left the living room and retreated to the back of the house so that she wouldn't hear or see him approach the front door. He watched as she drank her water, tapping away on her computer. She was getting close. She was on to him. Figuring him out. He could feel it.

She flicked her head and brushed the long, sweeping bangs from her forehead just like his mother used to do.

Ah, Ma Mère, he thought, I picture you happy, content, sitting at the table working your needlepoint and chatting with my sister, all of us safe from Father. Like so many descriptive words and creative ideologies he discovered as a boy visiting the museum, Ma Mère was one of the most profoundly appropriate, albeit his mother had not an ounce of French ancestry. His reminiscences filled him with a warmth he hadn't experienced in many years, even in the solitude of his long soaks in the tub late at night. He had not recognized the similarities between Ma Mère and Awakening until now.

And he wasn't sure how he felt.

Ma Mère had believed he was special, hadn't she?

She didn't tease him about his need to be alone for hours, although she punished him when it became excessive. She didn't mock him for his need to dress like a magician for six straight months when he was twelve, but she had shredded his cape in a fit of rage one night after he refused to eat his dinner. She understood that the torture he inflicted on his little sister was merely a unique plea for his mother's attention, which she gave him through each lovingly painful beating. She nuzzled and cradled him with love for each and every nosebleed that followed.

Despite her unpredictability—scolding then praising him for the same behaviors, beating then rewarding him for the same hard-earned grades year after year—her belief in him was constant and her understanding of him had transcended that of all others. Yes, he was sure of that now. She had understood him, accepted him, treated him as the brilliant prince he was.

Ah, Ma Mère, how I miss you.

She was the one who had introduced him to the fine arts, to culture, to his inner genius. She had taken him to the museums of St. Petersburg rather than the sunny beaches Florida was so well known for. It was at one of these museums that he found his calling, his passion, his life. He discovered an artist who, like himself, could think like a madman without being mad. He prophetically shared the same birthday, six decades later, the same capability of fantasy, the same appreciation for surrealism, and the same manic craving for solitude. His mother had fostered his newfound freedom by encouraging him to describe and draw his dreams, to fantasize, and to contemplate what he imagined and pictured in the clouds, rock formations, and ocean waves.

The development of his creativity and imagination had further blossomed upon Ma Mère's death a few short years ago.

He had her to thank.

For all he had become.

And for what he was about to do.

Awakening rose from the desk and headed down the hall, presumably to the bathroom or even to take a nap in her room. In either case, she would be a long way from the front door.

He slipped on his sunglasses, zipped up his coveralls, and tugged his cap low over his eyes. He started the engine and drove the truck farther into the cul-de-sac, eventually backing up into the driveway. He opened his door and quietly closed it, taking in the surrounding houses, cars, and sounds of the neighborhood. Two different dogs were barking, but not at him. They were much farther away. Four kids were playing in the green open space across from where his truck had been parked a few minutes ago. They were more interested in the football than they were in his comings and goings. No one stood at a picture window. No curtains moved or were askew in anyway. He walked to the back of the truck and popped open the window of the camper and lowered the truck's tailgate. He worked quickly to retrieve the syringe and the toolbox from the back, leaving the topper window and tailgate wide open for his return.

He walked to the front door, which he knew would be unlocked, feigned pushing the doorbell, and waited the appropriate amount of time in case someone in the neighborhood had been paying attention. Not that it would matter if they saw him. He had on work coveralls as if he were a handyman or a repairman in uniform. He opened the door quietly and stepped inside.

He climbed the steps, set the toolbox on the floor, and retrieved what he needed from it. Like a cat, he was across the living room and halfway down the hall when the phone rang.

He froze.

Lisa stepped from the bathroom. Her breath caught in her throat and he watched her eyes widen for a brief moment before he closed the distance between them. She threw a punch that landed square on the left side of his lower jaw.

He staggered back a step, and then he felt his right eye explode in stars, her left jab having connected squarely with the fleshy socket. His hands flew to her neck, squeezing it tight. He hissed, "You're a fighter. Good."

Her hand shot up toward her shoulder holster, toward her weapon. He kneed her in the crotch and clocked her in the head. Her hands cupped her left ear, blood seeping through her fingers.

The sudden chirp of a phone caught him off guard again. It was her cell phone, and nearly his undoing. In the second he had lost focus she had freed her nine-millimeter SIG Sauer pistol from her holster and was pulling it up to fire. He charged and slammed her against the wall, driving the breath from her. Weighing at least twice as much as Lisa did, he pinned her to the wall with his shoulder and batted at her hands until he realized she was no longer holding the gun. He hadn't heard it drop.

She kicked his shins and with her one free hand pushed at his chin, her fingernails clawing at his cheek. He turned his head and chomped down on her finger as hard as he could until she screamed. The blood from her finger was warm on his tongue. Her cell phone kept chirping and chirping.

"You're messing up my picture," he growled, shoving his shoulder under her rib cage. He shoved again, digging his shoulder deep into her solar plexus. She struggled to regain her breath. He delivered a swift undercut and she slumped to the floor in a heap at his feet. The chirping of the cell phone stopped.

"Finally," he panted, kicking the pistol away from her unconscious body and pulling the plastic baggie from his pocket. He opened the seal, pulled out the needle, and shoved it into a vein in Awakening's right forearm.

She never had a chance.

"Crazy bitch," he said, giving her a swift kick.

He entered the bathroom, pulled off his latex gloves, washed his face and arms, and scrubbed the sink with wadded up toilet paper, assuring he would leave no blood in the sink or on the towels. He worked quickly, his mind racing through all the details. He turned his wrist to check his watch. Seven minutes. He'd been in the house for seven minutes. *Take a deep breath and take your time*, he told himself.

He looked in the mirror and liked the calm that had settled on his face. Better. He shoved the used latex gloves into one pocket of his coveralls and pulled a new pair from the other pocket, snapping them over his hands once again.

"You've got work to do," he said to his reflection.

He canvassed the spare bedroom on the right. Awakening had been neat. A place for everything and everything in its place. He ducked across the hall, stepping over Awakening's body. William Tell was a minimalist and tidy too. *Pathetic obsessive-compulsive types like me*, he thought. He rifled through Tell's belongings, finding little. He rifled through Liv Bergen's dresser drawers and surveyed the personal belongings on top of the dresser and hanging on the walls. Nothing caught his eye except a picture of an army of children surrounding their mother and father. A cluster of rocks encircled the picture frame.

He grabbed one of the small crystals and stuffed it in his pocket for later.

He stepped back over Awakening and walked down the hall toward the living room. Well away from the windows, he peeked outside and noticed no change in the neighborhood. He returned to Awakening and pulled off her shoes, her socks, her pants—everything—until Special Agent Lisa Henry was completely naked. He hefted her over his shoulder and carried her to the bed. He arranged her body so that her right leg was bent at the knee and her right foot was tucked under her backside. He turned her head to the right and splayed her hair on the pillow exactly the way he had envisioned.

Except for the nasty bruise where he had jabbed and kicked her in the ribs. He shouldn't have done that, he realized. The bruising would definitely detract from an otherwise perfect shot.

He tucked Lisa's hands beneath her head in a casual pose. He returned to his toolbox and retrieved a pomegranate from the large compartment on the bottom. Again in the bedroom, he slid the camera from beneath his coveralls and readied it to shoot some stills.

Then he grabbed the nine-millimeter SIG from the hallway floor where he had kicked it away from Awakening's body earlier. He turned it over in his hands several times, enjoying the coolness, the weightiness, before laying it on the bed to the right of Awakening's right arm.

"There now."

Awakening was beautiful, peaceful. She truly looked as if she were one second away from awakening from a dream, as intended. Surreal that he had brought the painting to life, to perfection. Her skin was remarkably pure and white. White. With blemishes. The dreamlike euphoria faded as the angry swelling and bruising around her left ear, the trickle of blood trailing down her neck, and the purple bruise along her left ribs colored his vision. Her neck was red, as was the soft area beneath her chin.

She had ruined the moment for him. By fighting back, she had nearly ruined it all.

He would need to make final adjustments to his newest work of art. He slipped into the master bedroom across the hall, and then into the master bathroom, pulling out the drawers one by one until he found what he was looking for. Genevieve Liv Bergen's makeup. He returned to Awakening and opened the bottle of liquid foundation. He poured some over the bruise on his model's side and dabbed it with a cotton ball until the bruise faded. Her friend's skin tone was apparently darker by a shade or two than Awakening's, but it was working. He did the same around Awakening's neck, stepping back and making a frame with his fingers to see how she would look through the camera lens. He dabbed some more on her neck and left ear, making sure he covered the trail of dried blood. Finally, he pulled the cap off the red lipstick tube and applied it to Awakening's lips.

She was perfect. Awakening was ready for her photo shoot.

He threw the foundation bottle, lipstick, and used cotton balls on the floor. He would clean up later. For now, he would enjoy the moment, bask in his own glory, revel in his superiority and artistry—snapping picture after picture after picture.

Some photos scattered across the desk in the living room caught his eye. A quick glance outside showed it was safe, so he decided to take a short detour through the FBI's collection of reports and news clippings. A few quick taps on the keyboard and up popped the document Awakening had been composing right before he had surprised her with a visit. His eyes scanned the computer screen. A slash of a smile split his face just before he punched the delete button.

"Smart girl. As in death, in life you were merely seconds before awakening to the truth of me."

CHAPTER 17

STREETER'S LUCK WAS CHANGING.

He had had a great afternoon so far and was looking forward to having a successful night, considering that he was going to spend it in bars. Four bars in particular. He hoped to come across the crowd of kids that, according to roommate Kari and sister Julia, Jill hung around with every Saturday night, and he also hoped to find out more about this guy named Jonah if any of them knew him.

But for now, Streeter was sitting at a coffee shop eating a quick bite while he reviewed his notes from his earlier interviews. He had called Henry to see if she would join him, but she hadn't returned his call yet. He turned his wrist to check the time, gathered his notes, and headed off to his next appointment.

Rebecca Pembroke had agreed to meet Streeter on campus in her office at one thirty. Jill's academic adviser had been helpful, sharing information with him about the one independent study and one class Jill had been taking that summer, and the four courses she had taken during the previous spring semester. Ms. Pembroke had given him the class schedules, the buildings and room numbers, the names of the professors who taught each class, along with the names of any TAs. Streeter had shown his age by asking Ms. Pembroke what a TA was, and he learned it was an abbreviation for teaching assistant, often a graduate student who was earning both credit and cash by helping to teach. The adviser had also given him the RA's—residence assistant's—name and dormitory room number; the contact information for the coach, assistant coach, and athletic director of the women's basketball team; and all the names of every student in Jill's classes, on her dormitory floor, and on the basketball team.

Even though it was a Saturday, Streeter had found and interviewed eighteen of the twenty-one coeds living on Jill's floor. Only eight of them knew her much more than by name or as a casual acquaintance. After spending two hours with those eight young women and Nicole, Jill's RA, Streeter was starting to get a good picture of Jill Brannigan. He'd also been able to question Jill's biology professor for an hour, as well as the basketball coach, Pat Beck, for about thirty minutes. Coach Beck was arranging for Streeter to meet with the entire team and coaching staff at the gym the next day. It was clear to Streeter that the halo that Jill's family and roommate had hung on top of her angelic head seemed to be justified.

He suspected that image would be confirmed when he met with Jill's art, computer science, and journalism professors on Monday. He would try calling them at home tomorrow on the outside chance one of them would take the time to meet with him on a Sunday.

He collected his notes and headed off toward his last stop on campus for the day. Jill's statistics professor's office was in the Mathematics Building, third floor, fourth office on the right. She had answered his call and said she happened to be working that day because of publishing deadlines. Publish or perish. Dr. Yolanda Fischer was oxymoronic: She was large and exotic, approachable and prickly.

"Zachary Rhodes," she was saying. "The boy who was all lovesick puppy around Jill Brannigan is Zack Rhodes."

"You're sure?"

"Of course I'm sure," she said. "The kid was crazy about her. Jockeyed to find the closest open seat to wherever she sat. Made excuses to talk with her. Paid no attention to my lectures, just sat and stared at Jill."

It would be difficult not to stare at Dr. Fischer, Streeter thought. She had the proportions of Ursula, the sea witch, but with dark skin and honey blonde hair. Nothing seemed to fit, yet it worked for her.

"And what about Jill?"

"Straight A's, studious. Statistics is—was—a breeze for her. Sorry, this whole situation with Jill. It's all so unreal." She cleared her throat. "She knew Zack and talked with him, was nice to him, but didn't see him in the same way he saw her. I could tell by her body language, how she pretended not to notice him, by the way she was polite toward him but not overly friendly."

"How was Zack as a student?"

She shrugged. "This was a fairly easy class for Zack, too, although I wouldn't have expected any less."

"What do you mean?"

"Zack's a graduate student. This was a class he didn't need for his program and had probably already taken in an undergraduate program somewhere."

"So why was he taking the class?"

Her basslike mouth pouted. "You ask me, I think it was to stay close to Jill. Bad crush. Really bad."

"How bad? Like stalking or I'm-going-to-have-to-kill-you bad?"

She shook her head. "No. Not that bad. More like annoying. Lost-puppy-dog bad. You know what I mean."

"Earlier you thought Zack might be part of Jill's circle of friends that she spends time with on occasion. What made you think that, if she tried to avoid him?" Streeter asked.

"I never said she avoided him. Just ignored his advances, or maybe I should say she artfully deflected his attentions toward her."

"Well put. I understand."

"As to your question about the friendship, my classroom was rather small. And not many students take this level of statistics, particularly athletes. As the kids congregate in my classroom, I normally sit at my desk and pretend to do paperwork or read. Sometimes, it's more than pretending. The kids talk among themselves and I can hear their conversations."

She winced, listening to her own confession, and caught Streeter's attention. "It's not like I'm eavesdropping or anything. I do have a life of my own and am not some weird prof living vicariously through my students like some professors do around here. I'm just a geeky stats professor trying to be better at my job. It interests me to know what the kids talk about each year so I can stay current with how to motivate them, make analogies, relate the material to their worlds."

Dr. Fischer's cheeks reddened when Streeter threw her a lifeline. "I bet the kids appreciate your efforts, even if they aren't aware that you're observing them."

"Jill Brannigan, Zack Rhodes, and Micah Piquette were always talking about their plans, their friends, where they were going. The other two would plead with Jill to break away from the team for a few hours to spend time with 'the gang.' That's what they called themselves."

"The gang?"

"Yeah. I got the impression they had a study group of sorts that carried beyond the library and out to the bars each week."

"What would Jill Brannigan have in common with a bunch of art students?"

Dr. Fischer chuckled. "You mean a jock amid the artsy? I wondered about that too, until I found out that Jill and Shelby Goodman had been what Shelby called 'BFFs' ever since they had arrived at CSU."

"BFFs?" Streeter asked.

"Best friends forever," Dr. Fischer said with a smile. "The world of texting has forced me to learn the acronyms."

Streeter gave a nod.

"Jill was not jocklike in any way. She was fairly shy, actually. Compliant. So I suspect she frequently acquiesced to whatever Shelby suggested, which was likely how Jill ended up in the art clique."

Streeter mulled that over and wondered if de Milo preyed on compliant victims. "Ever hear Jill or the others mention someone named Jonah?"

Dr. Fischer shook her head. "Doesn't ring a bell, but I didn't know all the kids' names. Sounded to me like there were at least a dozen or so that made up their gang. Have you talked with Dr. Bravo yet?"

"The computer science teacher?" Streeter guessed, not remembering which class he had seen the professor's name associated with on the list Rebecca Pembroke had given him earlier.

"Jill's art teacher," Dr. Fischer said. "That's the class she's taking this semester. Sculpting. I think that's where all the gang hooked up with one another. They had all taken a class with Dr. Bravo at one time or another. I think they were all in the same class this spring, if I recall."

"Tell me about Dr. Bravo."

Dr. Fischer added, "He's a popular teacher. Well liked. His art classes are an elective many of the students here at CSU take. Mostly because of Dr. Bravo's reputation. He really makes classes interesting for the kids and teaches a lot about the artists behind the art. Many undergrads take his classes for several semesters because they enjoy him so much."

Dr. Fischer's words were kind, but her expression was harsh. Streeter asked, "You don't seem to agree."

"Well, let's just say his teaching techniques are a bit . . . unconventional."

"How so?"

She stretched back in her chair and adjusted the colorful tunic that had crept under her ample breast by ironing it flat over her belly with her large hands.

"For starters, he holds class out in the courtyard on sunny days, in the library on others. When he is in the classroom, he lets them watch movies, like *Amadeus*. I hear all about it from kids like Zack, Jill, and Micah as they gather for my class. And he lets the kids call him by his first name. They all call him Dr. Jay."

Streeter sensed a hint of jealousy in her tone.

"And worst of all, he fraternizes with his students."

"How so?" Streeter encouraged.

"He goes to bars with them, goes to the library on weekends, hangs out with them whenever he can. Even dates a few of the students on occasion, or so I've heard." Dr. Fischer blushed again. Streeter was beginning to think Dr. Yolanda Fischer was a bit prim despite her sexually alluring appearance.

"Do you think he dated Jill?"

She shook her head. "Zack would have killed him." She slapped her hand over her mouth. "That was such a stupid choice of words. When I say Zack would kill Dr. Jay, I don't mean that literally, of course; just a figure of speech. Zack was protective of Jill and wasn't a fan of Dr. Jay's, even though he was the TA for the sculpting class this summer. I heard Zack and Micah talking this week in my advanced statistics class about Dr. Jay and a student named Trina, or Trisha, when they weren't all consumed about Jill's murder and this horrible de Milo character."

"Isn't it against some code of conduct for a professor to fraternize or act inappropriately with his students?" Streeter asked.

"Of course, but how are you going to prove something like that? He's going to get away with it until one of those bimbos wises up and files a complaint against him. So far, he must be treating them well, because he's like a celebrity, a rock star around here."

"Do you think Jill would have been one of the bimbos?"

Dr. Fischer shook her head. "Jill wasn't that way at all. She was different. I told you how she treated Zack with patience and kindness while staying firm. She wouldn't have crossed that line with Dr. Jay Bravo despite his dashing looks and slick tongue."

It was Streeter's turn to blush. He may have misunderstood what he had earlier taken to be Dr. Fischer's jealousy of Dr. Bravo. Maybe she wasn't jealous of the students liking his class more than hers. Maybe she was jealous that he hadn't made a play for her. Streeter noticed there was no ring on her left hand.

"How could Dr. Bravo get by all these years as a professor here at CSU and not have one student file a complaint?"

Her eyes widened. "Oh, I should have told you. Dr. Bravo arrived at CSU just last year. He moved here from Florida. He's part Cuban or something. Couldn't be more than thirty or thirty-five. He's a real looker."

Dr. Fischer looked away, shuffled some papers on her desk, and glanced up at the clock. "Oh, forgive me, Agent Pierce, but I have another appointment I must be dashing off to. Anything else I can help you with?"

―――――――

As he rounded the corner from College Avenue onto Drake, his cell phone rang.

"Pierce, we have a problem." Detective Doug Brandt's voice was unsteady. "What's your location?"

"I'm about four blocks from the house. Why?"

"Get here." Brandt said, cutting off the line.

The Overland light was green, which allowed Streeter to pull into the cul-de-sac within less than two minutes. As he turned onto the street where he'd been staying, the two black-and-whites had their lights flashing, as did the ambulance in the driveway at Liv Bergen's house.

Streeter's stomach lurched.

His mind flashed to the moment Lisa Henry had told him about staying with a friend of hers in Fort Collins. He had reluctantly agreed—it would save him the sixty miles from Denver and another forty miles to Conifer round trip each day—because it was time better spent on the investigation. But all along he had not liked the idea of staying at Liv Bergen's house for fear of endangering an innocent citizen. Now something had happened to her.

He parked behind Brandt's Mercury and bounded across the drive and up the front steps onto the porch. Police were huddled in the entryway and nodded toward the back bedroom when he flashed his credentials at them. Streeter saw Brandt at the end of the hallway, holding his hands against his temples, staring into the spare bedroom.

"Brandt?" Streeter said. "What is it?"

He shook his head and stepped aside for Streeter to see for himself.

It wasn't Liv. It was Agent Henry.

The medical personnel were trying to revive Lisa, who lay still on the bed. Her lips were dark blue and her skin had a gray hue. He saw patches of something smeared on her skin, something light and tan. It was makeup. Foundation. To cover fresh bruises on Lisa's dead body, bruises that were not there when he had left her just a few hours ago.

Why?

She was naked, exposed to the strangers who worked the electric paddles on her chest. He resisted the urge to push them aside and wrap the comforter around her, protecting her from all the probing eyes and indecency. But at the same time, he knew it didn't matter.

None of this was making any sense.

"Lisa?" Streeter called to her, taking a step toward the bed.

The medical team turned to him and shook their heads. They removed the paddles, lifted the oxygen mask away from her face, and packed their equipment before retreating from the room.

It gave him comfort that her eyes were closed, and he tried to imagine the last image she saw before she died. She had no bullet wound, no blood underneath her on the bed, no obvious signs of asphyxiation.

Hearing the thud behind him, Streeter looked back over his shoulder in time to see Brandt slump to a sitting position on the floor in the hall and hang his head in his hands, moaning.

"How? When?" Streeter asked.

Brandt said, "I got here twenty minutes ago. No one answered the doorbell. Lisa's car was still outside. The door was unlocked so I let myself in, just like yesterday. Didn't think much of it until I went to use the bathroom. I just . . . I found her like this. Called an ambulance. Called you. That's all I know."

Streeter's breath caught. "And Liv Bergen?"

"Not home yet," Brandt said. "She doesn't know."

"Let's keep it that way." Streeter punched numbers into his cell phone. "Get the crime scene techs up here right away. It's Lisa Henry. And tell Phil Kelleher to get up here as soon as he can with an overnight bag." He gave the address and looked at his watch before closing his cell. "Brandt. Brandt?"

Brandt hadn't moved. His eyes were glazed over, dazed. Streeter had seen that expression before. This was not the first time Brandt had witnessed a murder scene, but probably the first time he knew the victim, Streeter thought.

Streeter leaned down next to him in the hall and put a firm grip on his shoulder. "Brandt, we need to help Lisa. We've got to get all these people out of here and secure the crime scene. Use your people to cordon off the cul-de-sac and interview the neighbors. My techs will be here within forty minutes. I need you to watch for them. Show them where the crime scene is. Where Lisa is."

Brandt blinked at him and roused himself a little. Streeter nodded at him. "Okay?"

"Okay," he said.

Streeter helped Brandt to his feet. "And check on Liv Bergen. Make sure she's still at work or wherever she's been all day. Just make sure she's still accounted for without alarming her. If she is still at work, come up with a reason to stall her from coming home. She doesn't need to see this."

"Neither did I," Brandt croaked.

CHAPTER 18

ZACK CALLED MICAH AT six. "Are we still meeting at Washington's tonight?"

"Yeah," Micah said.

"Want to go with me?"

"Nah. I'm going with Alicia and Shelby to Tate's for dinner. He's having a house party for some of his frat buddies and invited us as their dates."

Zack groaned. No wonder Jill and the other girls from the gang never paid any attention to him. The competition was stiff. Grad students trumped frat students only when grade tampering was involved. And most students didn't need a TA's help with an art grade.

"But we're going to make it there by eight; no later than nine. So save us a seat?"

"For Tate and his buddies too?" Zack said, holding his breath.

"No, just the three of us. You okay, Zack?" Micah added.

Zack let out a breath, relieved he wouldn't have to deal with the testosterone all night. At least not the *rich* testosterone. He'd still be in competition with the rest of the guys in their gang.

"Not really," he answered. He hadn't been right since Monday night when he saw Jill at the library. "I'm just missing Jill."

"Me too," Micah said. "But the gang will all be together again tonight, and we'll lift our glasses high to her, okay?"

Zack didn't answer.

"She'd want us to, Zack."

"I know," he said.

But he wasn't so sure. There was something a bit perverse in toasting a dead friend two short days after her mutilated body had been found. What would people think? Would it draw attention to them? To him? Shouldn't they all be in mourning? Didn't they respect the significance and gravity of this event? The fact that one of their own was dead? The fact that de Milo had struck again? The fact that it could have just as easily been one of them?

"See you there," Micah said, and hung up the phone.

He resisted the urge to throw his cell phone against the wall. They weren't taking this seriously. They weren't taking *him* seriously. They had turned this into a celebration, a party. Was it just Micah, or all of the girls? They should be afraid.

Zack dialed another number. "Jackson, what's up?"

"Nothing, dude. What's up with you?" Jackson sounded like he'd started happy hour early. Zack frowned. Hoping Jackson was drinking to drown his sorrows rather than to party again, Zack wondered if he, too, should be seeking the answer for all this at the bottom of a bottle of Jim Beam.

"Want to grab a pizza?" Zack didn't want to be alone. He was itchy. Very itchy. The harrowing emotional roller coaster he'd been riding this week hadn't set well with him. He needed normalcy.

"I already ate, man. I'm just sitting here with my roomie listening to some Bob Marley tunes. Want to join us?"

"Yeah, I do," Zack answered, desperate to find company. Company that wasn't partying or yucking it up. Who were mourning the loss of Jill's beauty as he was. "Let me grab a pie and I'll be over in a few."

He walked across the street from his dorm and splurged on a large sausage-and-black-olive pizza to go from Sporty's. Zack waited on a tall stool, watching the second hand tick through the minutes, imagining the pie baking, the cheese melting, the crust crisping. He recalled the last time he had eaten pizza with Jill; he could picture the blue shirt she had worn with her faded jeans. She had pulled her hair into a ponytail and had worn a Broncos cap. She had picked off the olives and sausage from the piece he'd offered her and eaten the slice plain, just sauce and cheese.

She had smiled at him Monday night when he'd walked up to her at the library. Smiled because she'd been *happy* to see him.

"Zack?" a familiar voice called.

He turned on his stool, nearly toppling from the sudden movement. "Dr. Jay. What's up?"

"Just grabbing a bite. What are you up to, bud?"

"Same thing." Zack said. He pointed to the empty stool next to him. "Want to join me?"

"Happy to. Not feeling much like being alone, you know?"

Measured across the chest, Dr. Jay was almost twice Zack's size; otherwise, they were very similar in stature. They were also nearly the same age, Dr. Jay not much older than Zack. That and an appreciation for art were the only similarities they shared. The differences between them were far more numerous. Dr. Jay possessed an agility and Cuban smoothness that Zack admired, even coveted. A babe magnet. He certainly didn't need Zack to keep him company. He could have any woman on campus.

Zack answered, "Yeah, me too."

Dr. Jay sat down on the stool. "Order already?"

"Yeah," Zack said. "A large. Want some?"

"I ordered a large, too," Dr. Jay said, ignoring the coeds in tight exposed-midriff T-shirts and short shorts seated at the nearby table who were snickering and pointing at him and Zack.

Anyone he wants, Zack thought once more. *What a life.*

"I guess I was hoping to find company by ordering a large, hoping to attract a broke and hungry friend, right? You know, 'Build it and they will come.'" Dr. Jay smiled, his pearly teeth perfectly offsetting his tanned skin and dark eyes. The pencil-thin mustache didn't seem so outdated as it did when Zack had first met him.

"Yeah, right." Zack agreed. "I was headed over to Jackson's dorm with mine. Want to come?"

Dr. Jay nodded. "Sure."

The girls at the table rose, making sure to command Dr. Jay's attention by working what they had on their way out the door, then turning to wave and giggle. Zack was surprised to find Dr. Jay's attention was on him instead of the vamping coeds.

"How are you doing, Zack?"

"What do you mean?"

"For starters, you haven't been to class this week."

Zack tensed. "Considering the circumstances, I didn't think you'd mind."

"I do mind, Zack," the professor said, sipping his soda, pinching the straw as if it were the molding clay he used in the sculpting class. He raised an eyebrow and added, "I understand, but I mind."

Zack stared, dumbfounded. Why would he care whether Zack missed a couple of classes this week? Was he insane? Jill was dead. Murdered. What could be more important than that?

"I mind because the students look up to you," Dr. Jay explained, his dark eyes sparkling with intensity. "You and I need to be their rock during their journey across an ocean of grief. Do you follow me?"

Zack's shoulders relaxed. He hadn't been aware of all the tension he'd been carrying in his back, his neck, his shoulders.

"Don't you think I'd prefer to skip class?" Dr. Jay continued when Zack didn't answer. He patted his TA on the shoulder. "Missing Thursday, okay. But again yesterday? That was too much. We can't miss any more classes, got it?"

"Are you going to report me?" Zack blurted, wishing he hadn't said it the second the words left his lips.

Dr. Jay shook his head. "No need to have you lose your grad student status over a few missed classes. I wouldn't call that egregious in light of what's happened."

"Thank you," Zack sighed. He wanted to both punch Dr. Jay in the jaw and hug him. He had no idea why his emotions were so completely conflicted and out of control.

"Bravo?" the pimply college girl called from behind the counter.

Dr. Jay patted Zack on the back again and retrieved his pizza. Before he was able to sit back down beside Zack, the girl slid another box on the counter and called out, "Rhodes?"

Zack retrieved his pizza, smiling at the bespectacled brunette. She returned the favor, revealing a mouthful of silver. *Braces suck*, Zack thought, feeling sorry for the poor girl. In that short a time, a blonde had approached Dr. Jay and was talking with him about something. She had her back to Zack, so he wasn't sure whether to interrupt them. He decided to slide back onto the stool beside Dr. Jay and wait for them to finish their discussion so that he and the professor could walk across the street to Jackson's dorm together.

"Zack, you know Brittany," Dr. Jay said, touching her elbow as if introducing his wife at a cocktail party.

Renaissance Art History class. Tuesdays and Thursdays. Eleven o'clock. Third row from the back. Always by herself. "Yes, hi, Brittany."

Brittany blushed, her eyes widening. "I didn't know—"

"Relax," Dr. Jay said. "Zack here was just leaving. Right, Zack?"

Zack opened his mouth to correct him, to remind him that they were going over to Jackson's, when it dawned on him what Dr. Jay was doing.

"Oh, yeah. Uh, I was just on my way out the door. Just wanted to say good-bye to Dr. Jay. Bye," Zack said, standing and taking his pizza with him.

"Bye, Zack," Dr. Jay said, giving him a little wave and a smirk as Zack walked away. As he was leaving, Zack saw a second girl approach Brittany and Dr. Jay. A redhead. Tina. Same class. The same Tina that Micah had told him about yesterday. The one Dr. Jay was diddling. He heard Dr. Jay say, "I have enough for both of you. Are you hungry?"

The tinkling of the bell on the door drowned out their answer, but Zack knew what they'd say.

Lucky bastard.

CHAPTER 19

I HAD RESISTED THE temptation to go home all afternoon.

I had originally planned to be gone all day to give Lisa, Agent Pierce, and Detective Brandt some space and privacy to get their work done. It made me feel good to help the FBI and police find Jill's murderer, even if it was in such a small way, by lending them my home as their headquarters. But my original plans to keep my distance changed after I heard what the guys had told me about the novel *Crime and Punishment*, about Jill's conversation with them the last day she had worked, and about the ominous Jonah reference and its biblical significance. Or insignificance. Maybe I'd been fancying myself a bit too much like Nancy Drew or, more to my taste, Encyclopedia Brown, and I'd put too much emphasis on the importance of some of the things I'd learned.

But I would have expected Lisa to call me back long before now. Particularly considering the urgency of my message. Around two, when I hadn't heard from her, I became a bit concerned, but then I remembered that the cell phone reception wasn't that great up here in the foothills of the Rocky Mountains, considering the steepled mountains and the limited number of towers. And I convinced myself that I'd forgotten to give Lisa my work number.

Then Detective Brandt had called about three hours ago. Not only did that mean he and the FBI agents had my work number but also that Lisa was tied up in an interview, in the field, or in a mess of some kind; otherwise, she would have been the one to be in touch. When Brandt had reached me I was so excited to unload my mind of all the details I'd learned from the guys at lunch I hadn't paid much attention to his odd questions and his stiff, unnatural tone. Now that I had started my long journey home, I was reflecting on the ominous nature of his side of the conversation and becoming more worried about what was not being said.

"Liv, good," Detective Brandt had said when the call was transferred into my office around three fifteen. "Are you still at work?" he had asked, wondering if the transfer had been made on a landline elsewhere or to my cell phone with me in transit.

When I had told him I was in my office, he had asked how long I planned on working. I had told him as long or as short as he needed me to stay. He seemed relieved, judging by the long breath he exhaled. He said if it were all the same to me, he would prefer I not come home until six or later. I told him I would plan on being home at six thirty and that I'd bring dinner for all of them. Detective Brandt, lover of food, told me I didn't need to go to that much trouble.

As I rounded a corner of U.S. Highway 287 near Bellevue, it hit me that something serious must have happened. Detective Brandt was stalling, not wanting me to find out.

My foot got a bit heavier on the accelerator and I flew over the hill near Laporte and into Fort Collins. I was just fifteen minutes from home, my mind racing. I punched in Lisa's cell phone number, knowing I had clear signals now that I was near civilization.

No answer.

I punched in my home number and hit send.

On the first ring, a man answered. "Hello?"

"Who is this?"

"Who is *this*?" His voice sounded so prim and proper.

"Liv Bergen, the owner of that house." I knew I hadn't done such a great job keeping the annoyance from my tone, but I didn't care.

"Ah, Miss Bergen. Nice to meet you," the man said. "I'm Agent Kelleher."

He sounded more like an English butler than an FBI agent.

"Is Lisa—I mean is Agent Henry there, please?"

At first, I thought he was handing Lisa the headset. Then I realized from his soft breathing, he had simply not answered me. The pause was unsettling.

"Where are you, Miss Bergen?"

"On my way home," I answered. "Put Agent Henry on the phone, please?"

He finally admitted, "She isn't here."

"Agent Pierce?"

"Not here either."

He pronounced "either" with a long "i" sound rather than a long "e" sound. More so because of the concern that was roiling inside me, not wanting to admit I was scared to death about not knowing what was happening, and afraid to admit I was inexplicably filled with dread, I was really getting annoyed with this man.

"Let me talk to Detective Brandt then."

"Gone," the man said. "I will fill you in on everything the moment you arrive, Miss Bergen."

"Stop calling me Miss Bergen," I snapped and instantly felt ashamed. I didn't even know this man. He was in a stranger's home trying to do his job investigating a murder, and here I was yelling at him about my name. I took a deep breath. "Liv, please. And I look forward to meeting you in person."

"Likewise," Agent Kelleher quipped.

Oh, I had really pissed off this one. How to win friends and influence people—*not*! Way to go, Liv, I told myself as I closed my cell phone and slipped it back in the charger.

Within minutes, I pulled into my garage, spotting one unfamiliar car at the curb outside my house. I closed the garage door and turned the knob to the door into my house from inside my garage, but it was locked. I never locked this door. I figure if a burglar breaks into my garage, he'd break the lock or the door or both from the garage into my house. So out of convenience, I leave it unlocked. Something about locked doors keeping honest people from entering, I suppose.

I tried the knob again, hoping for a different result. No dice, and I couldn't for the life of me think where I had a house key since I so rarely used it. The key to my house was my garage door opener.

Before I had a chance to retreat to my Explorer and dig through my key rings, the door opened wide. A tall black man in a gray pin-striped suit, starched white shirt, and maroon tie stood inside my house. His short hair was gray around his temples, and he wore a very tight smile.

"Miss Bergen?" he said, sticking out a long, lean hand.

I gripped it and shook. "Liv. You must be Agent Kelleher."

He stepped aside and I walked up the stairs into the living room, glancing around, stunned. Everything had been rearranged, put back in place where it had been before Lisa had come to stay with me. Before my house had been turned into FBI headquarters. The couch was back where it belonged. The table. The desk. The computer was gone. No satchel, no files, no papers, no crime scene photos. Nothing. The entire house looked as if the prior two days had been nothing but a dream. And it reeked of ammonia.

I blinked twice. I turned around and squared off with the FBI agent, glaring at him.

Agent Kelleher's smile had disappeared and his face was pinched. "Have a seat. Please." He motioned to the couch.

I didn't move. Fear crept into my chest. I balled my fists and stood my ground. I was afraid. I wanted to believe I was afraid because I didn't know who this guy was that was giving me orders in my own home. For all I knew, maybe he was de Milo.

"Show me your badge." I didn't recognize my own voice.

He slipped his hand into his suit jacket. For a split second, I thought he was going to pull out a gun, just like they do in the movies. He pulled out a wallet and showed me the shiny gold emblem and identification. Special Agent Phil Kelleher. The picture was old, obviously taken in Kelleher's much younger days. He was thinner now, grayer, eyes tired compared to the mischievous eyes in the photo.

"Credentials," he said.

"What?"

"It's not a badge. Police carry badges. FBI agents carry credentials." He motioned me to the couch a second time.

I sat. He chose the armchair closest to me.

"Miss Bergen," he started, clearing his throat.

"Liv, damn it," I said for the third time.

"Liv," he said. "Agent Pierce called me today and asked me to meet with you. He's very sorry for not being able to meet with you himself and wanted to thank you for all your hospitality."

My eyes were pinned on his face. This wasn't about thanking me for using my house. There was more. Much more. And I wanted him to get to the point.

"Where is he?"

"He's not here."

"I *know* that. Where is he staying?"

"He's still in Fort Collins. At an undisclosed location," Agent Kelleher said.

He hadn't moved a fraction of an inch since sitting down. His erect posture made it look as though he was sitting on the head of a needle rather than on the softest armchair I owned.

"Undisclosed," I repeated.

He nodded.

"And Lisa?"

He didn't flinch. "That's why Agent Pierce asked me to come here."

My heart jumped. I had never even met Streeter Pierce, but right now I was angry as hell at him for putting me through all this weird veiled discussion about undisclosed locations with a tight-lipped, pretentious prick who acted like he woke up this morning to someone squeezing a lemon on his asshole.

"Where's Lisa?" I demanded.

For the first time, he shifted, casting his eyes to the floor. I pinned him with my eyes and he eventually lifted his gaze to me. His eyes had softened. "She's gone."

"Gone?"

"Dead," he said, and his brows slackened.

My mouth fell open. I didn't believe him. I pushed myself up from the couch and marched back to the spare bedroom. As I stepped into the room, the smell of ammonia hit me. My stomach flipped. My eyes scanned the bare room. The bed had been stripped and all the pictures and mementos I had on the dresser were gone. Lisa's bag and satchel were missing. It was as if she had never been here.

I stepped across the hall. The master bedroom was the same as any other day. Bed made. Neat. Orderly. Nothing missing. Nothing out of place. I poked my head in the master bathroom and the spare bathroom in the hall. No Lisa. I shuffled back down the hall to the living room, confused. Agent Kelleher was still perched at the edge of the armchair, erect, his hands neatly folded in his lap. His eyes were still soft.

"She's not dead," I said.

He said nothing.

I eventually slumped back into the couch across from him.

"She was murdered," he stated. "We think it was de Milo, but we're not sure."

"How? Why?" I asked, stunned by the news and numb to the implication and meaning behind it all.

"We don't know yet. She may have been on to something. Her files were compromised."

"Compromised? Her files? She had left everything here, spread out on the desk and table I had set up for her. Why didn't she leave the files here? With everything else?"

He looked at me and blinked.

I didn't understand any of this.

In a steady monotone he said, "She didn't take her files anywhere, Miss Ber—Liv."

"But that means . . . " My eyes must have bugged out of my head, because his words came quickly.

"She was killed here. In your home."

I slapped my hand over my mouth, fighting the urge to blow chunks all over the man's custom-made suit.

"We think he came in through the front door. There was no sign of forced entry. We think he caught her off guard. Agent Henry put up a good fight. A great fight."

My head was spinning. Lisa was dead. She'd been murdered. In my home. If only I hadn't invited her to stay here. If only I had been more persistent about my phone call earlier. If only I had not resisted the urge to come home. Maybe I could have stopped this whole nightmare from happening.

I registered his words as though from a great distance. "Agent Pierce asked me to stay with you until this is over. He's concerned for your safety and regrets the FBI's presence here having compromised or endangered you in any way the past two days. He wanted me to share with you his appreciation and deepest condolences on the loss of your friend."

Was this really happening? One minute my employee is murdered, the next my friend is murdered. *In my house.* How could this be?

"I don't want to make you uncomfortable, but I have swept the house and prefer to stay in the room where Lisa was staying so I can be close to your room. I will be able to protect you best from there. Will that work for you?"

I was half listening. Lisa was dead. I had just talked with her this morning. Shared a cup of coffee with her. Agent Pierce was still sleeping when we two had talked. She had just rolled out of bed, yet she was still as beautiful as a princess with her long black hair in tangles and blue eyes heavy with drowsiness.

A flurry of thoughts rushed into my head. "Maybe it was a student."

"A student?"

"Maybe that's who killed Lisa. A student." My mind was racing. "The guy who left the book for Jill. Jonah. In *Crime and Punishment*, a graduate student killed someone thinking he would never be caught. Maybe Jonah's a student. Maybe he left the book as a way to flaunt his murders to the rest of the world, like he's smarter than all of you—all of us. Maybe the Venus de Milo murderer is a student, thinking he can get away with this."

Agent Kelleher looked at me as if I'd completely lost my mind.

Then I remembered the conversation I'd had with Lisa about Boeing and the carpet cutting methods. "Did she tell you about the water?"

"The water?"

"Cutting carpets with water. At Boeing, where I used to work. Was that how he killed her? With water?" I gasped.

For the first time, Kelleher loosened his tight smile and shook his head. He looked much younger now. "Agent Henry told Agent Pierce of your idea about water being the potential murder weapon."

I stared at him, willing him to tell me more. I couldn't bear the thought of feeding Lisa with the information that led her to being killed.

"You were right," he said.

My head was swimming. "I got her killed with that suggestion?"

He shook his head. "De Milo would have no idea we're on to that lead. You were right about the water being the murder weapon. The coroner is doing further lab tests to confirm the speculation."

"So it wasn't in her files? The files that were compromised?"

"We don't think so," Agent Kelleher said. "What we're missing are her latest additions to the profile she completed last night. The one that Agent Pierce read. We believe de Milo deleted Lisa's updated report from the computer."

It was hard to imagine de Milo having been right here. In my living room. Standing a few feet from where I was sitting, hunched over the computer in broad daylight, deleting Lisa's files from her laptop. Murdering Lisa in this house, my home.

I buried my head in my hands and cried, finally feeling the gravity of this situation.

Between sobs, I heard Agent Kelleher say, "Computer forensics will be able to recover what she typed," and "They think they might have a partial fingerprint lifted from the bathroom sink," and "But you're in no danger of de Milo coming back here again."

I didn't want to hear any of it. I understood now why Detective Brandt had called this afternoon, why he had sounded so strange. I understood why Agent Pierce moved out and found a new location to call headquarters, an *undisclosed location*, because clearly they could be in danger of being targeted by de Milo too. I understood why Agent Kelleher was here to protect me. I understood why Lisa hadn't answered my call.

I just didn't understand the destruction, the senselessness of murdering good people like Lisa and Jill.

I didn't understand why God made people like de Milo.

CHAPTER 20

THE LIVE BAND'S BASS pounded just like his heart had mere hours ago when Agent Lisa Henry put up the fight of her life. She was something. She had punched him in his jaw harder than any man had ever hit him. And the clawing she did on his neck and cheek had left angry marks. He'd been careful to conceal the bruising and scratches with makeup, but it stung.

Tonight his head pounded with exhilaration. His sensitive fingers slipped into his pocket, seeking his trophy. His fingertips brushed against the jagged edges of the crystal, the rock he had lifted from Liv Bergen's dresser earlier that day, just before the photo shoot of Awakening. It felt solid, fragile, healing, and dangerous.

The strobe light blinked in time with the melodic thump, and his barstool vibrated, sending an erotic wave through his body. That, coupled with the gyrating movements of the patrons on the dance floor, most of whom were scantily clad summer school students, made his excitement grow. His eyes were fixed on Shelby's tight ass and round tits, bouncing, rotating, spinning. *The beauty of youth and twenty-year-old bodies*, he thought. They were all splendid desserts for an insatiable appetite.

"The gang's all here," he shouted, lifting his glass of water with a twist of lime toward his friends, who were all out on the dance floor.

They responded with loud whoops and hollers, lifting their beer bottles and tumblers toward him.

Life was good. So good.

Agent Streeter Pierce was probably beside himself tonight. Blaming himself, cursing de Milo, pacing the floor as if that would provide him with the answers he needed. He hoped William Tell and Awakening had been lovers and he'd just killed Tell's only reason to live. He hoped Tell would be so distraught over Awakening's death that he'd collapse in a heap and die. But that would be too good for him. He'd hoped he could have sampled a little of Awakening, just as he'd wanted to with Nutrition. But he was smarter than that. He would never indulge his desires with his subjects, his models for the masterpieces. Not only would it lead them to him were he to leave such DNA evidence, it might alter the models and ruin the purity of their expression. For a genius such as he, work always came first.

What he really wanted was for William Tell to be his seventh work of art, right alongside Awakening on his wall. Awakening was such a beauty, and thanks to the makeup he'd borrowed from Liv Bergen, she looked nearly perfect in her pose.

Just as he envisioned what William Tell would look like on his wall of fame, the door to the bar opened and in he walked. Agent Streeter Pierce, soon to be his William Tell.

———

Streeter stood inside the doorway, daring the bouncer to check his ID and allowing his eyes to adjust to the darkness and the strobes. How he despised the life of a barfly. The dark, the smoke, the noise, the crowds, the desperation. He thought of the many nights he'd spent in bars after Paula died, how desperate he'd been to find the answer to life's mysteries by looking into an empty shot glass. Or more like how he'd used that shot glass as an escape hatch from reality, the sequence of chutes sending his player slipping farther from the finish line rather than climbing the ladders that would help him win the game.

He hadn't been in a bar for years, either to socialize or to drink away misery. But he had spent his share of nights in places like this, working the crowds in search of that special rock to turn over and see what slithered out from beneath.

Handing the bouncer his credentials, rather than his license, Streeter glared at the meaty young man. "You've got regulars?"

Baby Bull Bouncer nodded. His neck was thick, his hair cropped short. His eyes had brightened when he returned the credentials to Streeter. He was more than the typical bored big boy seeking a job that required little exertion, some authority, and the perk of sleeping in. This brawny youth liked security, Streeter figured, and he would work it to his advantage.

"I need your help," Streeter said in a lowered tone.

Baby Bull leaned toward him, excited, yet trying to pretend he was disinterested in case others were watching. Streeter figured him for not much older than twenty-four or twenty-five, probably from a farm, or he might just be a hobbyist mechanic, given the callused hands.

"Jill Brannigan," Streeter said, scanning the room. "Is her circle of friends here tonight?"

Baby Bull nodded again and stuck out his hand, palm up. Streeter hadn't a clue what he wanted. Was he expecting a bribe?

"We've got a five-dollar cover charge. You just want to fit in, right? Pay or my boss will be on me like flies on shit. He'll want to know why I gave you special treatment, and he don't like cops or giving up any information on our patrons. So keep up appearances for me and I'll do you a favor."

Streeter nodded and reached for his wallet, fishing out the necessary bill.

As he did, Baby Bull put his thick hand in front of his mouth as if rubbing his nose and cheeks, covering his words. "See the chick on the dance floor with the cutoff shorts and orange tank top? The one with the blonde hair piled high on her head?"

Streeter said, "Mm hmm."

"Her name's Shelby. One of the most sought-after chicks in Jill's clique. But if you ask me, all of them are babes. And Jill was the best. A natural beauty. Didn't need all that makeup or skimpy clothes. Best because she was sincere, not a flirt like the others. Good-looking. The guys ain't bad looking either, if you swing that way. I don't."

Streeter handed him the five-dollar bill and said, "Thanks." For added measure he asked, "Ever think of applying at the Bureau?"

The kid's face lit up, his hooded eyes brightening. "Think I should?"

Streeter nodded once and walked toward the least crowded end of the bar. He ordered a Wild Turkey on the rocks and sipped the elixir, keeping his eyes focused on the activities of Shelby: who she talked with, how she approached them, and her body language and facial expressions with each individual she came in contact with during a series of five dance songs, one of which she had chosen to sit out to talk instead to two guys sitting at the other end of the bar. Those two were part of Jill's circle of friends, as were the two girls next to Shelby on the dance floor: the brunette with braids and the Dolly Parton look-alike.

The man Shelby had been dancing with most of the time must have been someone she didn't know as well, judging by the distance he kept from her clan. She appeared to be playing coy, yet never let him out of her sight. A hard-to-get flirtation. Contradictory. Three other men and a woman with short black hair in a pixie cut sat at the table next to the two guys at the bar and were guarding Shelby's drink, presumably so it wouldn't get spiked by someone with ill intentions. But it was all speculation by Streeter. Five men, four women.

Kari had told Streeter about Micah and Shelby, the only two of Jill's friends she had ever met. Julia confirmed having met those two as well. From their descriptions, Streeter realized that Micah was the one with long braids, the exotic-looking young woman dressed in tight jeans and a sleeveless floral blouse. He wondered which of the five men was named Jonah. He was about to find out.

The band had just announced they were taking a short intermission, giving themselves and the strobe lights a quick break. A soft yellow glow settled on the patrons in its place. Micah, Shelby, and Quasi-Dolly found their seats at the table with the four others; the two guys remained perched nearby on their barstools.

Streeter drained his glass and flagged the bartender with a folded bill, leaving it on the bar to square up his tab. He rose and walked to the other end of the bar, pulling up a chair to the table of six. They all stopped talking and stared at him.

Streeter had to shout over the noise of surrounding bar tables. "You're all Jill Brannigan's friends?"

The pixie snarled, "What's it to you?"

Streeter reached into his jacket pocket and pulled out his credentials. "I'm investigating her murder. Mind if we talk?"

Pixie's eyes widened and her mouth formed a small circle. "Sorry."

"Not a problem," he said, looking at all nine of the men and women in turn. "Is this everyone?"

They looked at each other and nodded.

"Mind if we step outside, where it's quieter, and talk for a few minutes?"

One of the pimply-faced boys whined, "We'll have to pay the cover again."

Pixie hit him in the arm and said, "Geez, Jackson. This is for Jill. It's worth another five bucks, you tightwad."

He rubbed his arm and Pixie motioned toward the door, "Let's go, gang."

Streeter kept his eye on Pixie, the obvious leader of this clan. They waited for Streeter to lead them out the front door. He winked at Bouncer as he went by, slipped him a fifty, and said, "Mind if I borrow these guys for a few? This pays their way back in, okay?"

Bouncer grinned and held up the fifty. "No problem."

The night was cool and fresh, stars blinking in the dark, cloudless sky above. Traffic was light and the downtown area sleepy compared to what he imagined took place during the regular school year. Streeter gathered the group around a bus stop bench under a streetlamp, away from the front entrance, the noise, and the watchful eye of the bar's manager.

Two of the men sat on the bench, motioning the women to sit beside them or on their laps. Micah and Pixie sat on the bench; Quasi-Dolly and Shelby each took a lap. The other three men lingered behind the bench, Pimply Face slouching against the lamppost.

"My name's Special Agent Pierce," Streeter said.

"FBI. Cool," one of the guys said.

"I'm the lead investigator on Jill's murder and I would like to ask you some questions. Mind if we start by introducing yourselves to me?" Streeter pulled out a notebook and pen, unaccustomed to writing notes during an interview but having to, because of the sheer numbers.

Pixie leaned forward and stuck out her hand. "I'm Christina Jensen. I just met Jill this semester. We were in a class together. And I hope you nail the bastard who did this to her."

Streeter shook her hand. Her handshake was firm and confident. "I do too."

Shelby waved. "And I'm Shelby Goodman. I've known Jill since freshman orientation two years ago. We've hung out ever since."

The good-looking young man beneath Shelby had been wearing a dopey grin on his face ever since she'd plopped onto his lap. Shelby elbowed him playfully to indicate it was his turn. "My name is Grady. I met Jill through Shelby about a year ago or so."

Shelby jerked a thumb his way and added, "Grady Mullany." Streeter wrote it down as Shelby spelled it for him. Grady flicked the long dark bangs away from his eyes when Streeter looked up at him and smiled.

Micah rose to introduce herself. She extended her hand toward Streeter, her slender warm fingers wrapping around his hand in a light, sensual handshake. Her aqua eyes were large and smoky.

"Micah Piquette. Jill's friend for the past two years. And thank you for finding whoever did this to her."

Streeter gave Micah a nod. "Haven't found anyone yet."

"You will," she responded.

Sincere, polite, polished. Not flirtatious. Mature.

The Quasi-Dolly wiggled her fingers and said, "Alicia Smith. I'm a freshman, and I just met Jill this semester too. Same time Christina did."

The young man supporting Alicia in his lap nearly spilled her onto the sidewalk when he rose to shake Streeter's hand. He was the tallest of the bunch, hovering over Streeter by a few inches. "I'm Andrew Peterson. Nice to meet you."

Streeter shook his hand, a strong, confident embrace. "Likewise. How did you know Jill?"

While Andrew spoke, Streeter wrote, thinking, *No Jonah yet*. He was down to three men.

"I met her during rush last year and we've been friends ever since."

Streeter asked, "Jill was in a sorority?"

Andrew shook his head. "She never pledged. She decided it was too much with her class schedule and with basketball."

Andrew motioned Alicia to take his seat on the bench and he remained standing.

The guy behind Alicia stuck out his fist and Streeter bumped it. "Cameron Kelly. Senior. I met Jill through Andrew. We share an apartment."

The shortest male in the group, which wasn't saying much, since all of them were taller than Streeter, waved. "Zack Rhodes. Grad student. I've known Jill for about seven months. I met her in a class I was helping teach."

"Are you a TA?" Streeter asked, already knowing the answer.

Zack nodded.

"What class?"

"Sculpting 101. For beginners," Zack said.

"Was she any good?" Streeter pressed.

A smile reached the corner of Zack's mouth. "Yeah, very good."

The others snickered. Zack's cheeks reddened.

Streeter studied him for a moment. He wore his long, black hair pulled back into a ponytail, and a skullcap was perched on top of his head. He donned a loose, button-up bowling shirt, baggy shorts, and Birkenstocks with wool socks. Every inch the art student. By the way Zack was talking about Jill—or, more important, avoiding the subject—Streeter was hoping this was Jonah.

"What kind of sculpting? Clay, wood?" Streeter asked.

Zack perked up. "Wood, technically, is carved, not sculpted. For sculpting, we use traditional clay materials."

The others shot a glance toward Zack, who reluctantly added, "But we do sometimes carve rather than sculpt."

The twitch on Zack's lip was unmistakable. Reflecting on the one-piece crutch that had been used to prop up Jill's corpse, Streeter focused on Zack's sudden nervousness. He was about to probe deeper with his questioning when Pimply Boy, who was still holding up the lamppost, shivered and griped, "It's colder than shit out here. Can we get this thing over with?"

Or maybe this was Jonah and they could all go home now, Streeter thought.

"Shut up, you big baby," Christina shouted at the peevish group member. "That's Jackson Whaler. He's a complete ass, so just ignore him."

The others laughed. Streeter noted his name, wondering if Whaler had anything to do with the moniker Jonah, the biblical Jonah having been swallowed by a whale. It was a long shot, but hearing no one's name remotely close to Jonah, he had little else to go on.

"Nice to meet you, Jackson. And I'd love to get this thing over with, but I need your help. Okay?"

Jackson shot him the peace sign. Streeter gave him a nod.

"Is this everyone?" Streeter asked again.

"Everyone?" Christina asked.

"The circle of friends you hang out with," Streeter asked. "Is everyone here tonight?"

Andrew said, "The gang. Yeah, this is everyone. I mean we all have our own friends outside this group, roommates, high school friends, other classmates. But this is the gang."

"Jill's gang?" Streeter asked again.

They all nodded.

Cameron poked Zack in the ribs. "Except Dr. Jay, right?"

Zack jabbed him back. "I'm not his keeper."

"The professor?" Streeter asked. "Dr. Bravo?"

"Yeah," Cameron said. "He's cool. That's where we all met, really. We all took Dr. Bravo's art class this spring. Some of us have been friends longer, but we weren't a group until this spring.

"And then we started a business together."

"What kind of business?" Streeter asked, noting Zack's blanched face.

Andrew explained, "It's cool. Nothing serious. We carve walking sticks and sell them on commission through all the convenience stores, gas stations, and tourist stops throughout the Rockies."

Streeter noted Zack visibly shrink into the crowd of his friends. "And is the business doing well?"

Jackson piped in, "Selling them as fast as we can make them."

"But we don't make that much money on them," Cameron added. "Just spending cash for pizza. And looks great on our résumés."

Streeter's mind was racing. "Okay, let me see if I've got this straight. You meet in beginning sculpting class. And you're the teaching assistant for Dr. Bravo," Streeter said, pointing to Zack. "All of you, including Jill, were in that Sculpting 101 class this year, from January to May. And then you started a business selling hand-carved walking sticks."

They all nodded.

"And everyone but Micah is in intermediate sculpting this summer," Alicia piped up, her voice sounding like a cheer.

Streeter looked at Micah and saw a slight flicker behind those smoky eyes. "I'm working. Need to earn the money to pay for fall semester. Not enough in sticks."

They laughed.

"And Dr. Bravo is part of the gang?" Streeter repeated.

"He hangs with us from time to time; comes and goes like the wind," Cameron said.

"More like a tornado," groused Jackson. "Blows in, steals all the girls, and then disappears."

"Ladies man, huh?" Streeter asked.

The guys nodded. The coeds giggled. Except for Micah. Streeter sensed there might be something more between Micah and Dr. Jay, but he was surprised by Shelby's answer. "Not *all* ladies. Just some of us."

Grady gave Shelby a playful push. "Him too? Not only did you do the TA, you did the professor too?"

"The Professor and Mary Ann," Jackson crooned the *Gilligan's Island* theme song with a smirk. "Right here on Shelby's Island!"

"Shut up, moron."

Streeter was getting enough of the picture. He decided to pull his line of questioning back on track. "Do any of you know who would have wanted to see Jill dead?"

They all shook their heads. Micah added, "It doesn't make sense. Jill had an unblemished soul. Wouldn't hurt a fly. Loved everyone. Judged no one."

"Was she having any trouble with anyone? Afraid of anyone? A love interest she spurned?"

The gang was still. Zack's face turned crimson. Streeter added, "Any of you date Jill before?"

The men were still. Jackson blurted, "Dated or wanted to date her?"

The others laughed. A nervous laugh, Streeter thought.

"Okay. Any of you who wanted to date Jill?"

Streeter was surprised by all the nods. Every man except Zack, who looked down at his shoes.

"Any of you ever ask her on a date?"

"She wasn't into that. She was too busy, too focused on school, on B-ball," Andrew explained. "I might have hinted around at it, but she never gave me any indication she was interested in dating. Just in friendship."

The men all nodded. Zack looked up at Streeter.

"Zack?" Streeter pressed.

"Andrew's right. Jill wanted to keep everything at a distance. She just wanted to be friends."

"And did you?" Streeter asked.

"Did I what?" Zack spat back.

"Did you keep it on a friendship basis?"

Zack shrugged. "Did I have a choice?"

Micah said, "Jill didn't let anyone in. She was guarded."

Shelby wiggled on Grady's lap. "You mean a prude."

Zack barked, "Well, at least she wasn't a slut."

Shelby stood and slammed her fists on her hips. "What does *that* mean?"

Zack looked down.

"You were the one who was always trying to hump her leg. *You're* the slut, and she didn't want anything to do with you," Shelby sniped.

Zack's eyes burned through her. "Not every girl's like you, Shelby, spreading your legs the first time a guy pays any attention to you."

Grady popped to his feet. "Hey, cool off, Zack."

"Tell *her* to cool off. We've all had her and we all know it," Zack shot back, pointing at Shelby. "Jill was different."

Streeter stepped forward, placing his hand gently on Grady's shoulder. "Hey, hey. Have a seat. This is going nowhere. I'm not here to judge. I'm here to find out what happened to Jill."

Grady took a seat. Shelby shot daggers at Zack before turning her back to him and plopping herself onto Grady's lap again. Zack stomped off toward the bar, glowering back at them and calling over his shoulder, "I have to use the bathroom."

He was gone before Streeter could say anything; besides, he knew this crowd was restless and his time with them short.

Streeter studied each one's face, weighing whether this was the time to catch them all off guard and gauge their reactions. "Ever hear of anyone named Jonah?"

CHAPTER 21

THOU SHALT NOT KILL.

I lay there, eyes closed, wondering which commandment it was. Fifth? Six? I had cried myself to sleep last night because of Lisa, my heart full of sorrow that her time had been cut short at the peak of her brilliant life. I prayed to God my heart wouldn't be as full of hate as it was for de Milo and could hear Sister Delilah telling me I would go to hell for thinking such bad thoughts about him.

"What makes his sin of murder worse than yours of wishing him dead?" she would ask me if she were still alive.

"Because," I would reply.

"No sin is greater than another," she would insist.

"Bullshit," I would think.

I could hear Sister Delilah reciting the Ten Commandments, forcing me to memorize them. In order. The exact wording. She was tough. Third grade religion class was the first and only C I ever earned in all my years of schooling. It wasn't because I couldn't memorize and regurgitate. That was easy. It was because I challenged and questioned.

When we were studying Genesis, for instance—all about the beginning of time, of creation, of the world, and the Garden of Eden, with

Adam and Eve and all the subsequent generations begotten up, or down, to Noah—I had been sitting behind Jason, the classroom bully. I happened to have a crush on him, probably because he was the one person Sister Delilah disliked more than me, which made us kindred spirits. As I recall, he was sporting a black eye that week, and I imagined he had got it from Sister Delilah, which both tickled and frightened me.

The lightbulb went on when we read that Adam and Eve had two sons. Cain slaughtered his brother, Abel, in the field, and then Cain took a wife and had Enoch, and so on and so on. The question in my mind was, Who the hell was Cain's wife? His mother, Eve? Or was it a sister never mentioned in the Bible? Or, more accurately, never mentioned by Sister Delilah. Either way, unless God had created a bunch of Adams and Eves, wasn't there something terribly wrong with that picture of begetting?

I don't recall exactly how I broached the subject, but I do remember Sister Delilah's expression quite vividly, and the collective gasp in the classroom. Jason grinned and flashed me a grin, which cost him his recess for the next week.

Sister Delilah never answered my question.

Her eyebrows simply bobbed and wobbled above her thick, black glasses, her chins doubling in number as she banished me to the principal's office. And believe me, any moment with Sister Marie in her go-go boots was way scarier than catechism with Sister Delilah. And both were scarier than the prospect that we were all descendents of biblically unexplained incest.

I should have learned back then to keep my big mouth shut. But within a week, I was asking what was so good about Good Friday.

As the sunlight slipped into my room between the blinds, I squeezed my eyes shut, willing the darkness to return until I could rid myself of evil wishes and of desires to break several of the commandments on this wicked Sunday. To start with, I cursed God for taking Lisa.

A crash of broken glass pierced my thoughts. Not a lightning bolt, but certainly a sign nonetheless.

I bounded out of bed and dashed down the hall. Agent Kelleher was standing in my kitchen, a broken coffee cup at his feet, his face sheepish.

"I am *so* sorry, Miss Bergen," he said. "I will repay you. Did I wake you?"

I shook my head and retrieved the broom and dustpan, making short order of clearing away the mess. "I was awake anyway."

He pulled another cup from the cupboard. "You were awake most of the night."

I shot him a glare. "How would you know?"

He unabashedly answered, "I could hear you crying."

My cheeks burned. I dumped the broken glass into the garbage and put the broom and dustpan away. Agent Kelleher poured himself a second cup of coffee and retrieved a cup for me, filling it as well and offering it to me.

I thanked him and sipped, grimacing at the bitter taste.

"You don't like it," he stated.

"How many scoops did you use?"

"Three per cup," he said. "I like mine black."

His grin was pleasant. He was definitely growing on me.

"Well, okay, but does it have to be thick enough to chew?"

That converted his grin to a small smile. He regarded me and drank. At that instant I became aware that I was standing in my kitchen with a well-dressed man, perfectly coiffed and wearing a navy blue suit and wingtips, and me in nothing but an oversized T-shirt and panties. Agent Kelleher's eyes hadn't roamed, and he had had the decency to pretend not to notice.

I excused myself, gripping my coffee cup as if it were a shield, and retreated to my bedroom.

"Shit," I said, leaning against my bedroom door after I'd closed it. "Why, God? Why me?" I asked, staring at the ceiling.

I could hear Mom say, "Why not?" which always made me quit whining. Her point was always, if not you, then who deserves the challenges? God was indiscriminate and everyone had challenges of one kind or another. She would always tell me when I was feeling too sorry for my pitiful self to look around me and see how many had it worse than me. She was right. She was always right.

And she would never have asked Sister Delilah how Cain procreated. So much better mannered than her daughter.

I set my coffee cup on my dresser and sat on my bed to pray. I had switched from Catholicism to Lutheranism when I was in college, mostly because I struggled with the concept of transubstantiation. But I told people it was because all that kneeling, sitting, standing, and kneeling again wore me out. Kneeling to pray was brutal on my knees, so I'd been sitting to pray, like the good Protestant I was, for the past decade or so.

I prayed every morning for God to dull the edges of my sharp tongue and to help me to stop swearing, but that worked about as well as New Year's resolutions had. At least I never used the Lord's name in vain. Sister Delilah would be proud, wouldn't she?

I made my bed and had turned to grab my coffee cup before heading for the shower when I noticed the photograph of my family. All eleven of us huddled in the woods in our most colorful shirts and blue jeans. Something was amiss. I counted the cluster of rocks that encircled the photo, rocks I had collected from the various quarries we mined throughout South Dakota, Wyoming, and Colorado. Ten. One was missing. My eyes swept the floor around the dresser then swept across the circle of rocks again. I was missing the crystal, the one from the quarry at Livermore where I work. The crystal was the most fragile of my rocks, most of which were limestone, sandstone, iron ore, gypsum, or gravel. Where the crystal had been, I could see the tiny shiny pieces that had crumbled from it.

I pulled on my jeans and rushed down the hall. "Agent Kelleher?"

He stepped out of the kitchen and turned toward me, his gun drawn. The urgency in my voice must have signaled alarm for him.

I held up my hands, "No, I'm sorry. I'm okay. But I think I found something."

He followed me into my bedroom.

I pointed to the picture and the rocks. "One of them is missing. The crystal from my quarry, where I work. It's gone."

He stared at the rocks and at the picture. I could tell he wasn't following me.

"I have eight brothers and sisters. That's my mom and that's my dad," I explained, pointing to them as I spoke. "We're in the mining business. I like rocks. I have one for each of my family, a rock from different quarries. Mom's is missing. The crystal. The Beauty. It's gone. Someone took it. See how the crystal dust is all over the wood?"

I feared he still wasn't following me.

"The complete circle of rocks was here Friday evening when I changed the sheets for Agent Pierce. I remember seeing everything in its place. I made sure of it. I'm kind of a neat freak."

"Maybe Agent Pierce took it," Agent Kelleher said.

"Maybe," I agreed, "but if he or the crime scene people didn't, maybe the killer took it. Or Lisa hid it or placed it somewhere, as a clue."

Even as I was saying the words, I thought how silly I sounded. Again, I had become the really bad version of Nancy Drew's or Encyclopedia Brown's younger and idiotic sister. Agent Kelleher rubbed his chin and stared at the empty space on the dresser.

"Let me make a call or two," he said, leaving me alone in my room. "And don't touch anything on that dresser," he called over his shoulder as I shut the door.

I took a shower and enjoyed the feeling of the hot water over my aching muscles. I had been too tense to sleep last night and I was paying for it this morning. I quickly dried off, brushed my teeth and hair, and pulled on a clean pair of jeans and a button-down oxford shirt. I was no match for Agent Kelleher, but at least I wasn't in my sleepwear anymore.

I padded down the hall in time to hear Agent Kelleher say good-bye to someone on the cell phone. "The crime techs dusted in your room already, and no one except Streeter remembers seeing the rock. He said it was there when he was staying in your room; he had noticed you had a rock for everyone in your family."

"That was observant of him," I remarked, amazed at his attention to detail.

"He doesn't miss much," Agent Kelleher said.

"I'd like to meet him," I said, wondering if a guy this great at his work and handsome to boot could exist. Lisa had obviously been crazy about this guy, even though she'd insisted it was nothing sexual. I wondered how he was taking all of this. It couldn't have been easy for him or anyone with the Bureau; Lisa was one of them, a coworker, who had been murdered in the line of duty. I hadn't really given that much thought yesterday when Agent Kelleher had told me the news. In fact, I had been wound up so tight with self-pity and grief and irritation with him, I had been totally unsympathetic to his feelings. I really hadn't even given one thought to how Lisa's death might be affecting him.

"Agent Kelleher," I began, "I am so sorry for your loss. You must be devastated by Lisa's death. And thank you for being there for me yesterday and staying with me last night to protect me."

He nodded, folding his hands behind his back as if he were a soldier at ease. "You are welcome, Miss Bergen."

"Liv," I sighed. We stood in the living room, not sure of what to do next. He seemed less at ease than I was. I finally clasped my hands and said, "Well, can I make you breakfast?"

"That would be lovely. Thank you."

It was hard not to think back to yesterday, when I had spent the morning with Lisa Henry in this very kitchen. I recalled what she had told me about the case. And after we talked, she had mentioned again that I should seriously consider joining the Bureau. Her last words to me. I thought about what my last words to her had been. On my way out the door, I had told her to be careful.

"Agent Kelleher!" I yelled to him in the living room, startling both of us. I dropped the spatula I'd been using to stir the scrambled eggs. It tumbled to the floor, sending bits of egg in all directions. I didn't care. He was beside me in seconds.

"I forgot all about this. Yesterday morning I told Lisa to be extra careful. I was worried because I could have sworn I saw someone at my window Friday night; it was Saturday morning, really, at 2:00 AM. I had awakened to a noise. I was sleeping in the basement on the couch so Agent Pierce would have a comfortable place to sleep. The noise woke me up and I could have sworn I saw someone standing outside the window. I could see halfway up the shins, but for some reason my mind jumped to the conclusion it was a man."

I was embarrassed that I hadn't remembered that detail again until now. I must have thought it was more than a dream, because I had the inclination to mention it to Lisa before I headed off to work. And now she was dead. Murdered by someone who broke into the house.

"Maybe he was casing the house," I said, sounding more and more ridiculous every time I spoke. Casing? I'm surprised I didn't just jump off the deep end completely and tell Agent Kelleher that the perp was casing the joint.

Kelleher didn't find it as ridiculous as I thought I sounded. He turned toward the stairs and said, "Show me where."

I followed him down and showed him where I'd been sleeping the night before, pointing to the high window on the basement wall.

"Were there lights on outside?"

I shook my head. "No lights, but the moon was bright. Enough for me to make out two legs. And shoes."

"What kind of shoes?"

"I don't know exactly. I had rubbed my eyes to get a better look, and when I looked again, the man was gone. But I'm sure of what I saw. At least I must have been sure, because I had the sense to warn Lisa to be extra careful." I was starting to doubt everything. Maybe I hadn't seen anything at all. Maybe it was just an overactive imagination brought on by the situation and my houseguests. I couldn't be sure.

Kelleher rubbed his chin again and stood on his tiptoes to see out the basement window.

"Dirt," he said, walking up the stairs and out the front door.

I followed close behind him.

He rounded the house to the picket fence and gate, unable to work the latch.

"Here," I said, stepping around him and lifting the metal latch on the inside of the fence to release the gate.

He scanned the grass in my backyard and walked toward the basement window. When he approached the window, he scanned the dirt closest to the house and noticed a partial boot print right where I had said I'd seen a pair of legs. His eyes searched the area, and he stepped within inches of the partial boot print without compromising it and lifted his gaze upward. The guest bedroom window sat directly above the basement window. Kelleher was looking directly into the room where Lisa had slept. He was unable to see the four feet or so beneath the window, but he was able to see the rest of the room by stepping on his tiptoes.

Agent Kelleher flipped open his cell phone. "Streeter, it's Phil. We need to get the techs back and lift a boot print. Miss Bergen had warned Lisa yesterday morning about a prowler she'd seen earlier that morning around two o'clock."

He listened for a minute and pulled the phone away from his mouth, looking at me when he asked, "How sure are you of the time?"

"Very sure," I said. "I looked at the clock."

Agent Kelleher finished the call and closed the phone. He leaned over and kissed me on the forehead, something I would have never pictured this rigid man doing to anyone in his life.

He must have noticed my startled expression because he said, "Not me. It's from Streeter. He told me to do that and to tell you you're brilliant."

CHAPTER 22

SUNDAY MORNINGS WERE USUALLY his favorite time of the week. Not today. After Lisa Henry's murder the day before and the marathon of interviews he'd conducted since, Streeter felt like he'd been back amid the angry mob that flooded the streets of Mogadishu during Operation Gothic Serpent—expecting an ambush, edgy and hyped, amped to unhealthy heightened awareness. Both missions had left Streeter feeling a complete failure, with similar horrific endings: eighteen dead comrades in Somalia, one important friend dead in Colorado. Streeter was seething about de Milo's freedom as much as he had about Mohamed Farrah Aidid on that fateful mission in October. Three years as a Marine on a select military team had been wasted back then, but he was not about to waste any time now.

Streeter wasn't accustomed to interviewing so many people at once. Having to change his method wasn't helping his mind wrap around what was being said any faster than if he had interviewed each person individually. He felt pressured, trapped by the urgency of de Milo's murders. They were coming more quickly, more frequently than even Lisa had predicted. She had warned him of this, and now Lisa was dead. Lisa's murder had occurred in broad daylight within three days of Jill's murder and at the very home where the FBI had established temporary headquarters. Was de Milo mocking them, taunting them, he wondered? And when did he start thinking of Agent Henry as Lisa? He admonished himself for getting too close to her in death and wondered why he hadn't had the courage to in life. Streeter needed a break, but what he needed more was to make every precious minute count, pressing on with interviewing and investigating, with the pursuit of every angle. Lisa deserved at least that.

Buzzed on adrenaline and secretly worried about time running far too short, Streeter had asked Detective Brandt to join him last night, only to learn from Brandt's wife that Douglas had taken three sleeping pills earlier that evening and was knocked out cold in a deep sleep. *Warding off the nightmares*, Streeter thought. *Good luck.*

So he had interviewed Jill's circle of friends last night on his own. All nine of them. None of them ever having heard of a Jonah. And he had just finished interviewing Jill's basketball teammates this morning, thanks to Coach Beck. All thirteen of them, along with the assistant coach and the team psychologist. None of them was named Jonah or had ever heard of Jonah. And no one's expression changed much at the mention of the name.

Earlier that morning Streeter had also been able to reach two of the three professors he still needed to interview, including the infamous art professor, Dr. Jay, whose office he was on his way to now from the gym. Dr. Brian Miller, Jill's computer science teacher, said he could meet with Streeter that afternoon. Dr. Helen Dixon, Jill's journalism professor, hadn't answered her phone. He would try later. And he definitely needed to conduct a one-on-one interview with Zack Rhodes to learn more about the wood carving, a direct connection to the crime scene.

As Streeter walked across the green, he dialed his cell phone. "Where are we on the print?"

"They only got a partial. Most of the toe from the left boot," Kelleher answered.

"What did Linwood say?"

"He said we have a match from the shoreline at Horsetooth."

Streeter sighed. "Thank God."

"Jack also said he ran the tread through the database and found it's consistent with a hiking boot that only Cabela's and Jax sells."

"Nearest stores?"

Kelleher paused. "Cabela's would be Sidney, Nebraska, I think. Maybe three hundred miles. But Jax is a local store."

"To Denver?"

"No, to Fort Collins."

"De Milo's a local," Streeter concluded, piecing together the retailer for the boot, the hand-carved crutch, and his incredible intuition.

"Looks that way," Kelleher agreed. "Jack moved on to the items we pulled out of Lisa's room. I told him that was priority."

"Thanks. How's Liv?"

"Pretty shook," Kelleher said. "But she's hanging in there. She's running right now. Good kid."

"Smart kid," Streeter added. "Without her we wouldn't have found the boot print, figured out the probable murder weapon, or had the book from Jill's locker or the letter from the mysterious Jonah that no one seems to know anything about."

"She isn't through yet," Kelleher said.

"What do you mean?"

"She said there was something bugging her about the pomegranate we found under Lisa Henry's bed. Miss Bergen said she hadn't bought a pomegranate since her sister, a woman she referred to as Elizabeth, stayed with her a year ago. Said the pomegranate reminded her of something and she was going to run to get her mind wrapped around whatever was eluding her."

"You think de Milo was after Liv?"

"Don't know. Let's see what she comes up with."

"Kelleher, you shouldn't have let her go alone," Streeter fussed.

"I know, but it's not like Miss Bergen gave me a choice."

From Kelleher's tight tone, Streeter could tell Liv Bergen had become a handful for him. "Her name's Liv. Why so interminably proper, Kelleher?"

"Why do you call Miss Bergen by her first name, Streeter?"

Impasse. He decided to change the subject and give Kelleher a break. "Have you canvassed the neighbors about Friday night?"

Kelleher said, "One neighbor agreed with you about seeing a truck with a topper parked along the street, not in the cul-de-sac, just like you said. Another neighbor claimed he saw it parked in Liv's driveway yesterday around noon."

"Bingo," Streeter said.

"Tim Gregory is working on it with Jack."

"No, I agree with you that Linwood needs to stay focused on the evidence pulled from Henry's room. We're running out of time before de Milo kills again."

"And Tim's saying he won't have much luck on the truck without the plates, or even a partial number."

"It was too dark. It was late. I assumed it was a neighbor's truck," Streeter argued.

"Streeter, I wasn't blaming you. What I'm saying is that the neighbors didn't remember any numbers either. But we have the make, the model, the color, and the approximate year."

"And the tire tread, once we find the truck. If it's de Milo's."

Streeter was approaching the stairs to the College of Arts building.

Kelleher continued, "Chandler pulled some strings for you and he's got someone from DMV coming in today to access some information for us. At least we can narrow it down. We're going to get this guy, Streeter."

"I hope you're right."

Streeter closed the cell phone and slipped it into his pocket, bounding up the stairs two at a time. The front door on the far left was unlocked for him, just as Dr. Jay Bravo had promised, and the only light on in the building was Dr. Bravo's office on the second floor. Streeter's even steps echoed down the long marble halls. Just as he was approaching the office, out stepped a tall figure.

Streeter immediately likened Dr. Bravo to a cartoon character, so exaggerated were his features. His tall frame and delicately long fingers were what he expected of an artist, but his handshake was strong and his chest looked oddly larger than his frame would suggest as natural. But nothing about Dr. Jay Bravo seemed natural, starting with the weird, ponderous pose he had assumed just as Streeter neared. The professor held his left hand lightly to his cheek, his right arm crossing his body and the back of his right hand holding up the elbow of his left arm. Streeter half expected the man to call him Rochester in his best Jack Benny impersonation.

"Agent Pierce?" the man asked, extending the right hand, his left still resting against his cheek.

"Dr. Bravo?"

"They call me Dr. Jay," he said, his smile wide and bright next to his tan skin. He had dark eyes and an athlete's body. His jet-black hair was shoulder length, perfectly trimmed and tucked neatly behind his ears. *Must be an artist thing, particularly on this campus*, Streeter mused. The pencil-thin mustache was fifties vintage and oddly timeless on this thirty-something gentleman. Dr. Bravo's presence was somewhat off-putting, the way you'd feel meeting a model for romance novel covers, yet magnetic, as if he were everyone's long-lost friend. "Just like the basketball star of yore. Only I know nothing about the game. Just how to model clay."

He was as demonstrative and confident as Streeter would expect an American college professor to be, yet the slightest accent suggested his parents were not American, and his facial features hinted at classic Mediterranean.

"Come in, please." Dr. Bravo waved the FBI agent into his small office.

Streeter stepped past him and sat in the only chair available, directly in front of Dr. Bravo's desk. The bookshelves were filled with art books, and oversized books were stacked on the floor behind the professor's desk. Every book appeared to be well used rather than simply for appearance's sake. Dr. Bravo slipped around the edge of his desk and seated himself across from Streeter, angling his chair sideways to gaze out the window while they talked.

"What can I do for you?"

"I'm here about Jill Brannigan, as I mentioned on the phone," Streeter said, amazed by Dr. Bravo's peculiar behavior.

"Yes, yes, but how can I help you?"

Streeter studied Dr. Bravo's hands as he flailed them impatiently in the air. Long, lean fingers, curiously strong. Maybe from endless hours of sculpting, he supposed.

"Tell me about her."

Dr. Bravo leaned back in his chair and studied the ceiling. "Jill was a wonderful student. She was earning an A in my class."

"Intermediate sculpting?"

"Yes," Dr. Bravo said. "And she had earned an A in the beginners class as well."

"Spring semester?"

"That's right," Dr. Bravo said. "You must have her transcript?"

"Dr. Pembroke gave it to me," Streeter answered.

"Ah, Rebecca. Sweet Rebecca," Dr. Bravo said, twisting in his chair to gaze out his window toward the Administration Building, where she had her office.

"You two friends?" Streeter asked.

Dr. Bravo grinned. "Aren't we all, Agent Pierce? Academia is quite the clique. A close-knit gaggle, if I may say so. All of us seeking to impart higher knowledge to today's youth."

"Higher knowledge?"

Dr. Bravo arched his brows and sighed. "Must I spell it out for you?"

"That's what you call it these days?" Streeter said, resisting the urge to spring across the desk and wring this pretentious gigolo's neck for all womankind's sake.

Dr. Bravo turned to face Streeter and raised his hands in surrender. "I am nothing but a man and easy prey for the wiles of the lovelier sex. I love them all, and I choose not to discriminate."

Streeter drew in a large breath. "Tell me about your relationship with Jill."

"Ah, but alas, Jill was one of my serious students."

"Serious?"

"Focused, goal oriented. She was not one to stop and smell the roses," Dr. Bravo said. "You know the type. A go-getter, a type-A personality."

"You say that as if it was a bad thing," Streeter retorted, thinking of himself.

"Well, in the world of Art, in which I live, focus and goal setting are okay, but living life is more important." Dr. Bravo leaned forward on his desk and held Streeter in his fierce gaze. "You look as if you don't understand. Probably a type A yourself. Art comes from emotion, from life experiences. You must *feel* what you're doing, not think about what you're doing."

Streeter noticed the scratch along Dr. Bravo's jawbone and suddenly realized he'd just discovered the reason for the professor's odd Jack Benny pose and seeming fixation on the views outside the window.

Dr. Bravo had closed his eyes and was rubbing his fingertips together as if sensing something Streeter couldn't see. Streeter again used the opportunity to soak in every detail of Dr. Bravo's office. His desk was neat and organized, with three piles equally spaced apart: graded papers in one, papers needing to be graded in another, a third pile that looked to be administrative memos or letters. His two pens lay parallel to the piles. His books, obviously well read, were stored on the shelves alphabetically by topic.

As to the professor himself, Streeter noted his hair, although long and below his ears and shirt collar, was washed, neatly combed, and perfectly cut. His fingernails were groomed, his open shirt ironed, and his silk pants custom cut to his strong body. Everything about him was immaculate— maybe psychotically so.

"When you feel what you are doing, the art is natural, not forced as it is when you think you're way through it." Dr. Bravo's eyes fluttered open. "Jill's sculpting was forced."

"You said she was an A student?"

"She was," Dr. Bravo said. He gave a shrug and a crooked smile. "I never said she couldn't sculpt. I just said it was forced. She thought too much about what she was doing. She was good, but I would have liked to see her be great. If she could have felt her work, she could have been one of the greatest students I ever taught."

"You liked Jill?"

"Very much so," he said, twisting his body again to face the window. "Who didn't? She was smart, talented, strong. A regular Venus. That combination is an aphrodisiac for most of us men, don't you agree Agent Pierce?"

Something about the way he said his name bothered Streeter. "And was Jill one of the many students you'd slept with, Dr. Bravo?"

A smile slid across the professor's lips. He lifted his hands in surrender once again. "Agent Pierce. As I told you, I avoid confrontation of any kind.

Capitulate, not conquer. Kiss, not clash. Cuddle, not quarrel. So why do you choose to joust with me about something so personal?"

"Because it's my job when someone is murdered," Streeter said, measuring his words carefully.

Dr. Bravo chuckled. "I see. So, nothing is off-limits? Not even my love life? Well, normally I would say Jill Brannigan would be someone I was very interested in . . . sampling, shall we say? But she was an athlete and I have no interest in muscular women. A turnoff for me, I suppose you could say."

The muscles in Streeter's jaws were working double time. "You never hit on her? Pursued her?"

Dr. Bravo's head bobbed from side to side. "Maybe a little, in the beginning. That was this past January. Before I knew she was an athlete."

"Yet you hung out with her and other students from your class at the bars every weekend," Streeter pressed.

"Of course," Dr. Bravo admitted. "They are a wonderful lot. Full of life and wonder; brimming with energy."

"And have you 'sampled' any of them?"

"Agent Pierce," Dr. Bravo said with a cluck of his tongue. "You surprise me. A voyeur, are you? Interested in all that is so intimate, so personal? But if you insist, of course I have. Have you met the cute little cherub known as Alicia? Or the wild Christina? And that hot little Shelby . . . oh, what a man-eater!"

"You're disgusting," Streeter said.

"Maybe to you, but you're a thinker. If you lived life like I do, you would understand why feeling is so much better than thinking."

"You're just a lecherous opportunist." Streeter surprised himself with this uncharacteristic voicing of an opinion, warning him to regain control of his emotions.

"Lecherous?" Dr. Bravo mused. "So often that is coupled with *old*, Agent Pierce, and I am not old. Only a few years older than my students, as a matter of fact. They're old enough to know what they're doing—and to choose to do whatever they want with me, I might add. At least I treat them with the respect they deserve, as adults who have opinions and desires, unlike those of you who treat them as brainless tots needing parental advice at every turn. Your dismissive and pejorative treatment of these intelligent human beings is as useless as training wheels on a motorcycle."

"Who scratched you?" Streeter suddenly shifted gears and then gauged Dr. Jay's reaction.

"I told you, some of my lovers are a little wilder than others, like my little Christina. She likes it rough. As does Yolanda."

"Yolanda Fischer, the statistics professor?"

"Does that shock you?"

In truth, it further disgusted him. Streeter wasn't getting anywhere but angry during this interview. "Do you know of anyone who might have wanted to hurt Jill in any way?"

Dr. Bravo leaned back in his chair and closed his eyes once more. Streeter took the moment to scan Dr. Bravo's office again. Books were everywhere, of course: on art, on artists, on the masters, on romance, on Italy and France. An empty champagne bottle and flute sat on the windowsill, together with a small glass replica of the globe and a romantic greeting card that was too far away for Streeter to make out the name of the sender, but he saw the heart drawn under the signature. Dr. Bravo had placed a tiny blue ceramic songbird, an agate with purple crystals, a heart-shaped piece of glass, and a rock formation of clear crystals next to a photograph of himself in a graduation gown standing with what looked like his mother, who was laying a kiss on his cheek.

"This is a difficult question you ask me, Agent Pierce, because of course you are looking for the murderer. But I am seeing it from my view as a friend," Dr. Bravo said.

Streeter perked up. "Which friend?"

"My assistant."

"Zack Rhodes," Streeter said.

"Zachary was quite infatuated with our little Jill Brannigan. Enough so, that he would stalk her. In fact, on Monday night when I was dropping off some art books at the library, I saw him hiding behind a pillar in the library, watching Jill as she worked in a cubicle nearby."

"Why didn't you tell the authorities?"

"About a college boy infatuated with a college girl? You can't be serious, Agent Pierce," Dr. Bravo said.

"About seeing Jill at the library with Zack Rhodes Monday night, the last time she was ever seen alive," Streeter growled.

"You sound like you swallow barbed wire for sport, Agent Pierce," Dr. Bravo mused.

Streeter contained his simmering anger. "Why didn't you tell the police once you learned that Jill had been murdered?"

Dr. Bravo waved a dismissive hand. "Not everyone thinks as you do, Agent Pierce. As I have told you, I'm a lover, not a fighter. And I pity Zack for loving someone incapable of seeing his attributes. I certainly don't see him as a murderer. I only suggest he may know more about what may have happened to poor Jill that night. Maybe you should talk with him instead of prying into my love affairs?"

Streeter wanted to reach across the desk and punch this Romeo's lights out.

"And what were you doing there that night?"

"As I said, I was dropping off some art books. And I had a student consultation, if you must know.

"I must. Give me a name." Streeter clenched his teeth.

"So you can verify my alibi? His name is Barton. Collin Barton."

Just as he was deciding it might be a good idea to poke Dr. Jay in the nose after all, Streeter's cell phone chirped. He punched the buttons to silence the ringer.

"Before I go, what kind of car do you drive?"

"A Maserati, of course," Dr. Bravo said, smiling widely at him. "A coupe, actually. *Nero carbonio.*"

"That's the model?"

Dr. Bravo chuckled. "The color. Black as coal. I can see you are no connoisseur of the automobile."

That was an understatement. Streeter couldn't care less what type of car he drove. It was a means to an end: something to get him from here to there. But he did know that owning a Maserati coupe meant Dr. Bravo came from money. A college professor's salary wouldn't support the man driving such an expensive luxury car.

Dr. Bravo added, "Unique, sporty, muscular styling."

"Let me guess," Streeter said. "Like you?"

"Why, yes, Special Agent Streeter Pierce. You catch on quickly."

"And who's Jonah?"

Dr. Bravo looked puzzled. "Jonah? Who's Jonah?"

"I'm asking you."

Didn't so much as blink or hesitate, but Streeter thought he saw the slightest flicker in his eyes. "A jealous boyfriend? Husband?" Dr. Bravo ruminated. "Maybe he's a thinker like you."

Streeter excused himself to answer the call that was coming in for a second time.

CHAPTER 23

JACK LINWOOD LIFTED HIS eyes from the scope and rubbed them with the back of his wrist, using his lab coat sleeve to avoid the fine latex dust on his gloved hand. Dr. Berta Johnson had stopped by on her way to the autopsy of Lisa Henry to see if he'd learned anything from the evidence the techs had driven down from Fort Collins the previous afternoon. Linwood had worked all night, sleeping for only a few hours on a small couch in the break room. He had helped with prep work on the boxes of evidence and, since midnight, he and Tim Gregory had been on their own, poring over the slides looking for some clue, an anomaly. The only items the techs did not prep were the bedding materials, which were now splayed across the lab counters.

Linwood knew how important this was to Dr. Johnson and to the guys upstairs. He knew how important this was to Streeter. He knew how important this was to the Henry family. He knew all too well how important this would be to him, if he were Lisa Henry's father. He knew all this, but he didn't know yet how the evidence would help them find de Milo. And he didn't know what to tell Berta Johnson this morning on her way to the autopsy other than he had an even stronger conviction that de Milo was indeed a monster.

Linwood focused on the cotton bedspread, knowing Tim Gregory was on his way back after having gone home to catch a quick nap, a bite to eat, and a shower. Linwood lifted hairs and fibers from the fabric and swabbed the few areas where blood had spattered or dripped—not much, because Lisa hadn't been stabbed or shot or cut in any way. From what Dr. Johnson had told him, Lisa Henry had either been poisoned or asphyxiated, but she wouldn't be sure until after a long day and dozens more tests and procedures.

Wrapping more masking tape around his fingers, Linwood dabbed at the spread and, inch by inch, lifted anything that would stick to the tape. So far, with nearly three-quarters of the spread done, all he had found were long black hairs, presumably Lisa Henry's, and a few fibers that had not come from the bedspread. Dabbing, rolling, lifting, he worked his way across the spread, using tweezers to pluck the fibers and hairs from the tape and place each carefully between two plates of glass, marking each slide with unique numbers and quadrant and grid coordinates to indicate what part of the spread the item had been lifted from. Linwood was in the final quadrant, the area where Lisa's left buttocks and leg had been. Dab, roll, lift, pluck, mark. Dab, roll, lift, pluck, mark. Tedious, yet critical. Dab, roll, lift. Another black hair, only this one was about half as long as the others, maybe eight inches or so. Any other lab technician may have overlooked the subtle difference in sheen, but Linwood saw it immediately. He carefully lifted the hair and placed it between two slides, marked it, and set it aside.

On the very next dab, roll, lift, he found another interesting mass on the masking tape. Again, another tech may have missed the significance, but Linwood remembered seeing this at Quantico in one of the lab exercises only a year earlier. He studied the tiny ball of tissue, noticing its similarities to a miniature slice of orange peel that's cut in a spiral as one continuous piece, curling without a break. But the mass was smaller than the tiniest of peas. He plucked the delicate tissue from the tape and carefully straightened the curl of tissue. Sliding a glass over it to lay the tissue flat, Linwood knew instantly what he was seeing.

Excitedly, he took the slide to the scope, bypassing the step of marking the slide. He peered into the lens and adjusted the focus. Skin tissue. This was a scraping from underneath a fingernail. Hopefully, it was from

Lisa's fingernail and thus, beneath this scope, he was looking at the DNA of de Milo.

Linwood hurriedly marked the slide and grabbed the one he had set aside earlier, the shorter hair with the slightly different sheen. He slid the glass under the microscope and peered in to study the follicle. He compared it to one of the many others he'd been finding all morning. The hair was coarser, thicker, and was indeed a slightly different shade of black than the others. One end had a root and the other was cut, not broken or frayed.

He grabbed the phone and dialed.

"Jack Linwood. Put me on speakerphone so Dr. Johnson can talk to me. Please," he said, waiting until he could hear her voice. It sounded distant.

"What's up, Jack?"

He knew she was up to her elbows in her work, dissecting every organ to find out how Lisa was killed. And she'd need her full attention so as not to miss a single clue. He'd make it quick.

"Lisa's fingernails. Did you get any scrapings?"

There was a pause and he heard Dr. Johnson mumbling something about the nails. "Why, Jack?"

"Had her fingers been recently scraped? Fresh, maybe even tissue damage from too deep a scraping, like someone did it for her?"

"How did you know that?" Dr. Johnson asked. "What did you find?"

"So I'm right?"

"Yes, what did you find, Jack?"

"I think he missed one. A scraping. I have the tissue under a slide. It's most certainly skin tissue," Linwood explained.

"Great work, Jack." Dr. Johnson's level of excitement had reached his own. "You know what you're looking at?"

"De Milo," Linwood said.

"Lisa must have clawed the hell out of him. It explains the clean fingernails, the tissue damage near the quick. We need to start that DNA analysis, Jack. ASAP."

"There's something else," he added. "I might have found a hair."

"Does it have a root?"

"Yes, ma'am."

"God bless you, Jack Linwood," Dr. Johnson said.

"Might be the home owner or another guest."

"Might not."

"Did Streeter say what color hair the homeowner has?"

"Never met her," Dr. Johnson said. "But get that test started too. Composition, PCR, and RFLP, the works."

Linwood knew the prosecuting attorneys in sensitive cases like this preferred the restriction fragment length polymorphism because the tests would help differentiate or validate the DNA samples taken from the other de Milo crime scene, but he didn't know how to get the tests expedited. "I'm on it. RFLP has been taking six weeks lately."

"That's why I want a polymerase chain reaction done too. The amplification of the DNA will take far less time than the RFLP. We can at least draw some conclusions and get moving. You'll have the results by when . . . Tuesday?" Dr. Johnson guessed.

"Maybe I can get that going now. We've got the equipment for the PCR, but it'll mean I can't process the rest of the evidence."

"We'll need the RFLP since you've only got one hair and one skin tissue sample. Any blood?" she asked.

"If she scratched him, some of the drops might be his. That'll take time to sort out too."

"Think protocol on this one, Jack. We're going to need you to follow it to the letter. Think unassailable trial evidence. That's how we're proceeding," Dr. Berta Johnson announced, as if this were her case, as if it were her personal responsibility to nail the Venus de Milo murderer. Linwood understood how she felt and appreciated the direction.

"Fast tests for Streeter, slow and defendable tests for trial. Got it," Linwood summarized.

"If we can catch the bastard, we've got him dead to rights."

Linwood smiled, happy he could help.

Dr. Johnson added, "And Jack?"

"Yes?"

"As soon as you prep everything, give Streeter a call, will you? Tell him what you've found and ask if he wants you to process the rest of the evidence or if he wants you to work up the PCR on the tissue and hair. Might as well confirm what color hair the homeowner has, just to see if your test is worth running."

"I'll give him a call."

"Also tell him the perp's definitely using high-pressure water to kill the victims."

"Lisa Henry too?"

"No. If I had to guess, he ran out of time with Lisa."

"But you're sure it's de Milo?"

"Absolutely."

"So you know how Lisa died?"

"Initial screening tests, DAS, GDS, and ANS all indicate high barbiturates. We'll need further identification and confirmation on the specific toxicants for each biological specimen."

Linwood was anxious for Dr. Johnson to get to the point. He heard both her sigh and the sound of metal clinking against steel. Had she dropped a scalpel?

At length, Dr. Johnson blew out a long breath before adding, "She was killed with an injection of heroin, just like Jill Brannigan and the two in Platteville. Heavy dose. My guess, four or five milligrams; maybe more. He wanted Lisa dead. She just stopped breathing. She didn't have a chance."

"Holy mother," Linwood whistled.

"Yeah. And we lifted a print from Lisa's arm with the argon-ion laser."

"A fingerprint? From her body?" Linwood asked. "That's a new one on me."

"We got lucky because she was brought in so quickly. And de Milo must have taken off his gloves at some point, or someone was with de Milo who wasn't wearing gloves."

"Why would he be so careful, only to slip up by taking off the gloves?"

"That's your job to figure out," Dr. Johnson said.

"Maybe he cut himself, had to clean up, couldn't perform a specific task with latex on his fingers. Something. But whatever the reason, he was probably thinking he wouldn't leave prints on her naked body."

"Right. Maybe to wash up after he was done with her," Dr. Johnson speculated.

Linwood remembered something he had seen in the prep area. "They brought me the catch basin for each pipe from the three sinks in the house. Want me to look at the slides the techs prepared last night to see if I find anything?"

"You can't do it all, Jack."

"But I can try, Dr. Johnson." He smiled.

I hadn't run this hard since coach made us finish four miles under twenty-two minutes the last season I played for the University of Wyoming. For a track star, that would be nothing. For a big-boned girl like myself, that was quite an accomplishment. Running these days was more like jogging—and eventually walking—but today I was trying to jog something free in this gray matter of mine that I couldn't quite grasp.

It had to do with that stupid pomegranate they found beside Lisa's bed. That, combined with the hole carved in Jill's body, the scene from the photos Lisa showed me. It was all so macabre, but something about it was tugging on my mind. Something that should have made sense but was eluding me.

All I could think of was Elizabeth, my sister the graphic artist. Maybe it was because she loved pomegranates. She'd introduced me to them one day after school when we'd splurged on a couple, then drove around in her skin mobile. That's what she called the flesh-tone four-door American jalopy she owned in high school. Elizabeth was a free spirit, a "do what you love, love what you do," "forever keep me unsatisfied" kind of person. She was constantly in search of a new Mount Everest to climb and would do so with ease, only to find she quickly tired of the view. Being her own boss as a graphic artist, at least for the current moment, allowed her to follow a host of different passions and interests.

The pomegranate made me think of her graphics studio and the hours I spent dropping by and chatting about nothing in particular simply because I found her so energizing. What bothered me is that the pomegranate shouldn't have reminded me of the studio. We'd never eaten a pomegranate together there. I never saw her eating one while she worked there, at least not that I could remember, so what was the connection between it and Elizabeth's studio?

The only thing I could think of was the hours and hours I'd spent flipping through her gorgeous library of art books. The naked body and the pomegranate. It meant something.

Elizabeth would know. She had a brilliant mind that she frequently draped behind humor so no one would suspect.

I'd been running for an hour and that was what I'd come up with. Call Elizabeth. I ducked inside my house, read the note from Agent Kelleher saying he'd be back by noon, which gave me an hour, then showered.

With my hair still wrapped in a towel, I pulled on my jeans and slid my arms into a white oxford shirt. I slipped a jacket on over the shirt and tugged on my socks and shoes. I came into the kitchen, grabbed a packet of string cheese and a glass of ice water, and picked up the phone.

"Hi, Michael," I said when he picked up after the second ring. Nibbling on the cheese, I continued, "Is Elizabeth there?"

Elizabeth picked up the other line and I heard Michael hang up.

"Hey, Boots. What are you up to?" Elizabeth's voice was comforting.

I almost started to cry and didn't know why.

Maybe it was because I hadn't been called Boots in weeks. The only people in the world who called me that were my eight siblings and Dad; a nickname my oldest sister, Agatha, gave me when I was just a toddler playing with our father's steel-toed boots. Of course, Mom never warmed to the idea and continues to be the only one in the world who calls me Genevieve, the saint she named me after. As a matter of fact, she gave each of us girls a saint's name, starting with an "A" saint for the firstborn, "B" for the second, and so on. I was the seventh born, so I got a "G" saint. The concession for Dad was that he could give us each a middle name of traditional Norwegian origin, and the boys would go by those names. Thank God, because it was bad enough we girls had old-fashioned names; my brothers would have been teased unmercifully if they had to go by their saint names, Dismas and Hubert.

Genevieve, the first name on my birth certificate, happens to be the patron saint of disasters.

And right about now I was thinking Mom must have had that intuition about me when I was born. And I must have had the instinct to avoid it, using my middle name Liv on the first day of school. Of course, *Liv* was much easier to spell than *Genevieve*, too.

Maybe emotion engulfed me, because for the first time since I'd moved down to Fort Collins, I realized how far I was from my family and how much had happened in the last few days that they knew nothing about.

"Elizabeth, I need your help," my voice wavered.

"What's wrong?"

"Nothing," I lied. I drew a deep breath. "Everything."

"Boots, you're scaring me."

"I'm sorry. I don't mean to scare you." The steadiness in my voice helped me recompose. I bit off another long piece of string cheese and nibbled away as if at the irritating fray that might unravel my emotions. "One of my employees was murdered this week."

"At work?" Elizabeth asked.

"No, while she was off work. She was one of my summer interns. A CSU student."

"Oh, I read about her," Elizabeth said. "The de Milo victim. It's all over the news."

"Yeah," I said, glad she was living nearby in Louisville. Only Elizabeth and my sister, Frances, lived in Colorado, both near Denver. Nevertheless, they still seemed so far away.

"Oh, sorry," she said. "I didn't know that the woman was one of your employees."

"Well, that's not the end of it. You wouldn't remember her, but I played basketball with a friend named Lisa Henry at UW."

"What about her?"

"She was staying with me this week, working on the case for the FBI."

"Cool," Elizabeth said.

"Yeah, well, she was killed too." There. I had said it out loud. I admitted Lisa Henry was dead. I admitted her murder had happened in my house, just a few feet from my bedroom. But it didn't make it seem any less surreal.

"You're joking," Elizabeth whispered.

"In *my house,*" I added, nearing tears again.

It was as if the gruesome truth that spilled from my lips opened the floodgates to my emotions. I heard my sister tell her husband to pick up the other line so they could both hear my story. Elizabeth repeated what I had told her so far.

"You want us to come up and stay with you for a while?" Just the fact that Michael was willing to do that for me was comfort enough.

"No," I lied. "There's an FBI agent staying with me right now. My bodyguard, I guess."

"Does he have a gun?" Elizabeth asked.

"Of course he has a gun," I answered.

"Do you have your gun, Boots?" Michael asked.

"Right where you told me to put it. Under my bed opposite the door, so I can roll off and grab it."

"Good." My brother-in-law was a man of few words.

"Boots, you want me to call Mom and Dad?" Elizabeth asked.

"Hell no, Elizabeth," I scolded. "And if you do, I might have to throttle you."

"Okay," Elizabeth shot back. "You don't have to get your underwear in a wad about it. I was just trying to help."

"Well, that's why I called. To get your help. These murders are twisted."

"I kind of gathered that from the news reports."

"Jill had a hole cut out of her midsection. Like somebody punched a rectangular cookie cutter right through her. Then wrapped her head in cloth. And staged some weird shit by the shoreline. A couple of dressers, a brown bottle," I babbled on.

Michael said, "Hmm."

"That is messed up," Elizabeth said.

"Well, what's been bugging me is that Lisa, the college friend who's been staying with me, was found naked on the bed in my spare bedroom, her hands resting behind her head. But there was a—and you guys promise not to say anything about any of this, because it's an ongoing investigation and this stuff can't leak to anyone, especially the press—"

"Yeah, yeah, we get it," Elizabeth said.

"There was a pomegranate found near her bed."

"A pomegranate? Like the fruit?" Michael asked.

"Yeah, bizarre, huh?" I said. "I didn't have any in the house and Lisa came empty handed. So unless she went out when Agent Pierce or I didn't know it—"

"Is Agent Pierce your bodyguard?"

"No, he's another agent who was staying here. He says neither of them had bought a pomegranate. But what's been bugging me is that the stupid pomegranate made me think of something. But I can't remember what I want to remember about the stupid pomegranate. It has something to do with you, Elizabeth."

"With me? What do you mean?"

"I don't know. I mean I know you love pomegranates, but that's not it. I've been thinking and thinking and all I can come up with is the image of the woman sitting up, a rectangular hole in the middle of her body. A naked woman posed on a bed with a pomegranate. And the Venus de Milo murderer. What does all that mean? Why are those images bothering me? I mean, beyond the obvious. They seem . . . familiar."

There was a long pause. I could hear Elizabeth breathing. "Because it should bother you. It bothers me. It's the right idea, but it has nothing to do with the Venus de Milo."

"Who, then?"

"You thought of me because you saw it in a book in my studio. A book of artwork by someone, a creepy guy. Who is it? Oh, Boots, I can't remember. Maybe Hieronymous Bosch. Or Giocometti, although he wasn't so creepy. My memory tells me it was someone more recent. I can't remember."

"I couldn't either, but now that you say it, I think that's it. A painting with a pomegranate. And something coming out of it, but I can't remember what it was."

"Tell you what," Elizabeth offered, "Michael and I will drive over to the studio and dig through my books, see what we can find. Would that help?"

"A bunch. I'll go over to the CSU library and do the same. I'll take my cell phone with me in case you find something," I said.

"Great. Glad we can help. Are you sure you're okay, Boots?"

"I'm much better now."

CHAPTER 24

STREETER'S MEETING WITH DR. Miller, the journalism professor, provided an account similar to the others'. Jill was responsible, bright, and talented. Not that Brian Miller wasn't fascinating in his own right, but Streeter admittedly rushed to get the interview over with and on to his meeting with Micah Piquette.

Streeter found her inside the bookstore on the corner across from campus, right where she had told him she'd be, sipping a large gourmet coffee and looking more exotic than he'd remembered from the night before.

"Hi," she said simply as he approached her.

"Hi," Streeter said back.

"I don't like him," Micah said without any prompting or preamble.

"Who?"

"Dr. Jay," she said with a shrug. "I saw the way you looked at me when everyone was talking about how cool Dr. Jay was and how he occasionally joined our gang for drinks and partying."

"What way did I look at you?"

"You were studying me, my reaction," she said. "That's why I called you. It's true I'm guarded and hide my emotions well, but when it comes to that pretentious asshole, I don't do such a great job. I don't like him," she repeated, emphasizing each word as she did.

"Why not?"

She ignored him and sipped.

"Want to go somewhere and talk about it?"

"What'd you have in mind?" she said, sliding her eyes toward the FBI agent like a practiced seductress.

"Not whatever you're thinking," Streeter countered.

Her smile was crooked. She motioned toward the park bench outside the bookstore. Streeter took a seat and stared at the greenway through the middle of campus.

"I'm a quarter East Indian, a quarter Cherokee. My mom's white," Micah said, staring at the same biker in neon spandex that Streeter was watching.

"What does that have to do with anything?"

"Everything," Micah said. "We're two peas in a pod, Dr. Jay and me. So alike, we can't stand each other."

"I'm not following," Streeter admitted.

Micah cocked her head to the side, watching the biker as he sped away on the sidewalk. "He doesn't trust me. I don't trust him. I know he uses his ethnicity to attract women: sometimes he plays it like it's a handicap to overpower; other times he uses it to captivate."

"Like you were trying to do to me a minute ago?" Streeter asked without apology.

Her smile widened. "Yeah, just like that, like me. It's how he plays the game, but for someone like me, it's nauseating because I see right through it. I think all these women are stupid to fall for such a weak ploy."

"Yet you have your game on the same channel," Streeter said.

"Right. That's why I can't stand him." She turned toward Streeter, adding, "And he can't stand me."

"Just because you both have the same game on? The exotic, mysterious foreigner game?"

"Not just. Mostly," she said. Then, grinning, she added, "Sexy, huh?"

"Oh yes," Streeter answered, never once looking her way. "What is Dr. Jay's background?"

"Half white, half Latino," she said. "He's Cuban."

"How do you know that?"

"He asked me and I asked him. I'll show you my scars if you show me yours kinda thing. When people ask him, he usually answers that question with some pathetically glib line, like 'I'm one part tiger and three parts Energizer bunny.' And for some sick reason, the women eat that shit up."

"But not you."

Micah shook her head. "He's disgusting. So, anyway, one night when we were three sheets to the wind and I was off my game and so was he, I asked him flat out what his ethnicity was and he asked me. For some reason, we chose not to lie about it that night."

"Does he consider you one of his many conquests?"

"A little personal, don't you think?"

"So is murder." Streeter answered flatly, watching a couple walk across the grass and then lie down to stare at the clouds.

"Never, as if it's any of your business," she answered, following his gaze to find the lovers holding hands and pointing at the sky.

"What about the others in your circle of friends?"

"What? You mean have I slept with any of them?"

"That's not where I was going," Streeter said. "But is that the thing with these . . . gangs nowadays?"

"*Nowadays?* You act like you're an old fogy. How old are you, anyway?"

"Almost forty," Streeter said, amused by her straightforwardness.

"Hmm," she said, draining her coffee and throwing the cup into the nearby trash bin. "Well, *nowadays* kids just hang out in groups, so you don't have to get stuck with one friend or with the dating scene. It's more exciting to have several people to talk to, a crowd to lean on, rather than just one person. Several of our gang have enjoyed each other's company in the privacy of their own dorm or apartment, but that's not my thing. And Dr. Jay is certainly not my thing."

"Was it Jill's thing?"

This got Micah's full attention. She turned toward Streeter and commanded his attention. "Jill was not at all like that. She was just nicer about it than I was, particularly with Dr. Jay and Zack."

"They both hit on her?"

"Who didn't? Jill was amazing and super nice to everyone," Micah said, slouching on the park bench and crossing her jean-clad legs. She dangled her bejeweled sandal from her right foot, twirling her ankle nervously. "Jill had told Zack to back off, only she was so nice about it, I don't think the dweeb really got the message. He was all mushy over Jill."

"And Dr. Jay?"

"He was too narcissistic to think she really meant it when she told him she wasn't interested in him. He thought she was always playing hard to get," Micah said.

"How can you be so sure she didn't like either one?"

"Oh, I never said she didn't like them. She liked them both. As friends," Micah explained. "She just didn't want it to go any further with either of them."

"You seem so sure," Streeter persisted, watching as a dog ran out in front of a young girl, stretching the leash until she could barely restrain him.

"Well, let's put it this way," Micah said. "One night, maybe a week or so ago, Dr. Jay and Zack and Jackson were all giving Jill a particularly hard time. Mostly about her being a prude."

"Because she wouldn't sleep with any of them," Streeter concluded.

"Right," Micah said. "Only, their egos would never allow them to admit that it was because she found them unattractive or didn't see them in that way, so they started questioning which side of the plate she swung from."

"Her sexual orientation?"

Micah covered a laugh with her fist. Mimicking his words, she said, "Yeah, her 'sexual orientation.' Dr. Jay went so far as to say Jill must be gay if she was willing to pass up a night swinging from his dance pole."

Just thinking about how repulsed Jill must have been made the muscles in Streeter's jaw work overtime.

"Well, that was the first time I ever heard Jill say anything remotely bad or swear in any way."

"What did she say?"

Micah grinned, recollection filling her smoky eyes. "I'll never forget it. She looked right at Dr. Jay and said, 'Oh, Dr. Jay, you misunderstand. I've always said what a nice ass you have. It's just too bad it's on your shoulders.'" Micah doubled over with laughter, holding her gut as if Jill were right there saying it again and seeing the expression on all the men's faces.

"That must have shut him up," Streeter said.

"He was at a loss for words. First time for that too." Micah chuckled still more. "Go, Jill, is what I said. That was such a good comeback."

"And Zack Rhodes? How did he respond?"

Micah's chuckle faded. "Dr. Jay stood there with his mouth open like a docked fish. Jackson roared right along with me. And Zack blushed. He was mad, but I got the impression he was mad at Dr. Jay, not Jill. At least that's what I thought."

"And Jackson Whaler laughed."

"Yep. It was hilarious," Micah added.

"When was this? When Jill made you and Jackson laugh so hard with her comment about Dr. Jay. Do you remember?" Streeter pressed.

Micah leaned back on the bench again, laying her head on the wooden slats and staring at the blue sky. She stretched her legs out and twirled both ankles, pink sandals sparkling in the sun. "Actually, I think it was last Friday night. We were at Nate's around closing time. Everyone was kind of wasted."

"Wasted? As in drugs?"

She shook her head. "Booze. Lots of booze."

"Does the gang ever do drugs?"

Micah gathered herself. "What is this? I thought we were just talking?"

"We are," Streeter said. "I'm not with narcotics. I'm investigating a murder. I'm just curious if maybe there was any connection to drugs."

"Jill never did any of that shit. She really was a Girl Scout. Cool, but she never touched that shit or swore or had sex or nothing. She was a really good kid."

"Not like the rest of you," Streeter said, answering for her.

"Hey, I'm not ratting anyone out if that's what you're after."

"Just tell me this. Which one of the gang provides the rest of you with drugs?"

Micah sat up straight, pulling her knees together and folding her hands neatly on her lap.

"Let me ask it a different way, Micah. I'm trying to find out who killed Jill. Maybe the drugs and Jill's refusal to participate got her in trouble somehow. If you were me, and you were looking to find the answer to my problem, who would you focus on?"

Micah stared a long while at the couple lying on the grass, the girl playing with her cocker spaniel, and the geese flying overhead. The longer she stalled, the more convinced Streeter was that she'd eventually tell him.

"Who are you meeting with?" she asked in a small voice.

"When? What do you mean?"

"Today. After me," she said.

"Zack Rhodes."

Streeter could tell Micah was mulling this over, debating whether to tell him more or leave this discussion where it was. He was pleased with her decision.

"That's what I would have guessed," she said. "You already knew the answer to your own question, Agent Pierce. Your focus is right where it should be."

Micah stood up and, without ever looking back, walked slowly down the street toward the dorms.

―――――――

On the way to Zack Rhodes's dormitory, Streeter's cell phone chirped.

"Streeter, it's Jack Linwood. Did I catch you at a good time?"

Streeter stared up at the clear blue sky. "Sure, Linwood. What do you have?"

"What color hair does the homeowner have?"

"What homeowner?"

"Where Lisa Henry was staying," Linwood clarified. "What's her name?"

"Liv Bergen," Streeter answered. "And her hair is chestnut brown, her eyes, sea green." The second the words left his lips, Streeter regretted saying them. Such descriptive words to describe a stranger he knew only from her photograph. Whatever possessed him, he wondered.

"You sure?"

"Pretty sure, although I've never met her."

Linwood paused a long moment. Before he could ask, Streeter explained, "There were photographs in her house. Lisa pointed her out to me. Unless she's recently dyed her hair some other color, her hair is brown."

"Chestnut brown," Linwood repeated. "Interesting."

"Why?"

"Look, I need some direction. We've finished prepping everything. Dr. Johnson wants me to stop processing the evidence from Lisa's room and start performing a PCR on the tissue and hair I recovered from the spread."

"Hair?"

"Just one strand. With a root," Linwood explained. "And I was able to recover some tissue. Dr. Johnson confirmed my theory that it might be the killer's tissue."

"What kind of tissue?"

"Looks like skin, from underneath Lisa Henry's fingernail," Linwood explained. "Dr. Johnson confirmed that Lisa's nails had been cleaned by someone other than herself. This might have been a chunk the killer missed after he scraped her nails."

Streeter's mind flashed to the angry scratch down Dr. Jay's left cheek and neck. Alarm rang in the veteran FBI agent's ears. "What color was the hair?"

"Not chestnut brown," Linwood said. "It's black."

"Lisa's hair is black, Linwood," Streeter discounted.

"Yes, but this is definitely a different shade and texture from what I could see through the spectrograph and microscopically."

"Different," Streeter was starting to get that rush he often felt when the pieces were starting to fall into place. "Length?"

"About eight inches," Linwood said.

Streeter's mind went to both Dr. Jay and Zack Rhodes. Both had shoulder-length black hair. Artist's hair, in his opinion.

"Run it. PCR on the hair is going to give us more than RFLP analysis anyway," Streeter said.

"Means I'm going to fall behind on analyzing the rest of the evidence," Linwood reminded Streeter. "I have the traps on all three pipes from the house. If he cleaned up, I might get some blood or tissue samples."

"Save it for later, for court. For now, I need a name. Fast. He's going to kill again—soon," Streeter said. "It was only three days between Jill Brannigan and Lisa Henry."

"It might not mean what you think," Linwood said. "Dr. Johnson told me to tell you that she thought de Milo was rushed with Lisa Henry. He didn't take the time to cut her with the high-powered water like the rest."

"Well, he also killed Lisa in broad daylight, with me, Detective Brandt, and how many other law enforcement agents possibly dropping in at any moment. Of course de Milo was rushed." Streeter was fuming. The madman had killed a brilliant woman and his friend. And he did it within striking distance of where Streeter had slept that very morning. "He's getting bolder, taunting us, or Lisa Henry was on to something, closer than he wanted her to be. We need the computer forensic results."

"Which means you might be a target, Streeter," Linwood warned.

Streeter had thought of that. In fact, he hoped so. He would welcome the opportunity of de Milo taking him on. What worried him was that de Milo possibly had someone else in mind as his next target.

"Did Berta say anything about cause of death?"

"Dr. Johnson told me to tell you that it was the same as Jill's and the two from Platteville."

"Heroin," Streeter growled.

"And apparently lots of it with Lisa Henry, according to Dr. Johnson," Linwood reported. "Oh, and she got a print."

"You mean the boot print or the tire tread?" Streeter asked, wondering what Berta would be doing with either of those since Kelleher was working those angles with Gregory and Brandt. Then he remembered that Tim Gregory had driven back to Denver the night before to help Linwood, so it must be the tire tread they were discussing.

"No, a fingerprint," Linwood said.

"What?"

"I couldn't believe it either," Linwood explained. "But I guess Dr. Johnson was able to lift a print from Lisa's arm."

"Holy mackerel," Streeter whistled.

"She's something, isn't she?"

"Berta's something, all right."

CHAPTER 25

AS STREETER TRIED TO wade through the sea of empty beer cans and pizza boxes, Zack scrambled to tidy up his dorm room. He kicked a few piles of soiled laundry under his bed and parted the rest with his toe to make a path for Streeter to the lone chair. Streeter had to take the stack of books off the plastic chair before sitting down; he opted to put the pile on the floor rather than to fight for space on the small desk.

Zack plopped onto the bed, unfazed by his catastrophic surroundings. Streeter marveled at how "put together" Zack appeared, considering his clothes selection each morning must have come from the rumpled piles on the floor. Streeter was careful not to knock over the bottles of pomade around his feet, clearly the secret to Zack's slick look, the perfect ponytail.

"Shoot," Zack said, tossing a baseball from hand to hand.

Streeter couldn't help but notice how Zack eyed him sideways, never looking at him straight on, just as he had done the night before in the bar and out on the sidewalk. His demeanor would indicate Zack struggled with trusting people. Or he had something to hide.

"Zack, I need to ask you a few more questions about Jill, if you wouldn't mind," Streeter eased into it.

"Like what? We answered everything for you last night." The ball thumped, thumped, thumped against the palm of each hand.

"And you got a little miffed at Shelby, almost started swinging at Sean. You want to tell me what that was all about?" Streeter asked.

Zack stared at the floor. "No biggy. Happens all the time with those two. They hooked up and Shelby's not quite over me and Sean doesn't get why she was ever under me, *capisce*?"

"I'm old, not stupid," Streeter said.

Zack smiled. The first smile Streeter had ever seen on the man's long face. Zack's expression could only be described as forlorn or melancholy at best. A brooding artist. But when he smiled, Streeter could see the fire in his black eyes.

"Tell me about Jill," Streeter asked.

"What about her?"

Streeter tried to think like an artist. "Describe her for someone like me who'd never met her before and wanted to understand who she was."

Zack winced. Then his face mustered what looked like resolve. His voice was strong and sure. "Jill Brannigan was beautiful, smart, witty, kind, thoughtful."

All adjectives Streeter had heard before. Not much, coming from an artist, Streeter thought.

Zack's eyes dropped to his hands, tossing the baseball back and forth, back and forth to himself. Then he stilled the ball in one hand and stared at the stitching and picked at the red threads with a long, lean finger. His voice was quiet. "Her mouth was soft and inviting like a goose down comforter on a rainy day. Her smile reached the corners of your mind like a sunset stretching above the Rockies. Her eyes pierced the very soul you thought no one in the world could ever see."

Now we're getting somewhere, Streeter thought. The artist has emerged.

Zack picked at the red stitching, unable to find purchase. "Jill Brannigan moved like a dancer on the court, unlike those other Neanderthal basketball jocks. She was good. Strong and smooth, she played a game with finesse. Just like with everything she did in life. Thoughtful, tender."

"But not in her work," Streeter interjected.

Zack stopped picking at the ball and stared at Streeter. "What are you talking about?"

"Dr. Jay tells me that Jill Brannigan wasn't all that good at sculpting," Streeter pressed. He could see the muscles in Zack's neck strain.

"She was brilliant. Quite talented," Zack defended. "She was only half-way through her second semester and she'd started to show great promise with working the clay to imitate live models."

"Dr. Jay says otherwise. That Jill thought her way through class rather than felt her way through," Streeter continued. He could see Zack's ears turning red, the broodiness set into a thin line on his lips.

"Dr. Jay is—"

Streeter tilted his head, interested in why Zack caught himself. "Is what?"

"Dr. Jay is . . . a perfectionist," Zack chickened out. Jerking his head from one side to the other he cracked his neck before he continued. "Always seeking that perfect sculptor, the next Rodin."

"Tough grader, huh?" Streeter asked. "And you had to smooth it over with the students like Jill as his teaching assistant? Make sure they didn't lose interest in sculpting? Get disenchanted with it all?"

Zack's eyes slid in Streeter's direction, giving him just enough time to note the yellowing of his whites. Zack resumed casting the baseball back and forth in his hands.

He started in a mumble. "More like I was there to make sure no one ratted him out, didn't lose interest in the great Dr. Jay Bravo, get disenchanted with all his bullshit."

"Not a fan of Dr. Jay's?"

Zack hesitated before answering. "He gets my bills paid, you know?"

"You mean the school," Streeter said.

Zack eyed him again. "Huh?"

"The school gets your bills paid. You're a TA. Doesn't CSU pay your bills?"

"Oh, yeah, that's what I meant," Zack nodded, the ball moving faster and faster between his hands.

Streeter knew Zack was lying.

"You know, you're going to worry the leather right off that ball, Zack."

Zack tossed the baseball onto his desk and it landed in a heap of clothes. He lay back on his bed and draped one arm over his forehead. It had been so long since Zack had spoken, Streeter thought he'd fallen asleep.

"The professor decides whether the TA works or not. The school pays, but the professor has us by our short hairs," Zack finally said.

"And Dr. Jay has you by yours," Streeter concluded.

"Yeah."

"So you don't have a choice but to love the one you're with." Zack dropped his arm and scrunched his face up at Streeter, giving him a "what the hell?" look. Streeter grinned. "You know, the song? If you can't be with the one you love, love the one you're with."

"Oh, I get it. If I can't choose the professor, I better learn to like being the TA for a professor who wants me. Right."

Streeter thought Zack would be faster on the uptake, but he wasn't. Streeter added, "Nice ass; too bad it's on his shoulders."

That got Zack's attention. He sat up on the bed. "Where did you hear that?"

"Micah," Streeter said. "When did Jill say that to Dr. Jay? Do you remember?"

"Last Friday. A week ago this past Friday. Nine days ago," Zack answered. "We were all at Nate's doing shots of tequila and schnapps. And Dr. Jay deserved it."

"That's what Micah said. How long have you been in love with Jill?"

Zack stared at Streeter. His eyes were wide and for the first time unprotected by the hooded, sideways glance. "What the . . . Who—"

"No one. I figured that out all on my own."

Streeter stared at Zack in silence.

"Since the first time I saw her—January of this year—she took my breath away," Zack answered openly. Then, just as quickly, his expression collapsed into distrusting sullenness. "But I wasn't good enough for her."

"According to her?"

Zack shook his head, offering a corked smile. "She wasn't like that. I wasn't good enough for her from my view. She was so much better than me in so many ways. I made some bad choices. She never did."

"Did you ever fight with her?"

"Fight? No, why?"

"Did you argue about her not wanting to date you?"

Zack lay back on the bed. "I never asked. Like I said, I wasn't good enough for her. She wasn't too good for me. There's a big difference."

"You were the last person to see her alive, Zack. Did you fight with her Monday night?" Streeter needled.

Zack shot up again, sitting erect, his hands on the edge of the bed as if he were preparing to propel himself forward at Streeter. "What are you talking about?"

"Monday night, at the library. As far as anyone knows, you were the last one to see Jill alive, Zack."

"I didn't kill her," he moaned.

"The last one to see Jill before she was found butchered to death two days later."

"I didn't kill Jill. And I never told you I was at the library. Never."

"No, you didn't," Streeter admitted.

"Then who said that I was?" Zack's jaw was jutting back and forth, his teeth grinding.

"Why does it matter?"

Zack studied Streeter askance. He must have agreed with what he saw in his demeanor, because he eventually answered, "Because how would anyone know I was following her? *I* didn't even know I was going to follow her. Only the killer would have known I was following her that night."

"To the library?"

"Yeah," Zack said. "I followed her to the library."

"Were you stalking her, Zack?"

"I wasn't stalking her," he scowled. "I was just concerned. I saw her walking across the green by herself. It was late, dark. So, I decided to follow her."

"Because you were concerned," Streeter repeated.

"Yeah."

"Then why didn't you just make yourself known? You were a friend, part of the gang."

Zack sat up, lowering his head into his hands. He mumbled, "Because it would be weird."

"Weird?"

"She'd think I was weird, showing up in the middle of the night to walk her to the library. She'd think I was a cretin or something, thinking she needed protecting."

"You were seen at the library Monday night, watching her from behind a column. Why were you in the library, Zack?"

"I told you," he spat, his eyes fixed on Streeter. "I never went *in* the library. I followed her *to* the library, waited until she made it inside, and then went back to my dorm. That's it. End of story."

"Why should I believe you? That you aren't Jill's killer?"

"Because I loved her," Zack barked. He cradled his head in his hands. "I wouldn't kill her. Wouldn't hurt her. Wouldn't even ask her out. I wasn't in the library Monday night, but I did follow her to the library. Don't you see? The murderer saw me follow her to the library. I watched her go in. And never saw her again . . ."

Zack was crying.

Streeter regarded him, studied his face, his body racked with sobs. Streeter lowered his voice. "What if I told you I had a witness who swears you were there at the library watching Jill from behind a pillar?"

Zack wiped his eyes with the back of his hand. "I'd tell you that it was a lie."

Streeter had no reason to believe him, but for some reason he did. His instincts were telling him to pursue more. "Zack, will you humor me and take off you shirt?"

Zack gave him a funny look.

Streeter lifted his hands in surrender. "Nothing kinky, believe me. I just want to be able to trust you, to know you're telling me the truth."

Zack said nothing.

"Please."

Zack hiked his T-shirt over his head.

Streeter said, "Turn around."

Zack did. No scratches anywhere to be seen, and Streeter was not about to ask Zack to take off his shorts. Lisa Henry had not scratched Zack Rhodes.

"Okay, you can put it back on," Streeter said. "I believe you. So, you weren't there Monday night *in* the library, but you were *at* the library."

Zack squinted as if disbelieving Streeter.

"I believe you, but you can change all that with how you answer my questions," Streeter said. "First, what made you so edgy last night when we discussed the walking-stick business?"

Zack blew out a long, defeated breath. "It's an off-book business. A cash business."

"So you don't report any income or pay taxes?"

Zack nodded.

"Who all was involved? Was Jill?" Streeter pressed.

"No, no," Zack insisted. "That's what I'm telling you. She warned us that what we were doing wasn't right and what might happen as our business grew. She didn't want any part of it. That's when Dr. Jay started taunting her about being a goody-goody."

"Dr. Jay Bravo was in the walking-stick business with you?"

Zack swung his feet to the floor, sitting on the edge of his bed. "Well, yeah. It was his idea. He's the mentor who taught us all how to carve. He's a master with his hands. The school didn't approve his request to add the carving class to the curriculum, so we use the sculpting class to introduce students to carving."

Streeter's mind homed in on Dr. Jay Bravo as the lead suspect, noting how every path continued to lead straight back to him.

"Zack, this is important. You have to trust me and you have to be truthful with me," Streeter started. "Do you deal drugs? Provide for your circle of friends?"

Zack glared at him. After several seconds, he lifted a hand in surrender.

"Okay. Did you ever sell to Jill, provide any drugs for Jill, see Jill take anything?"

"Never," Zack answered quickly. "She wasn't that kind of girl, I told you that."

"Last question, Zack. And don't lie to me like you did last night," Streeter said, leaning forward in his chair toward Zack. "Do you know who Jonah is?"

Zack nodded.

———————

Streeter punched the buttons on his cell phone as he ran across campus to the Fine Arts Building. "Phil, I need you to get a search warrant for Dr. Jay Bravo's home, car, office, whatever you can get."

"Hard to find a judge who will come in on a Sunday, Streeter."

"Try."

"What do you have?"

"De Milo, I think. He's got fresh scratches on his left jawbone and neck. He had access to Jill Brannigan."

"That's it? Streeter, we're going to need more than that," Kelleher chided.

"Hear anything from DMV on the pickup truck with the topper?"

"Not yet."

"Well, call them back and find out how many and what kind of cars Dr. Jay Bravo owns. Or Jonah Bravo," Streeter added.

"Jonah?"

"That's what one of the kids thinks," Streeter said, pushing open the far left door to the Fine Arts Building, relieved that it was still unlocked. He bounded up the stairs two at a time and hurried down the hall to Dr. Jay Bravo's office. He turned the handle. It didn't give. He knocked.

Streeter said, "Call DMV, Kelleher, and then find out which judges are around."

Kelleher offered a reproachful groan, which only made Streeter want to end the call even sooner.

Streeter knocked again, drawing his gun with his right hand, switching the cell phone to his left.

"Where are you?" Kelleher asked.

Streeter knocked for a third time, noting that no light was coming from beneath the door.

"Got to go," Streeter said.

He closed the phone, slipped it in his pocket, and looked around the empty, deserted hallway before slipping a credit card past the latch of the door. The door popped open. Streeter stepped around the desk and stood facing the diploma on the wall. J. Stephen Bravo was the name on the college diploma.

Zack was right.

It was Dr. J. as in the initial, not Dr. Jay as in a first name. And the diploma read Bachelor of Arts Teaching Certificate from St. Petersburg University.

Streeter snatched the phone from his pocket again. It rang before he even opened it up to dial.

"Pierce," he answered.

"Hi, Streeter," the familiar voice greeted him. "It's me, Misty."

Misty Asante worked with Jon Tuygen in the computer lab on the floor below Streeter's.

"Asante, not now."

"Now, Streeter," Misty insisted, her voice stern, unyielding.

Streeter wasn't ready to play nice; he was tired of her advances and even wearier of trying to find new ways to make her understand no means no, but he had no choice. "What is it?"

"The forensics," Misty snapped. "On Agent Henry's laptop." Streeter's breath caught. "Jon said you needed it ASAP, and he's too busy to call you. So he asked me to call. Do you want to know what he found or not?"

"I do."

"The last thing Agent Henry did was look up a website."

He moved to the windowsill, noticing the crystal he had seen earlier. Lifting it, he noticed the dust that had gathered underneath. Lifting the surrounding knickknacks, he took note that the dust had gathered around and on but not under each item. The crystal must have recently been placed on the windowsill. He studied it again, realizing it was the rock that was missing from Liv's dresser.

"What website?"

Asante harrumphed. "What, no foreplay, Streeter?"

"I don't have time for this, Asante."

"You never do," Asante shot back. "She did a search on Salvador Dalí. Hunted and pecked around until she landed on a museum dedicated to him. The Salvador Dalí Museum. In St. Petersburg, Florida."

Streeter hung up without even saying good-bye.

He didn't have time. He was conducting an illegal search and hoped not to be discovered at it. Plus he needed to find Bravo as quickly as he could.

Streeter fumbled with the books on the shelves, pulling three out with Dalí's name on the spine of each. Thumbing through the pages, he found a color print of a painting that mimicked Jill Brannigan's murder scene. He leafed through more pages and saw the bizarre renditions of clocks and men and warped faces. He found the naked woman awakening from sleep, posed just as Lisa had been lying.

The surreal image featured pomegranates.

CHAPTER 26

"HI, ANN MARIE. HI, Pam," I greeted the women at the front desk, tucking behind my ear the loose strand of hair that had fallen from my ponytail. After taking the library steps at a dead run, I was winded briefly and welcomed the time to catch my breath while catching up with my acquaintances. "How's that grandbaby, Ann Marie?"

Ann Marie reached under the counter and within seconds, she flashed a photo of a pink, wrinkled mass of newborn baby flesh. "Trevor William Trotter. Eight pounds, ten ounces," she said, her grin stretching from ear to ear.

"Whoa, that's a big boy!" I said studying the picture she'd handed to me. "And he has your smile."

"I think that's gas," Ann Marie said with a wink.

"Yours or his?"

Both Ann Marie and Pam laughed, then hushed me for disturbing the other library patrons.

Pam whispered, "Liv, you are so bad."

"Behave yourself," Ann Marie scolded, swatting the air with her hand before covering her lips to hold back another snicker.

"Trevor's a handsome baby," I said, returning the photograph.

"Did you make that phone call?"

I sighed, "No, Ann Marie. And for the hundredth time, I'm not going to."

Ann Marie hefted her ample breasts onto the counter and leaned closer to me. She whispered, "Hundredth? That's why you don't get any dates, dear. You exaggerate."

"Okay, okay. For the last time, I'm not going to call your nephew. It's too—"

"Too what?" Ann Marie glared at me over her glasses.

"It's too awkward."

Pam giggled. "That's the best you could do?"

"Well," I responded, "it's . . . it's just too weird. I don't even know the guy."

Such a command of the English language I have.

"Because you haven't called him yet. If you did you'd get to know him. Then it wouldn't be awkward or weird," Ann Marie theorized.

How in the hell do I argue with that logic?

"Besides, how will you ever get to have grandbabies of your own if you don't start getting busy?" Ann Marie concluded.

"I'll work on it," I conceded.

Pam got me off the hook by changing subjects. "What are you studying today?"

"Art," I said.

"Oh, that's a new one. What kind?" Ann Marie asked.

"Weird, creepy art," I answered.

Pam and Ann Marie started laughing again; this time the laughter was met with glares from all the students seated nearby. The librarians hushed me again and pointed accusing fingers my way.

"Stop it, Liv."

"What? You're the ones who are laughing."

"And you're the one making us," Pam chided me. Her reproving eyes darted around in case anyone was watching us. She wrapped her graying brown hair in a large knot at the nape of her neck and pushed her wire rim glasses up her thin nose.

"What kind of 'weird, creepy art' are you interested in, dear?"

"I was looking for art with fruit," I said, oddly uncomfortable about sharing the pomegranate word with them.

"Do you have a particularly disturbing fruit in mind?"

"Like an artist using bizarre combinations of people and fruit and images that conjure up bad dreams," I explained, proud of myself for finally verbalizing what I'd been ruminating about ever since the pomegranate had been found.

"Oh, of course, dear," Ann Marie said. "That would be Salvador Dalí."

Pam shook her head. "No, René Magritte."

"Dalí had distortions and bent clocks and never-ending staircases and people and animals and fruit and peculiar images."

Pam protested, "But Magritte used people and fruit too. Remember the man in the suit and derby with a piece of fruit for his face?"

"That was Dalí."

"That was Magritte. He painted the bizarre, the surreal."

"No one was more bizarre than Dalí," Ann Marie argued.

The two women reminded me of the three fairies in the Disney cartoon movie *Sleeping Beauty*, the two that were constantly changing Princess Aurora's dress from pink to blue and back again.

I decided to settle the argument. "Okay, okay. You've both been a huge help. Point me to the section and I'll take a look. Then I'll let you know which artist I think is more disturbing."

Pam cleared her throat. "That would be third floor. You'll be using the stairs, right?"

I nodded.

"At the top of the stairs, turn right, go all the way down the hall, and look on the shelves to your right. Third row from the back."

"Thanks, ladies," I said, heading for the stairwell by the bank of elevators.

Just as I started up the stairs, I heard the plump fairy call out once more, "Dalí."

Once I reached the stacks on the third floor it took me less than five minutes to find expertly bound books displaying the work of both artists. Both men were twentieth-century artists who epitomized surrealism. I flipped quickly through the bios: Magritte, Belgian born, had lived in

France for most of his adult life and died at nearly seventy years old in 1967. Dalí was a Spaniard who mastered his craft in Madrid. He had spent the WWII years in the United States, where he remained until his death in 1989 at the age of eighty-five.

Pam was right about Magritte and his obsession with people and fruit. With people and birds. With people and anything that would cover up the face. He even had a work of art where it looked like there were two heads in the painting, both wrapped in white cloth. Troubling. I thought of what Lisa had told me about Jill and how her head was covered by a dish towel.

Maybe de Milo was mimicking all forms of art. The first murders in Platteville were mimicking the Venus de Milo. The second murder victim, Jill, was in René Magritte's honor. The third, Lisa, who knows?

But it was Dalí who really freaked me out. The funny mustache, kissing his pet bat, throwing kids off balconies, teaching class in a wet suit. The guy was a regular P.T. Barnum of the art world. Born to shock. The greatest showman on Earth. Even Michael Jackson could have learned a trick or two from Dalí. Wacky. He was everything sinister, and based on the first picture I turned to, his artwork followed.

I was staring at Dalí's "Soft Self-Portrait"—the dark, warped mask of Dalí's face propped up with little crutches—when my cell phone vibrated, startling the shit out of me.

I whispered, "Hello?"

"Dalí," Elizabeth's excited voice boomed. "Salvador Dalí. I called Agatha and she told me."

Agatha is the oldest of us nine, or as Agatha herself likes to say, the oldest and meanest. She's also a talented artist. I wished I had thought to call her sooner.

"I'm looking right at it, Boots. A naked woman lying supine, with her arms under her head like she's sleeping. And there's a pomegranate next to her. A second pomegranate, a big one, is floating in the air like a freakish planet and a fish and tigers are coming out of it. There's a bayonet and an elephant on stilts. It's like it's a freaking nightmare that doesn't make sense."

I was rustling through the pages, desperate to find the image. "I can't find it. Does it have a name?"

I flipped to the index in the back and waited for Elizabeth's answer.

"Dalí called it 'One Second Before Awakening from a Dream Caused by the Flight of a Bee Around a Pomegranate.'"

"You've got to be joking," I said, scanning the entries under the letter O until I found it. "No, I guess you're not."

"See? See? Is that what you were talking about?" Elizabeth pressed.

I flipped through the oversized pages and found the image. My heart pounded. It was exactly what I was talking about. "Yeah, Elizabeth. This was what I was trying to remember."

I studied the image and thought about Lisa. My eyes started to pool with tears. I wiped them away quickly before they soiled the pages.

"Dalí was twisted," Elizabeth stated.

"I see that," I said, slowly turning the pages one at a time.

I recognized all the different paintings depicting warped clocks draped over stairs and edges. Probably what Dalí was most famous for, I thought.

"Well, thanks, Elizabeth," I said. "This is a huge help. Thank Michael for me too. And Agatha."

"What are you going to do now?"

"I'm going to see if I can check this book out of the archives and take it to Agent Phil Kelleher. He'll get it to Agent Pierce for me. Maybe it will shed some light on this guy's twisted mind."

I flipped to a new series of pictures with William Tell as the main character. I speculated that Dalí wasn't a fan of his own father, considering the painful contortions he painted of William Tell, depicting him as a monster in hideous poses, distortions, and angles.

"Liv?"

Elizabeth hadn't called me that in years. "Yeah?"

"Be careful."

"Thanks," I said, closing my cell phone and slipping it into my pocket.

Disturbed by the sick images of William Tell, I turned more pages, delving deeper into the sick psyche of Salvador Dalí. *Not a master, a monster*, I thought.

Then I saw it.

My heart slammed against my chest. The book was splayed open on the table, exposing Dalí's "The Weaning of Furniture—Nutrition." My head was spinning and I was sure I was going to throw up. There, in the picture in front of me, was a woman sitting up, her head slumped forward to her chest and covered with a white cloth. A rectangle had been cut from her center. Two wooden cabinets sat near the water's edge. It was Jill. Or what de Milo was using Jill for as a model in one of Dalí's sick paintings.

This was the answer.

The Venus de Milo murderer wasn't just mimicking works of art. He was mimicking Salvador Dalí.

I fumbled for my cell phone. I had to call home, talk to Agent Kelleher immediately. He'd be home by now.

I felt a hand snake around my head and snatch the cell phone from my ear. For the second time in as many minutes, my heart slammed against my chest.

CHAPTER 27

PANTING, STREETER ARRIVED AT the CSU library steps.

The agent in charge had told Zack Rhodes he'd be right back after he tried to catch Dr. Bravo in his office. Zack told Streeter the professor wouldn't be there. He said that Dr. Bravo never worked when he didn't have to and only during those times he could ogle the coeds in the halls and on the green below his window. Sunday wasn't one of the best traffic days around the Fine Arts Building.

Zack had been right, yet Streeter was glad to have had the office to himself in which to snoop around, despite the breaking and entering laws he had violated.

Back at the dorm, Streeter had found a note Zack had left on his door for him. There was a change of plans; he had to meet a student about a quick question on a homework assignment in one of the private study rooms at the library.

Having caught his breath, Streeter entered the library and asked the plump lady at the front desk where the private study rooms were. She explained where to find them on the second floor.

There were six rooms in the area where Zack had told Streeter to meet him. He knocked on the first door and a rumpled young man opened the door. Streeter could see the room was not much bigger than six by six and contained a small wooden counter and a desk chair. Not too comfortable, but soundproof. Papers and books were splayed across the counter and on the floor.

"Yeah?" the young man said.

Streeter waved. "Sorry, just looking for someone."

The man shut the door without reply.

The next two doors were locked and no one answered to Streeter's knock. The fourth door was closed and a light shown from beneath it. Streeter gave a loud rap with his knuckles.

A male student, half naked, peeked through the crack. A young lady's voice sounded, "Who is it, Trey?"

"Don't know," he answered her. He turned to Streeter and asked, "What?"

"Nothing," Streeter said. "I'm looking for someone."

"Well, she's already taken, dude, so take a hike." The student hurriedly closed the door. *Kids*, Streeter thought.

The fifth door was open just a crack. Streeter knocked on the door but got no answer. The light was on. Streeter pushed open the door with his elbow, careful not to touch the handle with his fingertips.

He wasn't surprised by what he saw. Maybe he would even admit to having had a premonition if it wasn't so damned embarrassing. He preferred to call it an incredibly strong instinct.

Zack Rhodes sat in the chair, head and arms sprawled across the small counter in the tiny space. Streeter tapped his shoulder. Zack didn't move. Slipping a finger beneath Zack's chin, Streeter felt for a pulse. Nothing. A band was stretched and tied over Zack's left bicep, a needle still protruding from the vein in his arm.

"Overdose, my foot," Streeter said aloud. "De Milo, you're slipping."

Streeter punched 9-1-1 on his cell phone, waiting for the ring, when he saw the note beneath Zack's head. The note was addressed to Streeter. He pulled out a handkerchief from his pocket and slid the note from beneath Zack's head.

He walked over by the window to get a signal and told the emergency response personnel to get an ambulance to the college library. Then he called Phil Kelleher.

"She home yet?" Streeter asked Kelleher.

"Liv? No, why?"

Streeter glanced around to make sure no one was within earshot. "No call?"

"Not yet," Kelleher said. "But the note said she was going to the library and would be back in a couple of hours."

Streeter's heart pounded. He spun around looking down the rows of books, wondering if he would recognize her from the small photo Lisa had shown him at Liv's home. "The CSU library?"

"Could be the city library," Kelleher said. "Why?"

Streeter glanced down and read the note. With shaky penmanship, Zack had explained that he'd killed Jill Brannigan because he loved her and she didn't love him back. Then he'd killed Agent Henry because she was too close to figuring it out. He was ending his life now because he just couldn't live with himself anymore.

"Horse puckey," Streeter said.

Kelleher paused. "Streeter?"

"Oh, sorry, Kelleher. I have another de Milo vic here at the CSU library. The victim left a suicide note. It's coerced."

"Who's the victim?" Kelleher asked.

"Zack Rhodes," Streeter said, plowing his thick fingers through his white crew cut.

"Who found him?"

"I did. I was just over in Zack's room meeting with him and had to run a quick errand. Zack left me a note that he was helping a student in the library. That note wasn't coerced. De Milo must have set Zack up, then when he got to this private study room the perp forced him to write the suicide/confession note."

"Confession to what?"

"The de Milo murders," Streeter said. "But he was forced by the real de Milo to write it."

"How do you know it wasn't something else? A wannabe? A copy cat?"

"Because Zack's note mentions using heroin to kill Jill and Lisa. We haven't told anyone about that yet."

"Why couldn't he be de Milo?"

"Because Zack left a clue, knowing I'd be the only one to understand it. He said—" Streeter paused, looking at the note. "'I killed those girls just as surely as I was in the library Monday night.'"

"What kind of clue is that?" Kelleher scoffed.

"A good one. One that Jonah Bravo wouldn't catch," Streeter explained. "Zack and I had just talked about it. He swore he wasn't in the library Monday night. I told him I believed him. That's when he opened up, told me Dr. Jay's real name was Jonah. Told me he got the drugs he sold around campus from none other than the infamous Dr. Jay."

"Heroin?"

"You got it. As well as several others."

"Need help?" Kelleher asked in his naturally tight tone.

"Yeah, I do. That's why I was wondering where Liv Bergen was, just in case. Have Brandt check out the city library. If you'll meet me down here, you can check out the CSU library for me while I'm with the paramedics," Streeter explained, watching the bubbled lights of the ambulance from his perch at the second floor bay window.

"I thought you said Zack was dead?"

"He is," Streeter said with a sigh. "Probably a hefty dose of heroin, just like the others. Needle's still in his arm, poor kid."

"I'll be right there. Oh, and Streeter? Brandt's been working the pickup truck all morning. When I called him about Jonah Bravo, he found a hit. He's heading to a local judge's cabin as we speak to pick up the search warrant for both the home and the vehicles."

"He's de Milo, and he's a sick man. I'll explain it to you when you get here."

———

Streeter pocketed the suicide note, along with his hanky, and walked out to the landing to meet the paramedics. The EMT team hurried up the stairs, followed by a small crowd of students and a campus security officer. Streeter pointed down the hall toward private study room number five. Within seconds, the paramedics had Zack on a stretcher, first performing CPR on him and then strapping the oxygen mask over Zack's nose and mouth. The commotion caused the occupants in study rooms one and four to poke out their heads, like prairie dogs in the spring.

The paramedics hustled Zack down the stairs, out the door, and into the ambulance, the onlookers gawking as they followed, leaving Streeter alone with the prairie dogs and a security guard.

"What happened here?" the portly man asked.

"Overdose," Streeter answered. Turning to the three prairie dogs, he asked, "Any of you hear anything, see anyone out here?"

"Besides you?" the grumpy, disheveled loner asked. "Nope."

Romeo and Juliet shook their heads. "Just you," Romeo said.

The security guard asked, "Who are you and what was your reason for coming here?"

Streeter stepped aside and flashed him his credentials so the students could not see. He whispered, "We don't want anyone to panic, do we?"

Security guard's eyes widened as he took a deep breath.

"What's your name?"

"Dan."

Streeter patted his shoulder and slipped the credentials back in his pocket. "Will you do me a favor, Dan, and wait right here for Agent Phil Kelleher? Tell him I'm taking a quick look around the library and I'll be right back."

"How will I know who he is?" Security Dan asked.

"Tall black man with gray around the temples. He'll be the only man in this place wearing a custom-made suit, probably gray or dark blue, and looking like he swallowed a prune."

Dan nodded solemnly.

Streeter added, "And you can tell him I told you the part about the prune."

Dan smiled and flashed Streeter a thumbs-up.

Streeter said, "And don't let anyone in that room. Clear out the other rooms, and don't let anyone down that hall until the techs come."

"They're going to dust for prints? The kid was murdered?" Security Dan whispered loudly.

Streeter glanced quickly around them and was careful to answer, "They're going to make sure they check everything out, just in case. Probably just another overdose."

Dan hiked his beefy shoulder to his ear. "What are you going to do? Kids."

"Kids," Streeter repeated. Security Dan cleared the two occupied rooms along the corridor and turned and gave Streeter the A-OK sign.

Streeter glanced out the windows at the sea of people who were gathering at the foot of the library steps and staring at the ambulance.

CHAPTER 28

BEFORE I HEARD EVEN one ring on my call home to explain to
Agent Kelleher what I'd discovered about Salvador Dalí and the similarities between his surreal paintings and the de Milo murders, he was there,
snatching the phone from my ear.

"Genevieve L. Bergen."

I wasn't fooled by his charming voice and his easy manner, nor was
I lulled into thinking I was safe because we were in a public library sur-
rounded by people. The feeling of danger was palpable. I was clinging to
the fleeting belief that crime is what happens to other people or in novels.
Not to me.

"Genevieve Liv Bergen," he stated again, emphasizing my middle
name in a mocking tone and extending his hand.

Hesitant, I grabbed it and pumped his hand slowly. "And you are?"

"I'm Dr. Jay," he said, a wide smile spreading across his lips. "I am . . .
was Jill Brannigan's art professor. Maybe she told you about me?"

I shook my head. "How did you know who I was?"

"Jill, of course," he said, scanning the page of the Dalí painting that
revealed how Jill herself had been found. He caught me staring at him and
his smile widened. He pointed at the reproduction. "Ah, Nutrition. One of
my favorites by Dalí."

My throat went dry. "You . . . like Salvador Dalí?"

"Don't you?" he mocked.

"I think he was incredibly twisted, sick, and sadly devoid of any compassion for life and the beauty that exists everywhere in this world," I said. And I found myself imagining how that poor girl felt during the Columbine High School shootings when she was asked if she believed in God, milliseconds before being executed for her answer. I swallowed hard.

He chuckled. It was low and menacing.

"I grew up only a block from the Salvador Dalí Museum in St. Petersburg, Florida. Ever been to Dalíwood?"

I was wondering if he'd noticed me slipping my hands into my jacket pockets, fishing for something to use as a weapon. Anything.

He must have seen something in my eyes, because before I even got my hands to my pockets, his hand shot out and he demanded, "What do you have in there, Liv?"

I hated the way he said my name. I just stood there like a bastard calf at the gate.

"Give it to me. Now," he growled.

I glanced around the small pod in this remote place in the library, praying for someone—anyone—to see us. I emptied my pockets. A pack of gum, a tube of ChapStick, and a pen. Not much. I didn't exactly know what he was expecting, but I doubt if he was feeling very threatened by my mighty arsenal. Strangely enough—probably because I was feeling scared shitless—my mind wandered to when as a kid I used to order that stuff in the back of comic books, then wait by the mailbox for my treasure: the smoke from your fingertips, the throw-your-voice gadget, and the trick pack of gum that snaps a trap on the taker's finger. Oh, if only I had that pack of gum instead of this pack of Extra.

A slash of smile appeared on his face. "We're the only ones on this floor, Liv. And if you run or scream or do anything to draw attention to us, I will hunt down your family one at a time and kill all ten of them."

My heart jumped into my throat. How did he know about my family?

"Do we have an understanding, Genevieve Liv Bergen?"

I nodded. He had certainly discovered my Achilles' heel. I would rather die a thousand deaths than let anything happen to my mother, father, or any one of my eight siblings.

"Good," he said, "because it's time to leave."

I stared at him, unable to move, unable to think, unable to act. So much for thinking I'd never need to take Tae Kwon Do lessons. They probably would have taught me what to do in situations like this, how not to let your brain freeze.

Dr. Jay leaned over and closed the volume of Dalí prints, covering it with one of the books about Magritte, then motioned with his hand for me to walk ahead of him. I didn't move. He lightly grabbed my elbow, the gentleman that he wasn't, and my feet started moving.

As we made our way to the exit, he leaned into me and said, "Make this look legit, Liv, or they're all going to die, starting with your youngest sister, the one that looks like a model. What's her name again? Ida?"

My heart caught in my throat. I refused to answer, shocked that he knew my little sister's name. Mechanically, I was walking beside him now, arm in arm, as if we were strolling along a riverbank. My legs felt like rubber and my stomach churned.

"Ida, yes," he said with a hiss.

I was walking and talking, but not fully aware of what was happening. I could feel us walking down the stairs, could see people on the second floor, but I had no idea what to do except stare straight ahead and resist the overwhelming urge to bolt and run. My family's lives were at stake. I couldn't think of anything but poor Mowgli in the coils of Kaa, mesmerized by that horribly debilitating trance, while being crushed to death by an awful snake that had pretended to be his friend.

"You're de Milo," I finally managed to say.

"I hate that name," Dr Jay said. "The Venus de Milo was so simple to sculpt, so obvious. Not like the works of Salvador Dalí, who was known for his symbolic complexity and unparalleled imagination. He was brilliant, an ever-evolving artist, working in various mediums, as I do."

My mind kept going to the distortions and mangled body parts, wondering what he had in store for me.

"Did you know we were born on the same day, Dalí and I? The eleventh of May. Not the same year, of course."

He chortled, as if we were long-lost friends catching up. It wasn't until then that I realized that by talking with him, I was helping with his cover:

two friends chatting as we walked arm in arm. We were nearly at the bottom of the stairs and I could only hope that Ann Marie and Pam could detect my predicament and call the police. I fell silent and prayed to God Dr. Jay would too.

He didn't.

"My dear deceased mother thought that was an omen. Perhaps she was right," he said.

We were a few yards from the front desk. My eyes kept sliding to Ann Marie and Pam, hoping they would notice my odd behavior, but not so much as to make mention of it immediately. If they said something, asked me what was wrong, I was afraid Dr. Jay might very well abort his plan with me and make good on his promise to maim or kill my family. I had no reason to doubt him.

"Did you know my mother was dead, Liv?" He whispered in my ear, leaning into me as he spoke. "I killed her, too."

My face must have blanched because I saw that Ann Marie was staring at me, quizzically. I managed a small nod and smile, hoping that would pacify her curiosity. All of a sudden, the front doors crashed open and in ran three paramedics with a stretcher. They bounded up the stairs two at a time. Ann Marie's attention and Pam's were diverted to the emergency personnel and away from me.

Thank you, God.

"Let's go, Liv," said Dr. Jay, hurrying his steps as we neared the door.

Just as we approached the doors, Pam called out, "Liv, your ride's here!"

The two librarians snorted as they laughed. I knew they were joking about the ambulance out front, but considering the circumstances, I was struggling to find the humor in their remark. I turned stiffly toward them and offered a silly wave. They said nothing more, and the de Milo murderer and I were out the door within seconds.

Outside, I drew in a long, deep breath, feeling as if a guardian angel was watching over me. I glanced over my shoulder up at the library and offered a quick prayer of thanks.

CHAPTER 29

STREETER WENT DOWN TO the front entrance, assessing the mob that had gathered to watch Zack being carted away in the ambulance. He was looking for Jonah Bravo's face in the crowd when he spotted Cameron, one of Jill Brannigan's friends whom Streeter had met the night before.

Cameron gave Streeter a fist bump as he approached, "What's up, Agent Pierce? Who was that kid, did you see?"

Streeter lied, "No, I didn't. But I'm glad you're here."

Cameron's face lit up. "Really?"

"Yeah, I could use your help with something."

"Me? Really?"

Streeter sized up Cameron and decided on his strategy. "Have you been here all day?"

"Most of it," Cameron said. "Since ten, anyway. After I woke up, I came down here right away to get my paper done that's due tomorrow. Why?"

"Well, I'm looking for Dr. Jay. I met him a little while ago and thought of something else I needed to ask him. Have you seen him?"

"Not since last night," Cameron said.

"Last night?"

"Yeah, he was at the bar with us last night. Left right about the time you showed up, come to think of it," Cameron said.

That didn't surprise Streeter. Jonah Bravo would have seen him coming and guessed his purpose.

"Will you do me a favor?" Streeter asked.

"Sure."

"I'm going to take a quick peek around the library and see if he's here. Would you mind waiting here by the front door and, if you see him, tell him I'm looking for him and I'll be right back?"

"You bet," Cameron said, planting himself just beyond the book detectors at the front door, stuffing his hands in his front pockets and rocking back and forth on his heels.

Streeter smiled and took off in the opposite direction. He canvassed the first floor quickly, eyeing the clusters of people at the tables and weaving down and around every row of shelves. The faces he studied barely noticed him. None of them was Jonah Bravo, and none of the women looked much like the picture of Liv among her large family that she had in a frame on her bedroom dresser.

Streeter did the same on the second and third floors, weaving around quickly and thoroughly to make sure he wasn't missing anyone. He checked out the men's restroom on each floor and hung around long enough at the women's restrooms to catch anyone exiting them. Exhausting any possibility that Jonah Bravo was hiding in a corner or a favorite haunt, Streeter returned to the second floor to find Kelleher and Brandt overseeing the activities of the criminalists, technicians, and photographers. Standing against the windows, arms crossed against his chest, the sullen-faced security guard suddenly brightened when he saw Streeter approach.

"He told me to stay out of the way," Dan complained with pouted lips, pointing to Phil Kelleher.

"Agent Kelleher?" Streeter said, his distinct, gravelly voice causing both Kelleher and Brandt to turn in his direction. "Didn't I warn you he swallows too many prunes?"

Dan laughed. Kelleher scowled. Brandt grinned.

Streeter draped an arm over Dan's shoulder.

"Tell you what, Dan," Streeter bargained, walking slowly toward Kelleher and Brandt so they could hear too. "I'm going to ask Agent Kelleher and Detective Brandt to come with me so we can check something out, and I'm leaving you in charge of security."

Kelleher's mouth dropped, a rare expression of surprise. Brandt chuckled.

"You stand right here and don't let anyone bother the techs as they do their job," Streeter said, guiding Dan to his station. "No one gets down this hall without your permission."

Dan grew an inch or two taller, proud to be in charge. Streeter slapped him on the back as he walked past him down the hall to notify the techs of Dan's new assignment. When Kelleher tried to follow, Dan wouldn't let him pass. "You don't have permission."

Kelleher's scowl deepened.

Brandt slapped Kelleher on the back good-naturedly. "Face it; you've been replaced, buddy."

"I fail to see the humor in *that*," Kelleher said.

Streeter poked his head into the small private study room. "Walker, you're in charge of this crime scene, okay. I'm taking Brandt and Kelleher with me to find de Milo. I've got a CSU security guard watching your backs. His name is Dan. I told him he was in charge of security. Be nice to him, please."

Margo Walker nodded.

Streeter walked back down the hall, motioned for Kelleher and Brandt to follow him down the stairs, and flashed Dan a thumbs-up before disappearing around the corner.

"Too many prunes?" Kelleher asked dryly.

Streeter smiled.

Cameron was still in position, rocking back and forth on his heels, hands stuffed deep in his jeans pockets.

"Anything?"

"Nope," Cameron said.

"I guess I'll have to catch him tomorrow," Streeter said. "Thanks, Cameron."

"No problemo," he said, fist-bumping Streeter as he left.

"Good luck on your paper," Streeter called out as Cameron headed toward the cluster of tables at the far end of the library. Streeter turned to Kelleher and Brandt and explained, "He was looking for Dr. Jay for me. Long shot."

"No Liv Bergen, either?" Kelleher asked.

Streeter shook his head, asking Brandt, "You?"

Brandt shook his head. "She wasn't at the city library. Only took me five minutes to check. Liv would come here, not the city library, if she was doing any serious research."

Streeter said, "You got the search warrant?"

Brandt nodded.

"Then let's get over to Dr. Jay's house." Streeter turned toward Kelleher. "You've got more coming?"

"Three others." He turned his wrist, checking the time. "One of Brandt's men and two of our agents and four techs. They told us to call when we're ten minutes out."

"We're ten minutes out," Streeter said. "But let me do one more thing before we leave."

Streeter closed the distance between the front door and the main library desk, giving a quick nod to the two women huddled over a computer. He greeted them casually. "Ladies."

They smiled.

The shorter, larger of the two women asked, "What can I do for you, dear?"

"Do you know who Dr. Jay is?"

They both nodded.

"Have you, by chance, seen him at all today?"

They looked at each other, and the taller lady said, "Yes, he was just here."

Streeter's heart raced. "Where?"

"In the library. Right here," the shorter one said, pointing along the main doors and stairs.

"Did you see where he went?" Streeter asked.

Kelleher and Brandt sidled up to the desk, listening intently.

"Well, he just left, dear," the short one said. "When did he leave, Pam?"

"Right after the ambulance got here," the tall one said. "Don't you remember, Ann Marie? I joked with Liv about her ride being here."

"Oh, yes," the short one said. "When she went all pale and stiff."

"Guess it wasn't that funny," the tall one said, grimacing.

"Liv?" Streeter's heart pounded. "You wouldn't happen to mean Liv Bergen, would you?"

The short one smiled and elbowed the tall one. "He knows Liv. And he's cute."

Streeter asked, "Where did she go?"

"Well, she left too," the tall one said. "She'd been here for . . . oh, what would you say, Ann Marie. An hour or so?"

"Yes, I'd say an hour, maybe less," the short one answered. "She was studying again. She does that a lot. Picks a subject she knows nothing about."

"Then studies about it, just so she keeps her mind fresh," the tall one added. "She's such a special young lady."

"This time it was about art," the short one announced.

Streeter felt sick. He could feel the sweat pop along his brow and upper lip. "Did she say what kind of art?"

"Surreal art," the tall one said. "Modern, bizarre. She was looking for art with people and fruit."

"A pomegranate?" Streeter asked, swallowing hard.

"Never mentioned that," the short one replied shaking her head.

The tall one shook her head too. "She was looking for art by people like Magritte."

"And Salvador Dalí," the short one added.

"And Liv's already left?"

"About twenty, maybe thirty minutes ago," the tall one said. Streeter felt the bile rise in his throat and looked at his watch. He must have just missed them. Right before he posted Cameron at the front door.

"She left with Dr. Jay," the short one added. "They left arm in arm, as a matter of fact. Is there something wrong, dear?"

CHAPTER 30

"**AREN'T YOU THE LEAST** bit curious where we're going, Liv?"

"Does it matter?"

"I think so," Dr. Jay said, moving at a good clip down the sidewalk toward a partially filled parking lot. No one was in sight. "You're going to love what I have planned for you."

I glanced over my shoulder again, willing the police to be chasing us, hoping against hope Agent Kelleher had followed me to the library and waited to pop out of the nearby bush at just the right moment. When Dr. Jay pushed me into the fancy sports car, I decided it might not be so prudent to wish for someone else to save my sorry ass from this crazy bastard.

I was on my own.

I scanned the car, looking for any kind of weapon. The car was devoid of anything except what came with it off the showroom floor. My father came to mind in that moment, or, more specifically, one of his many "life's lessons" statements did. He had told me that if I was ever caught in a situation where I needed to fight my way out of it, to use my head—and to use my keys.

As Dr. Jay was walking around the front of the car, I reached into my jeans pocket and retrieved my key ring: there were two large ones to my Ford Explorer and a small one to my house. I fumbled with the largest key, slipping it between my first and second finger and closing my fist tightly around the other two keys in the palm of my hand. Perfect. I had a makeshift knife. Dad would be proud.

The driver's side door opened and my abductor's face appeared.

"Want to take it out for a spin?" he said, wearing a sickening grin.

It occurred to me that Dr. Jay had likely fashioned himself after a young Elvis Presley, thereby hoping to attract women easily. A curled lip. Bedroom eyes. But with Dr. Jay, it was all wrong. Something about him seemed disingenuous, like he was a cheap copy. He was probably more like a love child conceived by Mr. Roarke and Tatu on Fantasy Island.

"Where are you taking me?" I snarled, happy to see that he was distracted for a moment as he was climbing into his car. I slid the keys into my right sock, deep beyond the ankle of my steel-toed boot, while he wasn't looking. He'd already made me empty my jacket pockets. It was just a matter of time before he asked me to do the same with my jeans pockets, once he thought of it.

"Somewhere very special," he said.

He turned the key in the ignition. The car hummed to life.

"You're Jonah," I just realized.

Big mistake. His hand flew to my throat and he started squeezing. "Where's the letter?"

I clutched at the long fingers of his strong hand, struggling for breath as he crushed my windpipe. I tried to answer, and my lips moved, but nothing came out except an unnatural gurgling. Was that my voice? I started to see stars and offered up a quick prayer for God to help me. Dr. Jay loosened his grip, his hand falling back onto the steering wheel, and I coughed, gasped, and spewed.

"What the hell are you doing?" I choked, protectively covering my neck with my hands.

"Where's the letter?"

I answered honestly, risking another death grip. "I don't know. I gave it to my friend Lisa."

He threw the car into reverse, pulling out of the parking spot. "Agent Henry. Well, look where that got her."

I shot him a sideways dagger.

"Dead," he said, staring at me and grinning. He turned back to watch the road.

"You killed her," I said.

"Lisa Henry was a beauty. I called her Awakening. She put up one hell of a fight." He turned the rearview mirror so it was reflecting his face. He stretched and twisted so he could see the angry scratches down the side of his cheek and neck. I silently cheered Lisa and Jill for marring him.

Dr. Jay was conceited, self-absorbed. *Study his weaknesses*, I told myself. Study and learn.

"Jill didn't fight at all," he said, as if hearing my silent cheer.

My stomach churned again and I fought back the desire to upchuck. Often, the motion of ordinary driving is enough to make me nauseated. Given Dr. Jay's erratic driving and my loyalty to both Lisa and Jill—let alone the fact of my sitting beside the very monster who had killed them both—it was all getting to be a bit too much. He talked as if it didn't matter that he took the life of these two special women, beautiful souls. Both were strong, amazing spirits, with brilliant lives cut short—by this reptilian freak.

"I told her if she fought me, I'd take it out on her little sister, Julia," he explained. "And I would have. In fact, I would have enjoyed taking my frustrations out on that little bonbon. So, Jill obeyed my every command. Right to the very end."

I imagined the center hole punched through Jill.

I lost it.

All over the front seat and dashboard of his fancy car. I simply leaned forward and hurled between my knees, all over the floorboards. The smell was powerfully bad. Dr. Jay immediately rolled down his window.

"What the—" he started and decided against whatever he had planned to say or do. He said, simply, "You cow."

"Sorry," I lied, wiping my mouth with the sleeve of my jacket. Secretly, I hoped that once he had killed me, little traces of my barf in his sporty car would be the evidence collected to nail this guy's ass. "I get motion sickness."

The truth was, I couldn't stop thinking about Jill and what he had done to her. How he must have used all her innards as chum for the freshwater fish at Horsetooth.

I lost it again, only this time I had tried to roll my window down first. But Dr. Jay had locked the power windows, so all I managed to do was barf all over the passenger side door and under the nice leather seat of his expensive car.

Oddly, a vision of Mr. Wagner and his can of magic sand came to mind. Whenever any of us students puked at the Catholic grade school, the kind old janitor brought his magic sand to soak up whatever smells and gunk had erupted from our little bodies. Mr. Wagner never let on if he was disgusted; he wore the same deadpan expression as when he'd wheel out the gurney with the four candles—three pink and one purple—on it during Advent to our mournful rendition of "O Come, O Come, Emmanuel." I hadn't thought about Mr. Wagner in years.

"My Maserati! You are such a disgusting *vaca*," Dr. Jay shouted. "I ought to torture you by suffocating you with your own bile, you filthy cow."

I stifled my glee. I had managed to piss him off and it felt good. The same kind of good I felt when the keys dug into my ankle. I would have my chance. If I was going to get eaten by this mountain lion I was at least going to make it as painful as if he were swallowing a feisty porcupine. Like Lisa had.

Dr. Jay pulled into the driveway off Whaler's Way. After my initial shock in realizing this was not a plush hotel, but rather his house, the irony of Jonah living on Whaler's Way settled on me like a terrible omen. I imagined the whale swallowing me as he tucked his car into the garage, quickly lowering the automatic door behind us. *In the belly of Jonah*, I thought. And felt a chill.

"Get out, you selfish pig," he hollered at me.

I grabbed the slippery door handle and hoisted myself out of the stinky car. He stepped out and stomped through the garage into the house. I stood staring at the organized garage, noting the old pickup with a topper in the second stall. I was scanning the space, looking for another possible weapon, when Dr. Jay emerged with a bucket of soapy water and a sponge.

He shoved the bucket toward me and said, "Get to work. I don't have all day."

I did as I was told, scrubbing away at the floorboard and the door of his precious Maserati. I eased up on the elbow grease, at least enough for Dr. Jay not to notice, particularly on the area under the passenger's seat. I would leave something for the forensic team to find and link to me after my mutilated body was found. A shiver skipped down my spine as my mind flashed to some of Dalí's other paintings. As brave and ornery as I pretended to be, I was still scared shitless by the prospect of being butchered with high-pressure water. I glanced over my shoulder at the beat-up pickup and realized the compressor, water tank, and hose must be hidden in there. De Milo's mobile butchering shop.

"Hurry up," he hollered, watching my every move.

I did as I was told, taking my time but not so much so that he might figure I was stalling, which I was.

"You're done," Dr. Jay said abruptly, jerking the sponge and bucket from my hands, leaving them by the doormat, and disappearing once more through the door to the house.

I darted toward the toolbox, drying my hands on my jeans, and fished for a screwdriver. Hearing the door open again, I leapt away from the toolbox and shoved the tool down my pants in one smooth motion. I covered my face with my hand as if I was woozy.

"What are you doing?" he demanded, a camera and a white bed sheet tucked in his arms.

"I think I'm going to be sick again," I said.

"Filth," he spat. Tossing the items into the back of his truck, he demanded, "Get in."

I stood, staring at him. Not the truck. Not the high-pressure water.

"Get in," he insisted, motioning with his head for me to get in the truck, his eyes boring through me.

I did as I was told.

CHAPTER 31

GUNS DRAWN, STREETER CREPT up the driveway along the hedge to the enormous house on Whaler's Way, Kelleher right behind him. The agent in charge had sent Brandt around back with Kyle Mills and Raymond Martinez. He asked Brandt's man, Andy Doughty, to hang back at the curb in an unmarked in case everything went awry and they needed to call for backup. The four crime scene technicians were waiting in a van parked around the block.

Streeter crouched low and leapt onto the porch landing without a sound, flattening himself between the front door and the bay windows. He motioned for Kelleher to join him and pointed to the other side of the door where he wanted him to stand. Ready to bust open the door or through the window if necessary, Streeter stole an instant peek through the bay windows. He leaned back against the house and squeezed his eyes shut, holding onto the flash image of the inside of Jonah Bravo's living room. Fireplace directly across from the bay windows, couch to the right allowing whoever sat in it to watch out the window or at the fireplace from the same place. An armchair was situated by the right side of the window; a lamp sat on a table underneath the windowsill. The lamp was turned off. Not surprisingly, the fireplace was cold. Streeter saw no movement of light from a television in the room.

He took a deep breath and opened his eyes, ready to take a closer look inside. He craned his neck to see through the window and verified his snapshot image of the room being empty. He looked around and saw no light spilling from the hallway or any other room from the house.

Streeter pressed a button on his two-way and talked into the clip mic on his collar. "Looks empty, can't hear a sound," he whispered. "Brandt?"

Brandt and Mills were at the back door by the kitchen. Kyle Mills's voice sounded, "Same."

"Martinez?"

"Same. I'm at the door to the garage. Maserati's inside."

"Pickup truck?"

"No pickup. Empty stall, though."

Streeter and Kelleher exchanged a glance. Both men's shoulders sagged.

"Doughty, are we clear?" Streeter asked.

"Clear," the young man's voice cracked.

Streeter took a deep breath. "On three, guys. One, two, three."

Streeter slammed his shoulder against the door alongside Kelleher and the door splintered at the hinges. The two men pounded the door again and it twisted to the ground. Shoulder to shoulder, the men rushed into the living room and cleared the area, sweeping around every large piece of furniture and every closed door. The house was full of silence other than the noise of the kitchen door crashing to the floor and the muffled sound of the garage door being rushed by Martinez. The only thing Streeter could hear was his own heavy breathing and his heart pounding in his chest. His mind's eye flashed to Lisa's naked body, to Jill's mutilated corpse, and to Liv's captivating smile in the photo.

Where was she?

He raced soundlessly up the stairs to the bedrooms, Kelleher covering his back. The second floor was dark, no lights on anywhere, and all doors swung wide open. Streeter crept up the rest of the stairs and swept each room. The first bedroom was empty, but Streeter noticed the deadbolt on the outside of the door and the steel grate welded to the steel window frame.

It was a prison. Probably where Jonah had held Jill between Monday night and early Wednesday morning.

He opened the closet door. Completely empty. He opened the dresser drawers. Empty. This was the spare bedroom, devoid of any signs of life except for what might be reflected in all the mirrors when the candles in the numerous candleholders scattered about the room were lit. He motioned for Kelleher to follow him down the hall to what appeared to be the master bedroom. They rushed the room, Kelleher darting off to the master bathroom to search and clear.

No sign of Jonah Bravo. Or Liv.

Streeter was relieved in one sense, hoping he wouldn't find Liv as he had Lisa. On the other hand, he knew Liv's time was running out.

He pushed the button on his two-way again. "Second floor clear."

"Main floor clear," Mills barked. "Basement too."

"Garage clear," Martinez answered. "He was just here."

Streeter and Kelleher exchanged a look, Streeter finally noticing the gallery of pictures on Jonah Bravo's bedroom wall. He slowly walked over to it, turning on the nearby lamp and shining it directly on the photos.

Kelleher moaned. "There's more."

"Seven dead, not four," Streeter counted. "Three we knew nothing about, including his mother and sister."

"And look at this." Kelleher pointed to the seventh empty frame marked "William Tell." "Who the hell was he calling William Tell?"

Streeter shook his head. His two-way screeched.

"Streeter, did you hear me?" Martinez sounded.

"Yeah, I heard you," Streeter answered. "He was just here?"

"Yeah, the hood of the Maserati is still hot. And I found a bucket with suds."

"Cleaning lady?"

"On a Sunday? Not likely. And was she driving his Maserati?"

"Put an APB on the pickup, Brandt. Can you do that?"

Kyle's voice sounded. "He's doing it as we speak, Streeter."

"Make sure they know Jonah Bravo is armed and dangerous. And he has a hostage," Streeter added.

Kyle clicked the two-way in acknowledgment.

Streeter never took his eyes off the photographs, studying each one, his eyes darting from one to another photo, and each gory detail.

To Kelleher he said, "We've got to figure out where he's taking her. It's a matter of life and death. He knows we're on to him and he's going to be like smoke after he kills Liv. He'll go back to Florida. Or worse, Cuba, and we'll never find him there."

Kelleher nodded, rubbing his forehead as he studied the photos alongside Streeter.

Mills's voice boomed. "Streeter, you've got to see this. Brandt found a darkroom in the basement."

Streeter and Kelleher bounded down the stairs, falling in behind Martinez, who had entered from the garage. All three descended into the basement. The sounds Mills and Brandt were making came from a large room encompassing a quarter of the basement; nearly six hundred square feet by Streeter's estimation. The largest darkroom he'd ever seen.

He rounded the corner to find Brandt and Mills huddled around a pile of photos scattered on the large table, several more pinned to the walls.

"Holy shit," Martinez groaned.

Kelleher's mouth puckered at the grotesque sight.

Dozens of photos of each crime scene were scattered throughout the room, different angles and distances, different lighting and focus. The best four to six were neatly pinned beneath a ten-by-fifteen-inch glossy photo of the corresponding piece of Dalí's bizarre artwork.

Going from left to right on the wall were Dalí's "The Enigma of Desire: My Mother, My Mother, My Mother," "Seated Girl, Seen from the Back (The Artist's Sister)," "Bather," all three photos of crime scenes with people he had never seen before, and "The Great Masturbator," with photos of the young couple from Platteville pinned beneath, a photo of Jill Brannigan's mutilated body next, and finally, a photo of Lisa Henry's naked body.

"Streeter, look," Doug Brandt croaked, pointing at the page that had been ripped from a book of Dalí's works and pinned next to Lisa's photographs.

"William Tell," Streeter read, repulsed by the painting of the man with other distorted figures—a horse, a man, a dead donkey, a woman, a lion head—floating around him. The man, dressed only in his underwear, was standing on one leg, resting his left foot on a bench and holding scissors.

His face was screwed into a look of sheer agony as he cried tears of blood, his privates dangling from his fly.

"What a sick puppy," Martinez whistled.

"Dalí or Jonah Bravo?" Mills asked, as if the clarification mattered.

"Both," Streeter answered. "This isn't art. This is trash."

"No, look," Brandt said, the urgency in his voice pulling Streeter from his trance of disgust as he studied the Dalí painting.

Streeter hadn't seen the photo pinned beneath the Dalí image until now. It was a photo of Liv Bergen's house taken from a distance. Streeter saw himself approaching the door.

"You were going to be his next target, Streeter," Kelleher realized. "You're William Tell."

"Jesus, Mary, and Joseph," Ray Martinez blurted, making the sign of the cross as he did.

"We have to figure out where he took Liv," Streeter said again. "And fast."

Kelleher noticed a book of Dalí reproductions lying on the counter near a computer. The book was open to a photo of a woman dressed in a toga, spread-eagled on rocks as if mocking the crucifixion.

"Streeter, look at this," he said.

The group of men all huddled around the photo, studying the bizarre depiction of the compromised woman, a woman with thick arms, limbs, and mountainous breasts.

"Dalí conquering a strong woman? Posing her in a sexually provocative way to reveal vulnerability?" Kelleher rambled.

"What are you saying, Phil?" Brandt asked.

"Liv Bergen. She's strong. She runs her own mining company. He wants to reveal her vulnerability," Streeter answered.

"That's why he derailed his plans for William Tell," Kelleher figured.

"Lisa was on to him, was researching Salvador Dalí, when he killed her," Streeter said.

"And Liv was researching Salvador Dalí when he kidnapped her," Kelleher added.

"He's rushed," Streeter said. "Hurried."

"Out of control," Kelleher added.

"Making mistakes."

"And pissed about all these smart, strong women messing up his plans," Martinez speculated.

Streeter said, "Where would he take her? What rock?"

"Gray Rock?" Brandt said, everyone turning toward him. "It's probably the most popular hiking trail around here."

"Too many people," Mills offered. "Witnesses."

"That didn't stop him at the library," Martinez chided.

Kelleher's eyes widened. "What about the rock Liv was missing from her dresser?"

"The cluster of eleven rocks," Streeter agreed.

"A rock for each family member," Kelleher continued. "Jonah Bravo must have taken it as a trophy or something when he killed Lisa Henry."

Streeter's eyes widened when he realized he knew exactly where Jonah was taking Liv. He bolted out the door. The others followed, chasing him up the stairs.

"Streeter?" Kelleher called after him.

"The crystal," he called back to them.

"What?" Kelleher asked.

"He took the crystal."

"I know. But what about it?"

"I saw it in his office, on his windowsill. He's taunting us." Streeter ran out the front door and headed to his Jeep. He called out to them. "He's taking her to the quarry. *Her* quarry. Anyone know where that is?"

Young Andy Doughty was standing by his car. "I do. My brother works there."

Brandt said, "I was just there on Wednesday morning, interviewing Liv."

"We'll follow you," Streeter said, waving at Kelleher to join him.

Doug Brandt jumped in with Doughty, and Martinez jumped into the FBI sedan. Mills called out to Martinez, "I'll work the subpoena with the technicians. Go, go!"

The three cars fell in line, Doughty popping a bubble out his window and placing it onto the top of his unmarked as they sped away.

Streeter punched the numbers on his cell phone. "I need an ambulance."

"Address?" the woman at the emergency services asked.

"Sweet mother of pearl," Streeter cursed. "Hold on."

Streeter keyed his two-way, hoping they were close enough to Doughty for reception. "Doughty, I've got the hospital on the line. Can you give them directions to the mine?"

Andy said, "Yeah, sure."

Streeter held the cell phone down by the two-way clipped to his belt while Doughty gave directions. When Andy Doughty was done, the hospital employee said, "Got it. They're on the way."

"Wait," Streeter called, pulling the phone up to his ear. "We need an antidote for heroin. You got something like that? A magic pill?"

The hospital employee was calm. "No magic pill, but the paramedics usually carry Narcan."

"What does that do?"

"If it's injected in time, it blocks the heroin from acting on receptors. Receptors for opioids."

"English?" Streeter asked.

"Revives the person almost immediately. If it's injected in time," she repeated.

"Will you make sure these guys have it? Lots of it," Streeter pressed.

The woman sighed, as if frustrated by Streeter's urgency. "All the vehicles are equipped with respiration devices. The OD will likely die because of an inability to breathe."

"I'm not talking about an OD," Streeter argued, angry at the operator's accusation. "This is Special Agent Streeter Pierce, lead investigator for the de Milo murders. This is an emergency situation. It's attempted murder, homicide. I need this on the q.t. And make it fast. Without sirens and lights. Detective Brandt's escorting us to the potential crime scene as we speak."

Her voice became more animated. "Oh, sorry, Agent Pierce. I didn't know. I'll get right on it."

CHAPTER 32

WE DROVE FOR NEARLY thirty minutes into familiar territory for me, although I wasn't going to share that realization with Dr. Jay. I drive this way to work and back home every day.

I stared out the window, noticing the beauty I'd never slowed down to see before. God's gifts came ever closer into focus. I guess facing death will do that to you. I would have thought I'd been more scared, but knowing what I had on the other side gave me peace.

And an odd sense of clarity. "You cut the middle out of Jill with water."

He turned toward me and cocked his head. "How did you know that?"

"I've seen carpet cut the same way. It leaves a different impression than other instruments do."

"I thought you worked at a mine," he admitted. "Not as an undercover agent."

"I do," I said with no further explanation. "You're posing all of us like models in a Salvador Dalí painting. But I haven't figured out why." I had hoped Dr. Jay would fill the pregnant pause that followed, but he didn't. "You talk as if you admired Salvador Dalí, but now you're mocking him with cheap imitations."

That earned me a busted lip. His backhanded punch to my face stunned me, his words even more so.

"I'm not *mocking* Dalí," he grumbled. "I'm *honoring* him. Besides, what would an ox like you know about it?"

"I know that imitation is the highest form of flattery but art is supposed to imitate life, not the other way around," I added, enjoying the contorted expression that appeared on Dr. Jay's face, which I glimpsed through my peripheral vision. "I believe the brilliant Dalí would have seen this as unadulterated mockery."

"Shut up," he growled.

I didn't. I realized I was having some effect on him. I didn't know what, exactly, but it was something. He was off his game, losing his composure, which I sensed must have felt like being caught flat-footed and letting me score an easy layup.

I dug deep into the recesses of my mind trying to find the words Dalí himself had used and which I had skimmed through in the introduction to the first art book I had pulled off the shelf earlier today.

"You have tried to make reality out of fantasy, whereas Dalí was all about tapping the world of fantasy, not reality," I said, seeing Dr. Jay's knuckles grow white as he gripped the steering wheel even tighter. "What is it he said? Something like 'I'm always perplexed by why man should be so capable of so little fantasy.' I think he was talking about you, Jonah."

He backhanded me again in the face. This time I saw stars, my world darkening into shades of gray. I almost missed the significance of the familiar turn right and the rumbling beneath the wheels of the truck as we rolled over a cattle guard. When I regained my bearings and recognized that we were just inside the entrance of my quarry, panic narrowed my throat.

"What are you doing?"

"I told you we were going somewhere special," he said, turning into the quarry entrance. "Ever hear of Dalí's 'Figure on the Rocks'?"

I shook my head. I didn't remember seeing anything like that in the books. I knew I was to be the "Figure," however. And I knew "the Rocks" would have something to do with my quarry.

"You will," he added. "Soon enough."

My heart pounded in my chest, knowing it was Sunday and no one would be in the quarry, shop, or offices. I prayed that one of the three plant people might be taking a load out to the quarry or might see Dr. Jay's truck as we ducked over the hill into the quarry before disappearing.

He parked his truck on the edge of a highwall and offered a heavy sigh. "Figure on the Rocks. Perfect."

CHAPTER 33

STREETER CLOSED THE PHONE and tossed it on his dashboard, struggling to keep up with Doughty, who knew the streets of Fort Collins better than did Streeter. What if he was wrong about where Jonah Bravo was taking Liv Bergen? It would be a deadly mistake, he realized. *Instincts, don't fail me now*, he told himself.

Kelleher's cell phone rang.

"Kelleher," he said, Streeter straining to hear what it was about. "Just a minute. Let me put you on speaker phone so Streeter can hear."

The voice on the phone sounded tinny and distant. "Hi, Streeter. Jon Tuygen here."

"Tuygen," Streeter greeted the caller brusquely, focusing on the road and all the hazards flashing by.

"What have you got, Jon?" Kelleher asked.

"Pandora," he said. "What a box you found this time, guys."

Jon Tuygen was one of the most brilliant at computer forensics Streeter had ever come across, not only in the Bureau but anywhere. A shy, cordial young man, humble about his incredible talent for data mining, Tuygen was likable and approachable, unlike so many computer geeks Streeter had crossed paths with over the years. Unlike Misty Asante.

"Pandora. Really?" Kelleher asked. "Tell me about it."

"Where do I start?" Tuygen asked.

"From the beginning," Streeter said. "And make it snappy. We're right in the middle of something."

Streeter was instantly remorseful. He had no business being curt with Jon. It wasn't his fault that Liv was missing or that Jonah was a step ahead of them. It wasn't his fault that Streeter had just gambled on a person's life based on his instincts. Tuygen was one of the good guys and didn't deserve the way Streeter had treated him. And he should be doubly grateful that it was Tuygen who had called and not Asante again.

"Sorry," Tuygen said.

"No, it's my fault, Tuygen," Streeter interrupted him. "We need your help and I appreciate you coming in today. What'd you learn about Jonah Bravo?"

Kelleher nodded his approval at Streeter's contrition.

"Well, starting from the beginning," Tuygen said. "Born in the Municipio of Colón in Matanzas, Cuba, thirty-two years ago."

"What's a municipio? A city?" Kelleher asked.

"No, more like a county. He's from the barrio of Guareiras, a town of about three thousand. There's only about thirty thousand in the whole county. It appears his father met Jonah's mother sometime while he was temporarily detained in Cuba after being arrested as an unauthorized driver of a rental car."

"So Jonah's Cuban?" Kelleher asked.

"He's been an illegal immigrant, technically, since he was three. He's lived like an American."

"How'd he get to America?"

"Looks like the mother's family was deep into farming. The father's name was Maury Bravo and he married into the Este family, the mother's family in Guareiras. Maury was gunned down in Miami when Jonah was three and his sister, Jacan, was eighteen months old."

"Miami? That's a long way from home in Cuba, isn't it?" Kelleher asked.

"Not really," Tuygen explained. "Only a little over two hundred miles, as the crow flies. Or as the small, unidentified aircraft flies," he corrected.

"Smuggling?" Streeter asked.

"That's apparently why Jonah's father was killed. Overstepped some boundaries into someone else's market. The execution of Bravo senior was supposedly a message to the Este family. Threatened to kill the rest of family too, so the mother abandoned her post as loyal daughter and sister to the patriarchs of the Este family and fled with little Jonah and Jacan, using her married name and Maury Bravo's American status to relocate in St. Petersburg."

"She wanted out," Streeter stated.

"Yep," Tuygen confirmed.

"Let me guess, they were farmers growing poppies?" Kelleher asked.

Tuygen ribbed, "They were farmers, but not of opium poppies. Instead, they were using their crops to legitimize the exports to the States as middlemen from Columbia. Connect the dots."

"Heroin," Streeter growled. "That's the connection. His mother's family must have recruited Jonah at some point. Probably when he came of age. They've been using him as a mule to transport drugs from Cuba, the transition point from Columbia to the U.S."

"Or to distribute," Kelleher added.

Streeter nodded. "Jonah Bravo. Family member who's an American professor. The perfect conduit between students who would be using and an abundant supply from relatives in Cuba. That explains the four thousand square feet of home, custom-made clothes, and a Maserati."

"Only, he's not really a professor," Tuygen added. "He went to school at St. Petersburg College and obtained a teaching certificate, but he never got a master's anywhere. Looks to me like he bought it from somewhere."

"How the hell did he get past the administration?" Kelleher asked.

"Well, right out of college he got a job in a couple of vo-tech schools near St. Petersburg. Skipped along quickly, staying only a few months to a couple years at the most in any one place. Looks like he gravitated up to junior colleges, then on to a college or two, and eventually the university in Fort Collins. Probably once someone hired him, they never really checked out his background. The hiring was likely based more on the reputation of the schools where he taught than on his credentials."

"Probably," Kelleher agreed.

"What's your gut tell you about how he got into the business, Tuygen?" Streeter asked, curious about the psychology of this man since he was about to meet him face-to-face. At least he hoped he would.

"Looks like the mom tried to protect her kids, Jonah and Jacan, kept them away from the family business and all the danger. They were raised in a luxury condominium along the western shore of Tampa Bay, prime waterfront property in the artsy district. Two major museums within a stone's throw of their building and the private school they attended."

"Pushed her kids into culture rather than cultivating poppies," Kelleher quipped.

"Seems so," Tuygen answered. "But to answer your question, Streeter, I think everything fell apart for Jonah's family once he graduated from college. Looks like his mother was murdered a year later. His sister overdosed six months after that."

"Let me guess again," Kelleher said. "Heroin?"

"Yes, indeed. The way I figure it," Tuygen continued, "St. Petersburg was the perfect place to set up a smuggling operation. Sleepy town compared to Miami. Largest city marina in the U.S. Great place, if you need to dock boats unnoticed. Nearly two hundred thirty-five miles of shoreline. How do you patrol that? Not to mention that the family's condominium was minutes from the airport. It would have been easy pickings for someone like Jonah Bravo."

"And a profitable outlet for the Este family," Streeter figured. "Based on the photos we've seen up here on his bedroom wall, looks like Jonah Bravo murdered his mother and sister. I'll get someone to scan and send them to you if you can compare them to what you've found."

"Yeah, sure. That doesn't surprise me," Tuygen responded. "He's wanted for questioning by the Pinellas County homicide investigators on the murder of Rosa Este Bravo, his mother, and on drug trafficking linked to the death of Jacan Bravo."

"So they suspected him," Kelleher summarized.

"Not right away," Tuygen said. "Or if they did, they waited until they had enough evidence before they posted the warrant for his arrest. In the meantime, he slipped away from them."

"To Fort Collins, Colorado," Kelleher added. "A long way from St. Petersburg."

"With several stops in between," Tuygen reminded him. "All told, Jonah has worked in better than half a dozen postsecondary schools since he graduated ten years ago."

Streeter squinted in the sun as the convoy of cops and agents drove north out of Fort Collins on U.S. Highway 287. "Tuygen, did you run across any unsolved, bizarre murders in any of the other counties that Jonah Bravo lived in during the last decade?"

Tugyen hummed as he thought. "Don't think I inquired about anything like that. I was focused more on where this guy came from and what he was made of. Want me to poke around?"

"Could you? It might be a mutilation or death involving a naked corpse," Streeter suggested, thinking of the photograph of "The Bather" that Jonah had hung on his bedroom wall just after the one of Jonah's sister.

"Anything else?" Kelleher asked.

Tuygen paused. "Nothing of real significance other than he worked during high school and college to put himself through school. He was a tour guide at the Salvador Dalí Museum, a block from where he lived, and in the summer of his senior year in college, he won the Salvador Dalí look-alike contest."

Kelleher closed the phone after thanking Jon Tuygen and telling him what an excellent, thorough job he'd done in such a short time. Streeter was lost in thought about Jonah Bravo's fascination with Salvador Dalí.

"Look, there's the mine," Kelleher said, pointing to his right just as Streeter pulled off the highway and alongside Andy Doughty's car.

CHAPTER 34

"GET OUT," BARKED DR. JAY

I looked to the east, out over the highwall to the foothills rolling into long stretches of prairie beyond. The Rocky Mountains were behind us, the piñon grove to our left. I knew every nook and cranny in this quarry like the back of my hand. As they say in tennis, "my ad, butt wipe."

The door of his truck creaked as I pushed it open and stepped out, feeling stronger with the limestone ledge as my foundation. Familiar ground. I heard his door creak open as well and watched as my captor walked around the back of the truck and opened the window of the topper. I took the opportunity to retrieve the screwdriver from my panties and slid it up the right sleeve of my shirt, practicing once as I bent my wrist, allowing it to drop into the palm of my hand for quick use. I nearly dropped it, panicked as I considered what might have been if he heard it clank on the rocks, and pushed it back up my sleeve.

Dr. Jay rounded the truck and approached me carrying a folded white sheet.

"Undress," he said, his voice mechanical, robotic.

I wondered where his arrogance had gone, his lilting accent, his exotic charm. I wondered if all that had been faked and this was the real Jonah

Bravo. I glared at him through my swollen eyes, gently touching my broken nose and bloody lip with the fingers of my left hand. I knew my only chance to defeat him would be to render him useless, unconscious. Or kill him. If not, he was going to kill me. Or worse, kill someone in my family. He was a twisted bastard and I wasn't about to leave anything to chance.

"Another demonstration of your inability to fantasize? Need the real thing because you're incapable of imagining?"

He didn't budge. His hands weren't clenching into fists, his jaw muscles weren't working overtime. He just stood there, staring at me. With dead eyes.

"Undress," he repeated.

Maybe I'd been unconscious long enough to miss where the pod people had overtaken this otherwise emotional basket case and invaded his body. I tried again to push a button.

"Is this what 'Figure on the Rocks' is all about? Dalí getting his rocks off by making defenseless, helpless women strip in front of him on a quarry ledge?"

Nothing.

The air was still and hot. And thin. My breathing was heavy. Fear more than anything. Or maybe it was adrenaline, my wanting to use the screwdriver I felt against my right forearm.

"Undress or Ida dies," he said, a smile playing around the corner of his mouth.

"Fuck you," I replied, planting my feet shoulder-width apart and rolling onto the balls of my feet, ready to launch myself. "You're nothing like Dalí. He was a sick fuck like you, but at least he had some balls. It took balls to be a controversial artist. You . . . you're nothing but an unimaginative dullard, incapable of anything besides bullying women, the weaker sex."

He laughed. I had finally reached some emotional core within the robot. I was trying to stall, trying to prepare for my moment to maim him, hoping against hope he didn't have a gun or a knife hidden beneath his shirt or tucked into his pants. Or under that stupid sheet.

I squinted, cocked my head. "What's so funny?"

"You are anything but weak, Genevieve Liv Bergen," he said, chuckling, taking a couple of steps toward me, and unfolding the sheet. "In fact, you might be more fun than Lisa Henry was."

That got my blood boiling. I offered up a quick prayer for God to give me strength, and I dropped the screwdriver into my palm, lunged toward him, and stabbed at his heart. Jonah darted away, my screwdriver glancing off his left bicep, ripping skin and shirt along the way. Before I could reposition and take another stab, his right fist connected with my chin in a powerful uppercut, hurling me backward. I stumbled and fell. The gray was crowding my vision, but I'm pretty sure I saw an upside-down view of the prairie and blue skies.

And the bottom of the pit.

The sound of my screwdriver crashing against the rock floor thirty-five feet below confirmed my suspicions and I panicked. Shit, I was dangling upside down over the highwall, about to plummet to my death, my head being smashed like a melon against the floor of my own quarry.

I felt a yanking on my ankles and heard him grunt as Dr. Jay pulled me back onto the ledge. Rather than focusing on how closely I had just come to dying, all I could think about was if he had felt my keys through the leather of my boot.

"You stupid cow," he said. "You nearly ruined my photo shoot."

I lay on my back, eyes closed, trying to make the merry-go-round of stars in my eyes stop spinning, the ache of my teeth and jaw stop pounding in my head. I was going to be sick. Once the stars stopped spinning and I remembered to breathe, I started to feel all the sharp rocks against my back where I lay. I pushed myself up to a sitting position.

He was still there. Staring at me.

"For the last time, undress," he said in a low voice.

I threw up my hands in surrender, staggering to my feet. We squared off as if in the gunfight at the O.K. Corral. Dr. Jay staring at me, me glaring at him. I had nothing left but the keys in my right sock, which apparently he hadn't felt while he was pulling me off the highwall, sparing my life.

This crazy bastard really needs the photo more than he wants me dead, I thought. I slipped off my jacket and unbuttoned and removed my shirt, tossing them at his feet.

"How's this going to work, Jonah?" I had resorted to using his real name rather than Dr. Jay, hoping to evoke the same outburst of anger and energy he exhibited in the car when I first used it. "Now that you've blackened my eyes, broken my nose, and split my lip," I taunted.

I untied my boots, careful to bunch up my socks at my ankle to conceal the bulge of my keys. I pulled off my boots and threw them at him, one at a time. He grinned and arched an eyebrow.

I continued, "What kind of a model do I make for your photo, all bloodied and bruised, huh, smart guy? Have you thought of that?"

"I've thought of that," he said. It worked. I got him talking again.

"And it's ruined, isn't it? The picture. Your perfect picture of 'Figure on the Rocks,'" I challenged him.

His grin was unnerving, but at least he hadn't asked me to take more clothing off. I was standing in my bra and stocking feet, my jeans the only real clothes I still had on.

"As you've already admitted, you don't know 'Figure on the Rocks,'" he said tauntingly. "If you did, you'd know her face is obscured, hidden."

My stomach dropped. If I had had anything left to hurl, I would have, but my stomach was empty.

"You didn't think of that, did you, you imbecile?" he jeered. "Now, get on with it. Take off the rest of your clothes."

At least his voice was no longer frighteningly robotic. The cocky, narcissistic Dr. Jay was back. I had a chance. I unbuttoned my jeans and pulled them down over each leg, careful to block his view of the keys in my right sock.

"What are you going to do, rape me?" I spat.

He laughed again. Louder and longer. He was greatly enjoying this and I was happy for the delay. "I wouldn't soil myself for a beast like you."

"Wouldn't or *couldn't*?" What the hell was I saying? I didn't want to provoke him into raping me, did I? Or would that be my only chance to stab him in the jugular with the key?

Dad's face popped into my head, showing me how to drive the tiny little bones in a person's nose back into their brains with the heel of my hand if I ever got in trouble, pretending not to be imparting such a wise strategy to such a little girl when Mom rounded the corner from the kitchen. I didn't forget, Dad.

"Did hell finally freeze over? The great Jonah Bravo is at a loss for words," I said mockingly, deciding I'd rather take my chances with a rape for the opportunity for close proximity to this monster. "I repeat, wouldn't or couldn't?"

He blinked once, the eyes going dead again. "And I said get undressed."

I tossed the jeans onto the heap of my clothes that lay at his feet.

"Everything," he said.

I pulled off my left sock, then started pulling off my right one, but I pretended to hear a noise and looked up past Dr. Jay's shoulder to the road cut in the rocks. He glanced over his left shoulder and as he did, I gripped the keys in my right fist.

He turned back toward me, eyes shooting daggers at me. At least they were no longer lifeless.

I stood and tossed the socks into the heap. "Thought I heard someone coming."

"You wish."

Lilt in his voice. It was hard to understand what made this man tick. One minute he had the lilt, the next his voice offered no inflection at all. Lively to lifeless.

I didn't have anything on now except my bra and panties. My feet were blistering against the sun-beaten rocks. For the first time, I felt defeated. He wasn't going to allow himself to get close to me again. I'd already proven I was not trustworthy. The blood trickling down his left sleeve brought a smile to my split lip. I was certainly a sight to behold. At least my family would be told by Agent Pierce that I had put up a fight.

I unclasped my bra and slid out of my panties, tossing both onto the heap. I stood up, straightening my spine and hiking my chin, offering up one final prayer, aloud.

"Thy will be done."

"What did you say?"

"It's an ejaculation."

"A what?"

"A quick little prayer," I explained. "The nuns taught me how to do that. How to ejaculate. Ejaculations are quick little prayers."

He laughed again, tossing the sheet toward me. "You are such a strange creature. Now, put that on. Like a toga."

I stared at the sheet.

"Didn't the nuns teach you about togas?"

I wrapped the sheet around my chest, happy to be covering my body, shielding myself from the world, from the blistering sun, from his dead eyes. I tied the sheet over one shoulder and tucked the long key into position between the first and second finger of my hand, balling both fists so he'd think I was angry, not hiding something.

We did the O.K. Corral thing again, staring each other down until one flinched.

"Now lie down on the rocks. On your back, head pointed toward me."

His words, lifeless.

CHAPTER 35

"**THE QUARRY'S RIGHT THROUGH** that cut, straight ahead on the road," Andy Doughty said, pointing at the crest in the hill.

Streeter assessed the landscape. An industrial plant on the left, offices on the right; both on the western side of the ridge, the quarry on the other side to the east.

"He'd be on the other side. In the quarry," Doughty explained.

"Any way he'd know we're here?" Kelleher asked.

Ray Martinez pulled up beside Streeter. Their cars were three abreast on the gravel road. Streeter rolled down his window so Martinez could hear.

Doughty shook his head. "No way. My brother works in that plant right there on weekday nights and he says he doesn't even know if someone's driving around out here unless he gets lucky and just happens to be standing in the right place at the right time when they drive in."

"Are there people working there right now?" Streeter asked.

"Quarry, shop, and office are closed on weekends. But a few work at the pulverizing plant to produce 24/7. Probably three, maybe four guys. That's where Jill Brannigan worked."

Everyone nodded.

"So, if Jonah Bravo is in the quarry right now with Liv Bergen, there's no way he would have seen us pull in here, know that we're here?"

"Only if he's crouched on top of that ridge somewhere, hiding in the rabbit brush and piñons. Not likely."

"If we keep going on this road, will he see us?" Streeter pointed straight east, toward the road through the cut right in front of them.

"Probably so. If I were him and didn't know much about this place, I'd have driven right over the top to be hidden from view from both the plant and the highway. He'd have the place all to himself."

Brandt piped in. "There are some houses and ranch homes to the east, but Bravo would look like an ant to someone who looked from that distance. They're way the heck out there on the prairie."

"Is there another way in?" Streeter asked.

Andy Doughty nodded. "There's a road they call the south cut. Just beyond that fuel station before you go through the cut. If you turn right, just past the fuel tank, there's a road that's about a half mile long on this side of the ridge. Then it cuts left, into the ridge, just like this road. It circles back along the lower edge of the quarry on the east side into this cut right in front of us."

"Like a big race track," Martinez said.

Doughty nodded.

"Martinez," Streeter directed. "Go clear the guys out of the plant. Tell them to buy a cup of coffee somewhere."

"There's a café a couple of miles north of here," Brandt said.

"Good," Streeter said. "Then come back and hold the ambulance here at the entrance until we give the all clear. Any other road out of this quarry besides this one?"

Doughty and Brandt shook their heads.

Streeter turned to Martinez. "Then shoot the bastard if he tries to escape."

Martinez grinned. "My pleasure, boss."

"Doughty, you take Brandt down to the south cut and wait for my signal. You still have the two-way radio?"

Brandt lifted it up and nodded.

"Kelleher's going to drive to the cut right in front of us, and I'm going to walk up that ridge and get a bird's-eye view of what's happening over there. You wait for my signal too."

Kelleher nodded.

"This guy's dangerous and out of control. Shoot first and ask questions later," Streeter said. "Just don't hurt Liv Bergen."

Martinez drove up to the plant and gave Streeter a wave as he walked under the silos to the stairs. Doughty and Brandt drove slowly on the road west along the ridge to the south cut. Kelleher pulled up to the north cut and Streeter stepped out of the car, drawing his gun and scrambling up the ridge.

The ridge was steep and tall, higher than he first thought. He was sure Jonah Bravo hadn't scaled the other side to watch for incoming visitors. It would be too much work. And Bravo was too lazy, Streeter thought.

Ten minutes later, just before reaching the crest of the ridge, Streeter looked back and saw Martinez escorting three other cars away from the plant. He saw the cars peel to the right and head for the café up the road. The ambulance pulled in, lights flashing, no sirens. Martinez flagged it down and pointed in Streeter's direction.

Streeter crawled the rest of the way onto the ridgetop and perched on his belly overlooking the quarry to the east, peering through cactus and rabbit brush. His eyes landed on a rock ledge about a hundred yards southeast of his position.

His heart quickened. Liv was still alive.

Jonah Bravo was standing with his back to him, Liv Bergen facing him, wearing a sort of toga. Jonah's pickup was parked nose to the east to the left of the pair.

"I see them. You were right, Doughty. He drove through the north cut and took the first right he could find, out of sight," Streeter whispered.

Streeter heard three clicks, acknowledgments from Kelleher, Martinez, and Brandt that they all got his message. The ridge was so high he couldn't see Kelleher in the Jeep at the north cut or Doughty and Brandt's car to the south. He looked back over his shoulder and saw the paramedics huddled around Martinez's two-way.

"Kelleher, you're about a hundred and fifty yards to the subject. When I give you the signal, go through the cut, take a sharp right, and drive a hundred yards. They're on the edge of a rock ledge. Looks like they're standing on a steep grade, maybe fifteen- or twenty-degree grade. The rock ledge drops off to the east about thirty or forty feet. Liv is backed up to the edge. No sudden moves, guys." Three clicks.

Streeter's gravelly voice was hushed as he continued. "Brandt and Doughty, you're a long way from the target. I can't tell if he could see you or not if you start driving around. What I'd rather you do is block that exit with your car, and Doughty, you start walking north, just past the cut on the east side. You'll have a steep climb at first, but you'll be above the target. Try to walk about a third of a mile. Don't let him see you."

One click.

"Brandt, you stay on the road. Walk the circle down beneath the quarry. Stay out of sight if you can manage. Don't let him get by you by going downhill."

One click.

"Martinez, stand by."

One click.

"Once in position, Brandt and Doughty, no one move until I give the word."

Streeter inched along the scratchy shrubs until he could see where he could crawl down the reclaimed slope of the mine, easing closer to where they stood. He needed to get closer if he were going to get off a clean shot.

He was within seventy yards when he saw Liv jerk to the left toward the pickup, Jonah Bravo sprinting after her.

CHAPTER 36

"I SAID, LIE DOWN."

Was he kidding?

Dr. Jay cradled a fancy camera in one hand; the other fished for something in his pocket. My mind flashed to the Dalí book, wondering if I saw anything depicting a woman in a toga on the rocks. Nothing came to me except the mangled distortions of his more bizarre work, the sick depictions of people like Jill. The water slicing through tissue and organs and bone. I remembered the truck, the mobile butcher shop. An idea flashed in my mind. We were both equidistant to the pickup. Both doors were still wide open. My view was straight through the body of the truck. His view was at an angle, closer to the back of the truck where he'd retrieved the sheet and the camera.

I was never a speed demon, often running faster backward than forward in our college basketball drills. The other girls made fun of me about that, coming in last when we ran ladders normally, coming in first when we ran them backward.

I was never fast, but I was quick.

There's a difference. It's what made me a good fast-pitch catcher, snapping the ball into the strike zone before the umpire's call, able to fake and break against defense in basketball.

"Lie down, now."

Jonah Bravo and I were facing one another, standing square.

I'd lost too much sleep over the years worrying about our equipment operators accidentally skidding on the smooth rock after material was stripped and down the steep incline off the highwall. And now I wished for it to happen. I assessed if I was really going to attempt this stunt and decided to take a chance, suspecting it very well may be a pistol he was fumbling around for in his pocket. I broke suddenly to my right, sprinting for the passenger door of the pickup, hurling myself through the door. I felt his fingers claw at my calves and ankles as I scrambled across the front seat, releasing the hand brake, throwing the gear into neutral and scrambling out the driver's side door.

I barely made it out in time as I watched the pickup roll off the edge of the highwall, crashing nose first onto the pit floor below with an earsplitting crunch of metal, settling upside down on its rooftop.

Dr. Jay was sprawled on the limestone ledge, stunned by the sight of his crumpled butcher shop. His eyes were wide and childlike when he turned to gawk at me.

I was sprawled on the limestone ledge nearby, panting and heaving from the adrenaline rush. All I could think was how I'd managed to destroy the killing machine, the high-pressure water that tore flesh and ripped through bone. When I saw the childlike expression on Dr. Jay's face, I realized I had also just destroyed his mode of transportation, his ticket out of this quarry after he killed me. Oh, and I was sure he would still kill me. He just couldn't torture me with the water.

And I was okay with that.

But Dr. Jay did something I didn't expect. He rose to his feet, camera still dangling from his neck, and he started clapping. Slow and steady at first. But he just stood there and clapped. Then he smiled.

A chill skipped its way down my spine. This man really was quite insane.

"Liv Bergen. I'm impressed. You are quite the handful." He stopped clapping and walked slowly toward me. I flinched when he reached out his hand, thinking he was about to clock me again. But he just stood over me, offering his hand to help me to my feet.

I took it and pulled myself up. He lightly held my arm as if we were walking into a debutante party, guiding me back to the spot where I was instructed to lie down.

In the gentlest voice I'd ever heard from him, he said, "Liv, will you please lie down right here. Feet toward the cliff, please."

I did as I was told.

I had stalled long enough, put off the inevitable. I dropped to the ground, realizing too late that the keys were still balled in my right fist. He had already moved away, toward the highwall. He was holding up his hands, using the first finger and thumb of each hand to make a picture frame. He was really going through with this idiotic photo shoot, I realized.

I lay panting, heaving, trying to regain my breath and composure, sweating profusely in the hot sun. I saw him smile at me through the finger frame.

"You know you did me a favor, Liv," he said.

I lay there, still, choosing not to talk with him anymore.

"I needed to get rid of that pickup. I'm leaving town, you see, and I needed to find a place for it." He walked toward me once again. "So, thank you."

I squinted up at him. His body was not quite blocking the sun.

"I saw the handful of vehicles by the plant when we drove in. I'll just borrow one of those. And if your workers would rather I didn't, I'll just pop their heads off. See what you've done, Liv? To Liv, or not to Liv. Isn't that clever?"

I squeezed my eyes closed, cursing myself for putting my guys in danger. The swift kick Dr. Jay delivered to my ribs wasn't nearly as painful as the thought that I'd endangered one of my employees. Tears burned in my eyes, my throat welling with sorrow.

I felt his hands on my arm. My eyes snapped open. He was crouching beside me, injecting me with something.

It was now or never.

I slammed my right fist into his face, hoping to gouge the key deep into some part of his pretty features. I felt my knuckles connect with bone, the key getting lodged in something fleshy. My hand dropped to my side, a heavy thumping noise against the rock. But I didn't feel a thing. My arm didn't hurt. My nose didn't hurt. My knees stopped stinging from my having landed hard on the limestone after diving through the cab. My lips stopped aching.

"You stupid cow," the words came slow and slurred, distorted by some thickness in my ears.

I could hear him, but I couldn't see him.

My vision was failing me, and my world was slowly spinning to a stop.

CHAPTER 37

STREETER SCRAMBLED TO HIS feet and bolted down the hill toward both of them, clutching the gun in his hand. The pickup rolled down the hill, off the rock ledge, and launched itself into the quarry pit below. Streeter saw both Liv and Jonah dive from the pickup just as it was tipping over the edge, and he scrambled behind a boulder so as not to be seen. He had closed the gap to twenty yards, still farther than he'd like for a good shot at Jonah Bravo's kill zone.

He panted as he whispered, "I'm within twenty yards. I need to get closer and will need backup. Doughty?"

A crackle sounded on Streeter's radio. Streeter jerked his head around to make sure Jonah Bravo didn't hear Andy Doughty's frightened voice sound across his radio. "Did you see that? Oh my Lord!"

Streeter squeezed his eyes closed briefly, willing himself calm, and pressed the radio to his lips, whispering, "Get as close as you can without being seen or heard. Turn your radio off. I'm going to do the same. If anyone hears gunfire, close in. Fast."

Streeter turned off the switch and peeked around the rock. Jonah was leading Liv back to where they'd been standing. He was making her lie down on the ground. Streeter crept around the rock and sprinted behind a closer one, then another. He caught his breath again and heard Jonah talking. He was too close to peek around now, close enough to get a shot off. He heard Jonah telling Liv how she had screwed up and that he was going to kill one of her employees or all of them and steal a car.

Just as he was about to peer around the rock, Streeter heard Jonah scream, "You stupid cow!"

Streeter jumped from behind the rock and fired twice into Jonah's chest, the holes blossoming into red. Jonah Bravo just stood there, stunned. Streeter was stunned too. Not because of the bullet holes he'd made in the man's chest or because the man still hadn't dropped like a rock from the hole that pierced where his heart should be, but because of the keys dangling from Jonah's left eye socket.

Jonah staggered backward two steps, then plunged over the edge of the rock ledge.

Streeter ran to Liv, a needle still protruding from her left arm. Dust from Kelleher's tires sprayed a wake as he screeched to a stop nearby. Doughty crouched beside Streeter, panting, just as the ambulance rounded the north cut heading for the group.

Streeter felt for a pulse.

He couldn't find one.

The paramedics pushed him aside and injected a shot of Narcan into Liv's right arm. Her eyes fluttered open. The paramedics quickly rolled her onto a gurney and into the back of the ambulance, strapping the oxygen over her nose and mouth. Spent as the adrenaline rush subsided, Streeter plopped onto the ground as the ambulance sped away.

Kelleher reached out his hand and helped him up. All three walked to the edge of the rock ledge and stared down at the twisted mass below. Next to the crumpled pickup lay Jonah Bravo's shattered body, his eyes wide open, the crimson blossoms on his chest, the keys still protruding from his left eye.

Doug Brandt at the base of the highwall walked up to the body and stomped the heel of his boot hard on Jonah Bravo's belly, once for Jill Brannigan and once for Lisa Henry.

CHAPTER 38

MY PRAYER OF THANKS for being alive was long and rambling, interrupted often by the fuzz in my head and frequent drifts in and out of sleep. Crazy nightmarish dreams come along with being doped up, and I don't understand why anyone would want to volunteer to be in that audience.

I never did meet Agent Streeter Pierce. But I understand from Agent Kelleher that he's the reason I'm still alive.

I'm getting released from Poudre Hospital today, four weeks after I was nearly killed by the infamous Venus de Milo murderer. The Narcan wore off way faster than the heroin did, so I lapsed into unconsciousness a few hours after I arrived at the hospital. I was out of it for three weeks, my body protesting the pollution of that nasty drug. I don't know what the long-term effect of that scary little episode will cost me, but I'm glad I'm still here to find out.

During the past week in particular, I've had a lot of time to think. And pray. I've decided that as much as I love working in the family business and want to help any way I can, life is too short to spend every waking minute working, and I want to spend more time with the people I love. Of course, Mom is thrilled, as we've had hours and hours to talk through how I could make that happen, starting with coming home for a couple of weeks to do my required rehab.

She's been keeping vigil by my bedside every one of the last twenty-eight days. In fact, she said that every one of my family members has been by to see me. Dad spent the first three days sleeping in my room in that tiny little chair by the window. It's hard for me to imagine since my dad is larger than life—and busy as hell!

Elizabeth's been by several times. Once, she lifted the sheet to check if I was wearing my steel-toed boots with my hospital gown, making me laugh, which hurt. And Michael had been by too. So have Frances and her husband, John. I appreciate each one's effort even though I don't remember a thing. One thing that's crystal clear, though, is that I missed helping Elizabeth with the fireworks on Mt. Rushmore this year—apparently I was unconscious for that entire Fourth of July week—and I don't want to miss that ever again.

Even Special Agent Streeter Pierce came by to see me a couple of times when I was in a coma. Mom said he's a nice man. That's a bonus. Maybe my path will cross with Special Agent Streeter Pierce's again someday. I hope it's not when I'm naked, draped in a sheet, doped up on heroin, and lying on the edge of a highwall. A girl can hope.

I will miss Lisa Henry. She was a good friend, a great agent, and an awesome human being. What a beautiful soul! I just lived through what she must have experienced, so I'm comforted a little knowing that she didn't die in pain. But she didn't deserve to have her life taken from her.

When Lisa told me for the third time that I should consider a career with the FBI, my last words to her were, "Maybe in my next life." I wish my last words to her had been something more profound, more heartfelt. I would have gone for even a simple "thank you."

My eyelids are growing heavy again, and my mind's eye has flashed on Lisa's stunning face that last morning. As if in a dream, I am standing shoulder to shoulder with her and Streeter, fighting off all the bad guys in the world.

And in between the barrage of gunfire, I am screaming the words, "Thank you, Lisa. Thank you!"

ACKNOWLEDGMENTS

AS A MINER FROM the Black Hills of South Dakota, I am a neophyte when it comes to knowing what it takes to get a book into a reader's hands. I am amazed at the intricacies involved and the talents required of the publishing world. To acknowledge everyone who contributed is nearly impossible since the team that has helped me with my breakout novel is quite large. For my peers out there, I'll use mining terms to shed some light on those who have helped me in my journey.

Auburn Rutledge was the prospector looking for that diamond in the rough amid the rubble of submissions. She was the person who first saw a glitter of hope in this story.

Jay Hodges, the assay expert, confirmed Auburn's find, and his enthusiasm and kind words of encouragement helped me step through the mine portal. Without these two, you wouldn't be reading this book.

Hobbs Allison Jr. wore the miner's hard hat with the light, shining the way for me as I traveled down into the belly of the mine. Because of him, I merely stubbed my toe on occasion rather than falling flat on my face.

Bryan Carroll's was the face of every miner we meet, hard at work in production so that everything runs smoothly. Underground—but not unnoticed, and very much appreciated—he is the workhorse behind the book in your hands.

Lisa Woods was the blast, the most fun part of mining. I have her to thank for this explosive book cover and interior design.

Carrie Winsett was the mine engineer, her keen eye trained to find the best method, approach, and presentation of any gems mined. Her marketing genius created a sturdy, precise, and effective platform for launching this book.

Kristen Sears, the railroad engineer, carried this gem out of the mine to the market, to all the stores that are willing to showcase them. Without her efforts and the book buyers' discerning eye, this book would have never made it to the shelves.

Lari Bishop was the mine supervisor, making sure everything was as it should be. Without her guidance, vision, and direction, my book would still be stuck in the rubble, dull and unpolished.

Linda O'Doughda was the jeweler, the expert at taking a diamond in the rough and making it shine brilliantly. If you enjoy this book, you have her to thank most of all! And so do I. Without her skills, this book would be nothing more than a shiny imposter.

And Julie Schoerke, JKS Communications, was the environmental engineer who made sure the mine was well taken care of, restored, and reclaimed so that everyone involved was happy and rewarded. Just so you know, she rocks!

For all those who were willing to read my book and who wrote endorsements, reviews, and kind words of encouragement, thank you. For bookstore buyers who took a chance on me, thank you. For the stores willing to keep my book on the shelves, thank you.

For all of you who bought my book, I know you faced so many choices, and I appreciate that you chose to read about Liv Bergen. Thank you! My heart is filled with gratitude and my life filled with blessings too many to count. And I count each one of you as one of them.

LOT'S RETURN TO SODOM

Second in the Liv Bergen Mystery Thriller Series

SANDRA BRANNAN

GREENLEAF
BOOK GROUP PRESS

CHAPTER 1

"**CAN YOU STAY?**" he asked her.

"Just until eight, Roy," Michelle answered.

"That won't give me enough time," he said, handing her another can of diced peaches in light syrup. "I'll never get this restocking done without you. And I wanted this done by yesterday. But with everyone taking off for the rally, I can't get ready. Make it nine."

"Eight, Roy. I don't have my car. Charlene borrowed mine because hers is in being fixed. She's picking me up at eight," Michelle argued.

"Charlene's old enough to drive?"

"Fourteen," Michelle said. "Learner's permit in this state, remember?"

"Forget your sister. I'll give you a ride home," Roy offered.

"I'm tired," she explained, tilting her head from side to side to stretch her weary neck and shoulders, tiring of his persistence. "I appreciate what you're doing for me, letting me work extra hours so I can afford to go back to college full-time this fall—"

"Which you've postponed for way too long," he interrupted. "You've always wanted to be a doctor, and it's about time you followed your dream."

"You know I couldn't. Now, with all my summer overtime, I'll have enough money to at least get my premed out of the way. I appreciate it, but you have me working the morning shift tomorrow, and I've been here since six this morning, or did you forget?"

"I never forget," he said, staring at her through his glasses. "You punched in at exactly five fifty-eight, two minutes ahead of time. You probably arrived at five forty-five, drank your first cup of coffee, and put your lunch in the employee break room refrigerator."

She glanced sideways at him and said, "Okay, that's weird, Roy."

It was if he wasn't listening. "You took your morning break at nine ten until nine twenty, shorting yourself five minutes," he continued.

She always knew he was a bit off, ever since she had first met him in high school. Maybe that's why they became quick friends: she felt sorry for him and he had a crush on her. Somewhere in the back of her mind she wondered if he'd ever truly outgrown that schoolboy crush. But after almost eleven years of deflecting his advances, she hoped he had moved on and was only an attentive friend. His account of her every move didn't give her confidence in that assumption.

"You took a lunch break from eleven thirty-five to noon, again shorting yourself five minutes. You ate your lunch while reading a book, probably a mystery," Roy described mechanically, shoveling can after can of fruit and vegetables toward Michelle.

"Stop." Michelle felt her breath catch as she realized Roy Barker was not kidding.

Her mind flashed to all the times in recent months when she and Jens had seen Roy around town when they went out. That time he happened by their table at the Millstone, hinting that he should join them for brunch. Catching a glimpse of him at Canyon Lake Park when they were feeding the ducks and thinking he'd been watching them before he jogged away on the bike path. Maybe Jens had been right about Roy's obsession with her, Michelle thought.

"You took a ten-minute afternoon break at four fifteen and haven't taken a break since. You expertly averted the advances of that wannabe biker dude shortly after, even though he was putting a full court press on you to become his lady."

"His lady?" Michelle shot back, disturbed that his creepy mania was spiraling out of control. "Roy, what are you talking about?"

Just as her mind raced to find an excuse to end this conversation, Michelle saw Roy's eyes narrow as he stared past her shoulder and down the aisle. She turned slowly to see what had distracted him from his bizarre fixation on the minutia of her life.

Three bikers were walking toward them. These were motorcycle club, or m.c., bikers, the real deal. The kind known for illegal activities like selling drugs. The bikers who often started trouble: mostly with other m.c. bikers, but trouble nonetheless. The bikers whom the police—the authorities who flew in by the hundreds from all over the country for the week—watched closely during the rally, jetting in authorities. And because Jens had pointed it out to her last year, she knew what it meant to be flying colors, and that the authorities generally disallowed it during the rally to help prevent knife fights and shootings. These three bikers, however, were most definitely flying their colors.

The well-worn black leather jackets had patches and badges across the front, and the skinny biker on the right was wearing a red-and-silver skullcap with Lucifer's Lot stitched neatly across the front. The scary-looking guy in the middle was staring directly at her.

Ray scuttled to his feet and stepped between Michelle and the men. She rose to her feet. Watching Roy draw in air to inflate his chest, Michelle thought he looked more like a puffer fish than the friend she'd known for so long, the friend whom she now wondered why she had kept all these years.

She barely recognized his tone when he barked, "What do you want?"

The scary biker in the middle, who wore his hair in a black-and-gray ponytail and had a black mustache, ignored Roy's question, never taking his eyes off Michelle. With a voice like Trace Adkins, the biker said, "Excuse me, ma'am. Can you help us find a few things?"

Roy shielded Michelle, but the biker had such an overwhelming presence that Roy seemed nearly invisible.

"Sure," Michelle said, relieved by the interruption. She definitely preferred a hardcore biker's attentions to Roy's unusual interest in her at that moment.

"Michelle, no," Roy said, grabbing her elbow as she stepped around him.

The two bikers flanking the ominous one growled like two guard dogs. Michelle turned to Roy, removing his hand from her arm, and whispered, "It's okay. Really. They just want a little help finding things."

Roy scowled. His disapproving eyes pierced through her.

Michelle turned toward the bikers. "These gentlemen, our customers, need some help with their grocery shopping. I'll be right back to help you finish stocking."

"My name's Mully," the biker said, cutting his eyes at Roy and walking alongside Michelle down the aisle, the two other bikers falling in behind them. She could almost feel Roy's glare burning a hole through her as she turned the corner with the strangers. She imagined his disappointment that she didn't wither or faint from the fear of it all, allowing him to protect her as the hero he was meant to be. Lord, he was getting to be so annoying. Two more weeks. That's all she had left to work here.

Welcoming the break from Roy, she replied evenly, "Michelle. That's my name. What do you need help finding?"

One of the guard dog bikers handed her a short list. She glanced at it and made quick work of finding the items for them. Needles, thread, fishing wire, matches, and rubbing alcohol. She wondered if they planned on sewing up a buddy's knife wound or something.

Michelle walked briskly toward the aisle of miscellaneous housewares with the three bikers in tow, the lead biker with the velvet voice falling in step beside her once again. She scanned the shelves for the items, the one called Mully standing so closely beside her that they were almost touching shoulders and arms. The other two bikers stood behind them. By the scruffy looks of them, she had imagined the three of them would stink. But the scent emanating from Mully was actually quite pleasant, suggesting a dash of expensive cologne perhaps.

"Where did they relocate the Harley Davidson dealership?" he asked.

"So, you've been here before? To Rapid City?" she replied, handing the scrawny biker his list, pointing to the shelf where sewing items were displayed, and watching him check the list while the other biker gathered items.

Up until that moment, Michelle had hoped the black leather jackets the three bikers were wearing were not their colors but rather a second riding jacket. When their backs were turned away from her, however, she saw the familiar grin of the chunky idiot in the skintight red spandex and evil horns, the bold rocker arcing above the cartoon. The bikers were definitely Lucifer's Lot, one of the motorcycle gangs that were from time to time banned from crossing South Dakota state lines because of the trouble they caused with the Fallen Angels, who were also banned occasionally from entering the state. She had read about them in the newspapers years ago and tried to recall niggling details about a gunfight or ambush that involved the two gangs near a small lake in Custer State Park. A drug deal gone wrong or something. The article had indicated that the authorities would escort known m.c. gangs straight through to the next state, disallowing the bikers from using any off-ramp within the state.

"Yeah," Mully answered. "I know the area fairly well."

"It's out on the corner of Deadwood Avenue and I-90. By the Windmill truck stop. You know where that is?"

Mully nodded. "I do."

Michelle pointed down the aisle to the camping section, and the two bikers were off to find the fishing wire and matches. She hadn't noticed before, but the youngest biker wore a jacket with the word "Prospect" printed on the back underneath the logo. Mully stood shoulder to shoulder with her, his eyes never once straying from her face. She pretended not to notice. She glanced over toward the checkout lanes and realized Roy was nowhere in sight, which made her more nervous than having this gang leader stare at her.

Michelle stole a quick glance up to the manager's loft and barely detected the light inside his office shining behind Roy's silhouette through the tinted window. She could feel his eyes on her and a shiver skipped down her spine. He would be angry with her for disobeying him and for showing kindness to these men. What did she ever see in Roy besides someone to be pitied, she wondered. They had nothing in common other than this workplace, and she concluded that pity doesn't make a very stable foundation for friendship. And she further concluded that feeling safer with Mully standing beside her, knowing what he represented, underscored her deeper concern about Roy.

The last of the items, the rubbing alcohol, was over with the first aid supplies, and she led the trio to the farthest aisle of the store. She pointed at the shelf and the young biker retrieved several bottles. Her suspicion that a wound was involved intensified. Mully beside her, she watched as the two struggled to redistribute the load of items between them.

She wasn't sure why Mully's silence made her more uncomfortable than their conversation did, so she decided to break it with small talk. "Are you here for the rally?"

He nodded once and said, "Starts tomorrow."

Before she knew what was happening, he had turned to face her, a kind smile on his face. She thought the look in his eyes was sad, maybe even lonely. She felt his groomed fingernails lightly drag across her left cheek as he brushed a strand of hair from her face, and she detected the faint smell of cloves on his breath when he asked, "Want to join me?"

Michelle took a step back, pushed the loose strand of hair behind her ear, and said, "No thanks, but I'm sure you guys will have a great time up there."

Just then, she felt long arms sliding around her waist from behind, a chin resting on the top of her head—the familiar hug of her boyfriend. She closed her eyes, turned around so she could return the cuddle, and said, "Hi, hon."

Michelle sensed Jens's tension then connected it to Mully and his minions nearby. "Jens, I was just helping some tourists find their way around the store."

When she turned back toward them to introduce Jens, Michelle saw Mully walking away with the bikers without even acknowledging Jens's arrival and without saying another word to her. She suspected Jens was reading the Lucifer's Lot rocker above the familiar gang emblem on all three jackets as they ambled toward the checkout registers, Roy scrambling down the stairs from the manager's loft to stand guard by the checkers.

"He asked you to go to the rally with him?"

Michelle nodded.

"You have to be more careful," Jens said.

"I know," she replied. "Thanks for the tip. By the way, what are you doing here?"

"Just wanted to see if you have time for a late dinner."

"Char's waiting, and I need to talk with her about something. Later?"

"Sure. Come by my house?" he asked, giving her a wave as he headed for the front of the store.

Before she could answer, Roy stormed toward Michelle and jabbed a finger at her nose. "What in the hell are you thinking?"

She saw Jens pull up short, noting Roy's tone.

"I was helping some customers," Michelle answered, glad that Jens had noticed and had stopped in the aisle.

"Why didn't you let me handle it?" Spittle flew from Roy's lips. "Why did you deliberately disobey me?"

"Hey, calm down, Roy," Jens warned, approaching from behind and laying his large hand on Roy's shoulder.

Roy glared at Jens. "Stay out of this, pretty boy. This is an employment issue. Subordination." He turned back on Michelle.

"Roy, come on. My last day is in two weeks. I've worked here for eleven years without a single reprimand," Michelle said, calmly.

"Lucifer's Lot, Michelle? Really? You won't help me, but you'll help them? Mean sons of bitches?"

Unfazed by Roy's temper, Michelle shook her head and said, "Good night, Roy. See you tomorrow."

When she turned away, Roy snatched her by the arm again.

Jens intervened, "Hey, hey Roy. I said calm down."

"What's gotten into you?" Michelle wrestled quickly from Roy's grip and checked her watch. "I have to go. Charlene's waiting for me."

Roy followed behind as she headed toward the back of the store. "Lucifer's Lot is a dangerous motorcycle gang, Michelle. Not nice. Killing machines."

"I know, Roy. All they wanted was a little help with their grocery shopping."

"You let him touch you."

Michelle ignored him and pushed open the swinging door that led to the cool storage and the employee break room. Roy turned and held out his hand like a traffic cop to stop Jens just outside the door marked "Employees Only." Jens shook his head and waited for Michelle as Roy followed her to the punch clock.

Michelle noticed Roy checking behind him, either making sure Jens hadn't followed or making sure the door had swung shut, leaving Roy and Michelle alone. His anger quickly dissipated and he almost pleaded, "Michelle, how could you?"

"How could I what, Roy?" Her anger mounting, she spun on her heels to find him directly behind her, too close. She felt trapped between the wall and Roy. His breath smelt like a sterile mouthwash.

"Touch you like that," he said, dragging his fingers across her cheek as Mully had.

With a shudder, she shoved at his chest, making him step back from her, and slammed her fists on her hips, hoping to snap him out of the hypnosis he seemed to have fallen under.

"What's it to you, Roy?"

Roy blinked. "He . . . he's nothing more than a filthy criminal."

"Haven't you ever heard of not judging a book by its cover?" Michelle argued. She grabbed her time card, keeping a watchful eye out in case Roy grew angry again as his creepy catatonia ebbed. "You don't know he's a criminal. And I didn't let him touch me."

He didn't seem to hear her. He watched as she slid the time card into the punch clock, still careful not to turn her back on him.

He cleared his throat and pointed to the small pile of belongings she was gathering. "Speaking of judging books, you're reading the newest John B. McDonald. It came in last week, right?"

Michelle looked down at her pile, scooped it into her arms, and said, "Not that it's any of your business."

Foolishly ignoring her indignation and warning, Roy continued, "At precisely three o'clock, and not a second earlier, you took a ten-minute lunch break and read a book in the employee lunchroom. Then you came back to work and relieved Sarah so she could eat lunch."

Michelle spun around and held up her hand. "Stop, Roy. Just knock it off, will you? You really are scaring me."

Michelle stared at the man she had once considered a friend, studying his glassy green eyes. She instantly recognized the embarrassment in them and felt sorry for him. In an attempt to push him back over that fine line between friendship, which would never be the same again, and obsession, Michelle cautiously inquired, "Why do you know so much about me?"

He lowered his eyes, pushing the designer frames up his nose, although they hadn't slipped since the last time he had done so. A nervous habit. She studied him as he contemplated his answer. His large hands hung limply by his hips, his long, lean body straight and strong, bent only at the neck. Roy's grocery store uniform was rolled up at the sleeves, the folded cotton barely fitting over his toned biceps. His arms and hands were bronze, as were his face and neck. He looked very humble in his pose and she wondered if she had gone too far by asking her question.

Roy looked up from the floor and smiled sadly.

"Because you're my friend," was the answer he settled on.

It was a blow. Maybe she had been too harsh, too judgmental; maybe it was a matter of his simply being socially awkward. Maybe she'd been the one to cross the line and was bullying him. Remorse swelled in her belly. She opted for being compassionate, yet truthful, by saying, "You're my friend too, Roy, but I don't make it my business to know every move you make every minute of your day. It's kind of freaky, like I'm being watched or something. Do you understand?"

She had avoided the word "stalker" so as not to further anger him, but it was definitely the word she would use to describe him.

He added, "I admire you, Michelle. You could have been anything, gone anywhere, but you stayed here after high school to watch after your little sister. That's admirable."

"Anyone would do that in my situation. Good night, Roy." She walked toward the hall and paused just before the swinging door. As an afterthought she said, "*Nightmare in Pink.*"

"What?"

"*Nightmare in Pink,*" she repeated, holding up the paperback and offering him a conciliatory smile. "That's the book I'm reading."

He stared up at her and she recognized the gratitude in his expression.

Casually, she added, "And yes, it's a John D. McDonald. D as in dog; not B as in boy. And it's not a new one. It first came out in the sixties, I think, but it's a new reprint. A very good one, I might add."

She moved toward the door, to Jens who awaited her on the other side. She could just make out his silhouette and was relieved to know he was nearby.

"I love you," Roy said quietly.

"What?" Michelle asked, turning on her heels, aghast by what she thought she heard him say.

"I . . . I love you," he repeated with less confidence. "I thought you should know."

"What are you saying?" Michelle gasped. She wondered what had possessed her to take pity on him just now. Her decision to show him a little kindness seemed only to have inspired him to go deeper into his fantasy about her. She had made a terrible mistake.

"I have never given you *any* reason to believe we were anything more than friends, Roy. At least we *used* to be friends until you started obsessing over every little thing I do, stalking me wherever I went this summer. Don't you understand? I'm in love with Jens. Not you. You know that. You've always known that. So why are you casting aside our friendship after all these years? Why, Roy?"

Roy stared blankly at Michelle, speechless.

She shook her head and added, "Our friendship must have been more important to me than it was to you. You must be crazy."

The anger rose to Roy's cheeks, an anger that touched his eyes in a way she had never seen before. She was used to his childish tantrums, such as the fit he threw a few minutes ago over her willingness to help Mully and his buddies. But she'd never seen Roy like this.

His voice was nearly unrecognizable when he demanded, "Do not call me that."

"Roy, this isn't—"

"You listen to me," he interrupted, closing the distance between them instantly, and gripping her arms in his hands, shaking her. "Never say that word again. Ever. Or you will pay for it. Do you hear me Michelle Freeburg? You will regret this for the rest of your life."

A shiver ran down Michelle's spine and she forced a smile to her face. "Roy, calm down. I didn't mean anything by it."

The door swung open and Jens was filling the space with his six-foot-four-inch, two-hundred-twenty-pound frame. He had overheard Roy and she was glad of it.

"You want to step outside and pick on someone your own size?" he said, nostrils flaring.

Roy froze.

Michelle shook free from Roy's grip and clung to Jens's arm. "Jens, listen to me. This isn't worth it."

Roy and Jens squared off in the tiny little space between the swinging door and the employee lunchroom, and Michelle was finding it harder and harder to breathe with every passing second of mounting tension. She had never seen Roy so angry before and she had never seen Jens angry at all. And she knew she'd find Charlene waiting for her outside, angry as hell at her for making her wait. This was turning into a disastrous night.

"Jens, please," she pleaded, pulling on his muscular arm, trying to make him follow her out the door and away from this place.

Through clenched teeth, he warned, "Stay away from Michelle, Roy Barker, or *you* will be the one who regrets it for the rest of *your* life."